❀ Created with Vellum

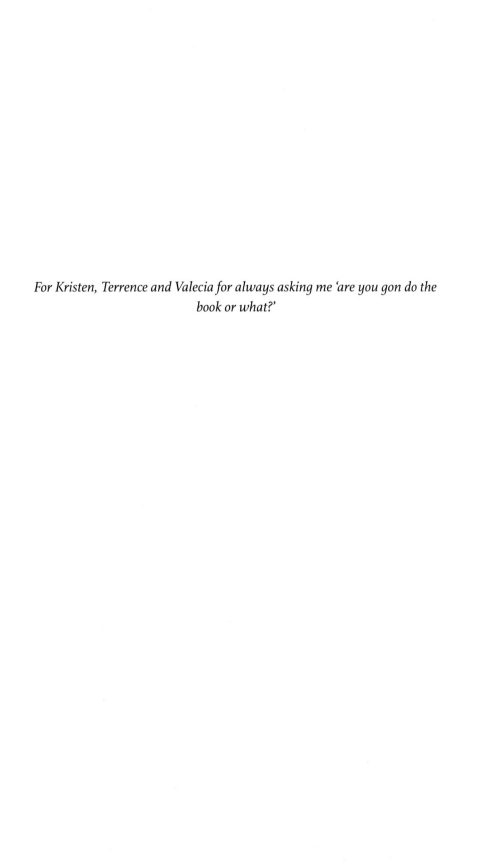

For Kristen, Terrence and Valecia for always asking me 'are you gon do the book or what?'

JESSICA WATKINS
PRESENTS

Mercedes

by

LOLA JOY

1

MERCEDES

A pretty face, hips, butt, thighs, and boobs... That's all you need to be successful in life, or so I've been told many times.

My fucked-up life coach, slash roommate, slash babysitter is standing in front of me with her hands on her own shapely hips.

"Mercedes! Are you listening to me?" Julissa, Jules for short, waves her hand impatiently as if she's trying to snap me out of a trance.

I'm not in a trance. I'm just *thinking*. Jules refers to my tendency to do so as "extra annoying." I can't help that my brain actually works.

"I was just listening to the song and trying to get into the mood."

Jules squints at me. "You hate this song."

"I do not hate it!" I sing a little bit of Katy Perry's "California Girls," doing a little foot work and snapping for emphasis. Okay, I might hate it.

Jules rolls her eyes. "You're going to have to be more convincing than that to pull this off tonight. Are you sure you got this? I can go without you if you don't think you can do this."

Um, that would be a hell no. I'm not staying in this house by myself, not after last time. It's not like I'm scared. I just don't want to have to shoot somebody. Also, I'm scared.

Jules widens her eyes and holds her hand out at me as if she's waiting on a response. "I've totally got this. You should stop worrying so much. You're starting to get lines around your eyes."

Jules gasps dramatically, her face a mask of horror. *Bull's eye.* I laugh while she rushes over to the vanity mirror and desk in my bedroom. I knew mentioning aging would get Jules out of my face. Otherwise, it's a complete lie. Jules has flawless skin. The only lines her face has seen are probably cocaine. She is stunning; sex in a pair of Manolo Blahnik pumps and a dress that is nothing more than a very thin layer of a second skin. The red dress sets off Jules' olive complexion, long, almost-black hair, and dark brown eyes perfectly. The dress sits just below Jules' butt checks, but they are so clearly outlined in the material that the length doesn't make the ensemble modest. Jules adjusts her boobs in her push-up bra while shooting me an annoyed look. I don't really get the push up bra thing. How high do boobs need to be, neck? Chin? Where are we going with this?

"I do not have lines, Mercedes. Stop being a little jerk before I decide to leave you here."

I walk over to the full-length mirror in the corner of my gray and coral bedroom.

"I was kidding. You know you look amazing and I'm ready for tonight." I appraise myself in the mirror as Jules moves behind me and starts discussing all the rules for tonight *again.*

My hair, which is normally a rich chestnut brown, has been lightened with blond highlights and chopped to a chin-length bob. The bob comes with a dramatic side part, which causes my hair to persistently try to blind me by stabbing me in the eyeball. Unconsciously, I move to tuck it behind my ear and Jules slaps at my hand.

"No tucking, Mercedes. Have you not heard anything I just said?" She's behind me in the mirror rearranging my hair meticulously. "Listen, this hair is perfect. It gives you just the sexy edge you need to make this work. One bottle of dye and a haircut and you look ten years older already." Is that a good thing? Twenty-five seems kinda old.

"Add the hair to your excellent bone structure." I assume she means my high cheek bones.

"With those full lips and your slanted eyes, the bouncers won't think twice about letting you in."

Slanted eyes? My eyes are not "slanted." I have almond-shaped gray eyes, which people have commented on since I was born. I have no idea where they or my hair—came from. I know for certain I'm at least fifty percent black. Beyond that, it's anybody's guess. "Anybody" includes my mother who could only narrow the list down to two men and a possible. Classy. So, I might be African-American and Hispanic, African-American and Italian, African-American and Vietnamese, African-American and Irish, or all of the above. My racial composition is the equivalent of a multiple-choice question on the SAT. When I asked my grandma about it, she just said, *"You're black. The rest don't really matter."*

"Well, that's if they even get to your face. Since you're an early bloomer, I'm guessing the bouncers won't even notice your face!" Jules gestures to my curves. They started popping up when I turned eleven and a half. Some girls got acne. I got B cups, which are already C cups. My butt and hips joined the party and now I get the kind of attention that ruins girls with daddy issues, girls like *me.*

Jules claps like a little kid might when her birthday cake with candles blazing is set in front of her. Her earlier doubts seem to have self-resolved. Good, because there's no way I'm staying in this house.

Jules wasn't living with us a few months ago when some meth head broke in. She was out on one of her missions to self-actualize, whatever that means. I will never forget the feeling of standing in our Southwest D.C. kitchen by myself trembling in fear. I couldn't even call the police. I knew it would have turned into a CPS case because I was home alone overnight. We're on our own in the world. My grandma works two jobs during the week and another one on the weekend, so I can go to a fancy private school with only a partial scholarship. I used to be in a public school honors program, but it wasn't challenging enough and I was fighting, defending myself, nearly every day. I'm tough, but I'm not meth-head-in-my-kitchen-eating-my-cereal-at-2am tough. I can scrap it out with hateful teenage girls who try to pin me down and cut my hair. Bet good money those bitches think twice before they try anything like that again. But I'm smart enough to hide too and that's what I did the night of the break-in. I stayed under the stairs with my grandma's glock and prayed until dawn when I finally came out and saw the back door standing open. My cereal was the only thing missing.

I never even told Grandma about the break-in. I didn't want her to worry. We got the back door fixed. I started keeping every light in the house on during the nights my grandma was working late and I would keep myself awake until I just collapsed in exhaustion. Needless to say, when Jules failed to self-actualize and returned to the basement apartment, I was thrilled.

I look at Jules who is now primping and rolling her hips to a Rihanna song. I'm always studying her, always trying to imitate her. Jules is older than me. She is on her shit and I want to be on mine too. I'm not sure how old Jules is, but I know she's old enough to get into a nightclub and old enough that my grandma thinks that leaving me alone with her while she works the night shift is a good idea. I guess it's better than me facing off with Captain Crunch-eating fiends by myself. Knowing Jules, she definitely would have shot the guy and asked questions later.

Jules has been around off and on my whole life. While she's "on," she's usually a tenant in the basement apartment. When she offered to stay with me overnight while my grandmother worked as an in-home nurse, grandma was pleasantly surprised. She thinks the responsibility is good for Jules. She says that Jules needs an "anchor" in the world, something to keep her from drifting away. Seems to me like that's a recipe for someone to find Jesus, but instead, she's stuck with me. Grandma's brother, Earl, found Jesus and has been on a mission trip in Guatemala for three years. On second thought, Jules is not at all cut out for Guatemala and therefore maybe not Jesus either.

Jules yanks on the skirt I chose from her expansive wardrobe of teeny tiny pieces. I would never tell her this, but the skirt is one of the few "decent" things I could find in her closet.

"If you're going to wear this long skirt, at least keep it where it belongs so some skin still shows."

"This skirt doesn't even come down to my kneecaps." *How is that long?*

"That's just because you're tall." Jules waves her hand in dismissal.

I'm 5'5", but I don't bother to point that out. I wind my hips to the music too, imitating both Jules' moves and her facial expressions. I really do think I've got this. The woman in the mirror is wearing a top that barely covers her breasts and a skirt that doesn't cover enough of her thighs. Her makeup is understated, but the smokey eye and the pink lip gloss highlight all her best facial features. Nobody would guess that earlier today this woman rode a city bus to high school dressed in a school uniform, carrying a purple backpack. *I'm a grown woman. I'm a grown woman. I'm a grown woman.* I keep up the mental chanting. As if she's reading my mind, Jules launches into another speech about the required etiquette for the evening.

"No acting like a little kid. Tonight, you are a sophisticated 20-something-year-old *woman* and every girl wants to be you and every man wants to be *in* you."

I frown at that. Too soon. The girls I know started having sex in the 8th grade. I'm one of the last virgins I know and I'm well versed in the topic of sex. But still, I'm not trying to do all that. My goal is to let Jules know I can hang so whenever she goes out, she'll take me with her.

"We only sit in VIP sections. We don't drink anything by the glass, so our hosts have to be able to afford bottle service. We don't dance to more than one song at a time because nobody wants the sweaty girl with the raccoon eyes when she leaves the club." Jules taps a long red fingernail on her chin as she always does when she's thinking. She snaps her fingers, signaling that she remembered something. "Oh, and pros before bros always."

"What does that mean?"

"It means we're looking for professionals, athletes, and enter-tainers who are at the top of the food chain and among them baseball and basketball players come first. Unless you come across a quarter-back or a successful running back, football players can't really afford us."

Honestly, Jules makes us sound like prostitutes. That might not be a stretch for the way she lives her life, but I'm a 15-year-old virgin.

"Where do you go to school?" Jules quizzes me.

"I'm a senior at George Washington I transferred here from Kent State." We had picked Kent State because it seemed pretty obscure to us and not the sort of place people might know people if I said I was from there.

"That's good but don't say George Washington. Nobody says that here. Just call it GW. What if they ask where you live?"

"I've been abroad for two years and now I live off campus. You're my roommate. We met at GW. We're both psych majors." I recite the answers Jules has been drilling into my head for days. I don't really know enough about any of the information I'm passing off as fact to know if it sounds authentic, but Jules seems pleased.

"I really wish Tiana could come with us," Jules scowls at the mention of my best friend.

"Mercedes, how many times do I have to tell you about girl-friends? If they're unattractive, they're jealous. If they're attractive, they're a threat. You really can't go right with women. It's best to keep them all at a distance."

And there you have it: Julesism life lesson number 112 and prob-ably the reason I have only one friend.

Despite her crazy "isms," I admire Jules. She lives a completely unselfconscious life. That's not me at all. I'm always worried about fitting in and the fact that I never do. Boys my age are both nervous around me and overly solicitous. *Solicitous or attentive, my vocabulary word from this week in language arts.* Girls are much worse. They either deliberately ignore me or do nothing to disguise their contempt. Besides Jules, Tiana really is my *only* friend. Jules is always lecturing me about how to live a life filled with designer clothes, accessories, and vacations, but that's not what I really care about. What I care about is *not* caring. I don't want it to matter that I don't fit in anywhere. Jules waves her hand and dismisses anything that doesn't go with her plans at the moment. I want to be able to do that. So far, I haven't been able to wave anything away.

I give myself a final once-over before I square my shoulders and jut my chest out as I've seen Jules do. *Winning life is 52 percent about tit visibility. Julesism number 97.* Grabbing my small clutch purse, I strut to the door of my bedroom. *Hip action is the other 48 percent of winning life. Julesism number 98. I really do got this!* Even Jules is giving me an admiring look as I strut towards the door. All I'm thinking is that I don't have to worry about being left at home alone.

I had no idea there were much worse things.

2

LOCHLAN, 7 YEARS LATER...

Adrenaline is a living, breathing thing. It's an electrical force firing through my bloodstream, amplifying sounds and sensation. I'm not on top of the world. I'm at the apex of the entire universe and everything exists for my pleasure. Hyperbole aside, my team is on the verge of securing a spot in the NBA finals for the first time in franchise history and anyone in this city would tell you that I'm a key part of that achievement.

My king-of-the-world complex seems justified as I walk into Vis Nightclub with three of my teammates. Two of us started our rookie year in the NBA together. Bryce Hardwick and I had come from the University of Southern Cal to the Wizards. Unlike Bryce, I wasn't a first-round draft pick. In fact, I wasn't drafted at all. I was picked up by the Wizards after grueling tryouts. I promptly became an enthusiastic bench anchor for the entirety of my rookie and sophomore seasons. There was no chance that bench was going anywhere with my ass firmly affixed to it. I was the guy who came in as a shooting guard when the fans were racing to the nearest exit in an effort to beat traffic before the game was officially over because it was pretty much over.

All of that changed during the summer before the start of the season three years ago when the starting guard shot himself in the leg during an argument with his girlfriend. I wasn't there and my official and often-repeated stance was "no comment." I couldn't tell you what happened, but if I was forced to base a guess on my predecessor's behavior during practice—whenever he showed up—I would assume that his temper was somehow associated with the event. The bottom line was it was my time. Everything came into alignment to give me an opportunity, and I took it. I'm now in the top 10 for nearly every important stat, including scoring, rebounds, and assists. My name is everywhere and the team is on the verge of its first playoff run in franchise history.

"It's like being at a buffet." Bryce rubs his hands together, sweeping his eyes through the throngs of scantily-clad female flesh.

Chris Taber, our other teammate, laughs in agreement. "Yes, yes… whatever you're in the mood for is here, gentlemen."

We're following one of the hostesses to our VIP section, flanked by our security, when Chris stops abruptly and stares at a woman at the bar. He taps Bryce on the chest with the back of his hand, stopping him in his tracks. "Hey, man, isn't that Jules' girl, Mercedes?"

Bryce and I look toward the bar where a woman is sitting in a short floral sundress. She is only illuminated by the lights on the bar, but even from the distance, it's easy to tell she is beautiful. Her hair is pulled back in one of those messy pony tails that women do on purpose. Her long tan legs are crossed and her feet adorned with simple flat sandals. I'm immediately struck by her appearance. There's nothing overtly sexual about her outfit. Nothing about this woman says "Take me home and knock my head against the headboard." She's not destined to become another faceless groupie, but I still want her. I want her more than a fun but forgettable night. This is something I've never even considered before. That's why she's so alluring. I don't just want her; I want her secrets. I want to know why I want her so much.

"Yeah, that's her. Damn, she's the stuff legends are made of." Bryce actually sounds a little awestruck.

Our VIP section gives us a direct line of vision to Mercedes and I have to ask, "What does that mean? What legends?"

Bryce shrugs. "Truthfully, I don't know much about Mercedes. She was on the scene all the time with another chick, Jules, for a while and then she hooked up with Clay Farrell and you never really saw her anymore. Jules was still around and upside down and any other way you wanted her if you could afford her, but Mercedes kind of disappeared."

I don't know why I'm gulping down every detail about this total stranger like it's water in the desert, but I know I need more. "Are you talking about *Clay Farrell*, Clay Farrell, the Ravens quarterback?"

"The one and the same. This is the first time I've seen her out in years."

As he talks, Chris stares at Mercedes with contemplative interest. I don't like it. I have no idea why I don't like it, but I don't.

Chris continues in a thoughtful voice. "Her friend, Jules, was in-your-face sex. Don't get me wrong, though. She was fantasy-level sexy, but Mercedes was something different, something less common, I guess."

Yes, that I can see.

"What happened with her and Clay?" I ask, hoping to distract him.

"They called it quits a couple of years ago. I don't know the story. I just heard they weren't together anymore."

When Chris calls for one of the bottle girls, I make my move before he can do anything to stop me. Chris is a veteran and the way the unspoken hierarchy plays out, the vets get first dibs on women. Truthfully, he doesn't need the logistical advantage. He's got the rugged bad-boy look down to a science and women eat it up. I have a feeling if I wait a minute longer, Chris will claim Mercedes for himself and that's just not how this night is going to end. Not while I'm at the apex of the universe and shit.

One of our two security guards who is accompanying us tonight, follows me to the bar, but before I can reach Mercedes, she begins walking through the crowd toward the exit. I follow her without once looking back at my teammates. The club is crowded; now I'm famous, so getting from one point to the next is not as easy as one might imagine. When I finally make it to the exit, I think I've lost her and my heart does this weird stutter beat. I'm not even sure why I'm chasing this woman. My heart reacting to her potential disappearance is not something I'm able to process at all.

The club is in Georgetown on the waterfront. I burst out onto streets, which are bubbling with the sounds and sights of excited twenty-something night wanderers out for a good time. After walking half a block in a direction I'd chosen, using an extended version of eenie meenie minie moe, I'm on the verge of admitting defeat and returning to the club when I spot her. She's entering a café on Wisconsin Avenue when I catch up to her and realize I have absolutely no plan.

MERCEDES

I have no one to blame but myself. If I hadn't expected anything. I wouldn't be disappointed right now and I know better than to have expectations.

No one came to my college graduation. I fought and clawed for that piece of paper through an avalanche of misfortune that threatened to bury me underneath it. Violation, dead babies, betrayal—I had survived all of it. But if this was a mountain I was climbing, there was nothing at the top but cold air and the task of getting back down.

B.S. in Nursing.

I first clutched my degree in my hand to the sound of the polite applause of strangers. I later walked through crowds of families oozing love and pride and snapping pictures like paparazzi. And there was just me and that piece of paper.

I came out tonight because the thought of going back to an empty house alone felt oppressive. I tucked my cap, gown, and degree into my over-sized handbag and hit the streets. It seemed like a good idea at the time.

The club is the marketplace. You're the goods and the seller. Julesism number 67.

I should have remembered that because tonight I was in no mood to be "the goods." So now, I'm in a café where I can get one of the best

Rueben sandwiches in D.C. with coleslaw and French fries. My current plan is to eat, belch, and add this day to the list of days I'll be sure to forget in the near future. It's a long list.

I'm so focused on my plan that I don't notice the man standing near me right away. What I do notice is the change in light caused by the large shadow looming over me. When I search for the source of the shadow, I'm temporarily stunned. The man standing next to my table holding a bag from the café is Lochlan Rait. I used to be a basketball fanatic, but after the river of blood and hurt, I developed a sports aversion.

Sports aversion aside, you would have to be Helen Keller to live in D.C. and be unaware of Lochlan Rait. Lochlan is more than a break-out superstar athlete, He's California-forest-fire hot. He's not just on the covers of Sports Illustrated and ESPN. He's on the cover of GQ too. And he's standing next to my table with a hesitant smile on his face.

"I'm sorry to bother you, ma'am." *That's right! He's originally from somewhere down south, Texas maybe?*

"I think they may have switched our sandwiches at the counter. I ordered the turkey and guacamole, but I have a Rueben with coleslaw here."

I tilt my head to the side in confusion. "You ordered a turkey and guacamole sandwich?"

He laughs a deep throaty laugh. I don't know why, but his laugh reminds me of mahogany because it's rich, deep, and smooth.

I buried my desire for men three years ago. Apparently, it was a shallow grave because deep in my belly intense *want* is resurrected with the potency of an explosion.

"So, you're going to sit there with my turkey sandwich judging me?" His beautiful slate gray eyes sparkle with amusement. Instead of answering him, I pull the white paper wrapped sandwich out of the bag. It's clearly marked 'TG' which I assume stands for turkey and guacamole.

Lochlan Rait pulls out the chair across from me and awkwardly folds his long legs under the table. I feel my eyes widen slightly. *He's sitting down?* He notices my expression and smiles an even more brilliant white smile. "You took my sandwich so you have to share your table with me."

I start searching through the bag and even bend over to look under the table.

"Uh, did you lose something?"

"No, no, I just... It seemed like you were quoting a rule you-take-my-sandwich-I-take-your-chair rule and I was just trying to find where it was written." I bite my lip to hold back a laugh, a real honest to God laugh. How long has it been since I felt that sensation?

"Touché." He puts my sandwich down on the table and assesses me with his cool gaze and a smirk on his lips.

"Are you going to give me my sandwich now?" I push it across the table to him because really, what else *am* I going to do with it?

"Thank you." He holds his hand out, gesturing for me to fill in the blank with my name.

"Mercedes."

"Mercedes..." He rolls the name off his tongue as if he is savoring the taste of it. Goosebumps break out on my arms. "I'm Lochlan. Thank you for sharing your table with me."

Sitting this close to him is overwhelming. This man cannot be the result of a bunch of random cellular divisions. He wasn't just made; he was sculpted. His face is chiseled with high well-defined cheekbones and a square chin that has a dimple that is only visible when he makes certain faces. There is sandy scruff on his cheeks, chin, and around his mouth that I want to rub against. His hair is short on the sides but a little longer on top with a slight curl. He reminds me of a *better-looking* version of the actor Paul Walker from the *Fast and Furious* franchise. *How is that even possible?* Lochlan is 6 feet and 5 inches of tanned, muscular flesh. He's wearing a plain black Armani T-shirt with light gray writing and plain blue jeans. He looks *edible*. And I'm annoyed by all of this. I came here to wallow in self-pity, not to be *titillated* by a professional athlete no less. *Ugh.* My day just keeps getting worse.

"Do you hate the name Lochlan?"

"What? No. Why do you ask that?"

"Well, I said my name and you just rolled your eyes." He unwraps his sandwich as he talks.

"It's not your name, which, by the way, everyone in the tri-state area would know without you introducing yourself."

He bites into his sandwich and his eyes roll back in his head. "Mmmm, that's so good."

I laugh out loud at his display of pleasure. The laugh sneaks up on me and rips out of my throat without my permission. I try to wrangle it back but it's too late. It's out.

Lochlan raises an eyebrow at me "What? It's really good. So, you know my name?"

I take a bite out of my sandwich. "Everyone knows your name. I rolled my eyes because of who you *are*."

He eyes me speculatively. "Who is that? A son? A brother? A leftie? A former flautist?"

"Wait, you play the flute?"

"I did until the fifth grade. My grandmother liked it. She died and I haven't picked up a flute since."

Why am I having this conversation? Why am I kind of enjoying this conversation?

"I meant a professional athlete."

Lochlan wipes his mouth with his napkin and leans back in his chair. It's hard not to notice the increasing number of people with camera phones out.

"That's because you didn't know any of those other things." He says it gently, but his point is clear and valid. I don't really know him.

"Touché back at you."

"Listen, I would like to keep talking to you, but it's going to get really difficult to do that in the next three minutes." He glances around at the gathering hoard of people whispering and pointing in his direction. "My back-up security just showed up. They can get us out of here. Would you come back to the Ritz with me? I'm staying there while my house is being built."

I'm just getting ready to tell him that I'm not going back to a *hotel* with him when he holds up his hand.

"Hear me out. I know it sounds like I'm asking you to go back to a hotel with me, but I'm not. I mean it is a hotel, but I live there. And for the record, I've brought other women to other hotels, but you would be the first woman to visit me someplace I call home even if it's only temporary. I would rather take you to sit in a park or go somewhere and get drinks or something else in public. Unfortunately, public places have become a little difficult for me to navigate so I'm asking you to come back to my very large suite where we can sit on the balcony and *just talk*. What do you say?"

3

LOCHLAN

I *can't believe she came with me.* Her body had been stiff, eyes
hard, and shoulders back. It'd seemed certain that she was
going to tell me "hell no," and then chastise me for even having
the audacity to ask. But then, something flashed in her eyes and she
just came with me.

The amount of success I've experienced in life has imbued me
with an enhanced sense of confidence. I'm usually sure that I can
handle any situation and come out on top. What I can't accomplish
with effort, I've always achieved with time. I've never failed. But that
look in Mercedes' eyes forces me to experiment with the idea of fail-
ure. She needs something, and I want to be whatever it is, but the
possibility that I'm not is palpable. This is new. God, I know I don't
talk to You often, but please let me have this woman.

Mercedes isn't beautiful. Beautiful is much too common. This
woman is an altar at which men worship. From a distance, her eyes
appear gray, but up close, they're like kaleidoscopes of color with
flecks of green and hazel. She has thick, pink lips, tanned skin the
color of very light honey, and hair that is luxurious even in her ponytail. Something about her features is indefinable. There is something
in the shape of her eyes and her delicate bone structure that would

distinguish her from any woman who was merely beautiful. Her body is something I want to mark to remind anyone who looks at her that I've been here. That's how strong my feelings are about the curves and lines that inspire an immediate physical response from me. Mercedes might have the face of an angel, but her body is something else entirely. She has full breasts and hips that flare out from her waist and long legs that show tone even in her flat sandals. I never knew exactly what I wanted in a woman until tonight. Before my criteria was just "pretty" or "sexy." But now, Mercedes will always be the standard.

"Are you chilly? I can get a blanket for us?"

It's May in D.C., but the weather is unpredictable this time of year and there's a breeze coming in off the water bordering the hotel. Mercedes is sitting on the patio of my hotel room with her legs stretched out on one of the chaise lounges. She took her hair out of the ponytail so it's now falling around her shoulders in gold and light brown waves. I tracked every movement of her fingers, every flip of her neck as she shook her hair loose.

"No, I'm fine. The breeze feels good." She seems shy now that she is here with me.

"So, what are you doing wandering the streets alone?"

She flinches at the word "alone." "I was just looking for something to eat."

"I have a confession to make."

"If you used to be a woman or have a urine fetish, I'm out of here. Fair warning."

"*What?* Has that happened to you before?"

"Yes."

"Which one?"

"Both."

"The same person?"

She laughs. It's a beautiful sound followed by that same shocked expression as if she wasn't expecting her own reaction. "No. Not the same person. That would've been something, though."

"Well okay, and no, neither of those was my confession. I was going to tell you that I saw you earlier at Vis and I followed you to the sandwich shop."

She tilts her head to the side and considers me carefully before speaking. "If you're some crazy psycho stalker, you should know that there are probably hundreds of pics and videos of us online already. If I come up missing, everyone will know where to look first."

I laugh at that. "Making you disappear is the last thing I want. I tried to get your attention in the club, but you were moving pretty fast so I followed you."

"Why?"

"Why what?"

"Why did you follow me?"

"I had to."

She gives me that considering stare again, and then nods as if my vague explanation was sufficient. "I had a rough day. I thought having a couple of drinks might help me to put things in perspective."

I want to reach out and touch her. I want to rub the back of my hand over her cheek and promise that her rough days are over. In the interest of not completely creeping her out, I remain in my seat.

"Tell me about it."

She raises her eyebrows at me and swings her legs over the chaise so she's facing me.

"You want to hear about my day?"

"Yes."

She's quiet for a long time; so long I think she's not going to answer. But then, she does.

"I graduated today, from college, nursing school to be exact."

I blink at her. That wasn't at all what I was expecting her to say. "Well, that's wonderful. Congratulations. Wait, did your uncle show up drunk? Or your parents got lost trying to find a place to park and missed the ceremony?"

She looks sad and amused at the same time. "Does that really happen?"

"Yes. It happened at my college graduation. My uncle passed out during the national anthem."

She smiles, but it's a pained smile. "Well that didn't happen to me. No uncle and no parents so that would've been a stretch."

"Are your parents alive?"

"I don't know about my father. I don't know who he is at all, but my mother is alive."

"But she didn't come to your graduation?"

She looks down at her hands. "No. Nobody came. I graduated *summa cum laude* and nobody was there."

And just like that, the sadness and pain in her expression make perfect sense.

MERCEDES

I have no idea why I told him all that. I'm a tragedy but I don't want *him* to know that. Jules would die if she knew I was sitting here with a wealthy athlete being pitiful. But Lochlan doesn't seem like he's either judging or pitying me.

"You deserve to be celebrated."

I shrug. "Maybe I don't. For all you know, I'm a total bitch."

He smiles gently and moves in closer to me. He smells spicy and sweet. Yearning washes over me and shocks the hell out of me all at the same time.

"Are you a total bitch?"

Before I can answer he waves his hand. "It doesn't matter if you are. Even a total bitch who graduates *summa cum laude* deserves to be celebrated."

That was sweet.

"What we need is a do-over." He jumps up from his chair as if he just thought of a really great idea. "We have to find you a cap and gown. I'm going to call the concierge."

There it is again—*laughter*.

"The concierge will *not* just have a cap and gown sitting around."

He seems to be looking for the phone and doesn't look up when he chides me.

"Don't be negative. Just help me find the phone."

I'm stuck in place. He is just... I don't know. He's kind of wonderful. I think. "I have my cap and gown in my bag and my degree is too. Everything is in my bag."

Lochlan stops searching and turns around slowly to face me with a smile that is spreading quickly. "Well, why didn't you say so, Mercy."

"*Mercy?*"

"Yes."

I furrow my brows and narrow my eyes. "Nobody calls me that."

"Good. I want to be the only one."

"Why?"

"Because I'm possessive."

"No, but we can come back to that later. Why do you want to call me Mercy?"

His gray eyes penetrate me. "When I saw you in the café, I thought to myself that if God was merciful, he would give you to me."

He could be telling me that it looks like rain outside. Although they are casual, the impact of his words is ocean-deep.

I know who I am, what I am. I'm sexy, pretty, and tempting, even "fuckable." But I'm nobody's prayer. And I'm sure as hell not the answer to one. I'm angry. I've been through a lot in 22 years, but it was *honest* trouble. It was the shit anybody would've guessed would happen to someone like me. I'm wiser now. I know what to expect. The last thing I need is someone messing with my certainty because at least when I know what to expect it's safe.

My glare is intense. "You don't know me, Lochlan."

"It's just Loch. I know I don't know you, but what I want is the chance to know you."

The glare doesn't seem to be effective.

"Cap and gown, Mercy." He's standing in front of me now. "Please." It's not a supplication the way he says it but it's a concession.

My body is stiff, the frown frozen on my face, but my feet are moving. The balcony is more like a deck in shades of white and blue with a hearth in the middle. You could have an entire party out here. I stand next to my bag where my cap and gown are housed and I look out at the water.

I shouldn't do this. I don't need this. I should leave.

LOCHLAN

Mercedes is upset and I'm not sure why. When she digs in her bag and begins to put on her gown, I realize that I had been holding my breath. When I see that she's not going to bolt—a distinct possibility a minute ago—I relax and breathe. As she puts on her gown, I aim for a neutral topic of discussion.

"So, which school did you graduate from?"

She looks up as she zips the black gown and takes out a gold overlay. "I graduated from Johns Hopkins."

I do a double take. "Isn't that one of the best nursing schools in the country?"

She nods. Why did nobody come see this beautiful girl graduate at the top of her class from such a prestigious program?

"Do you live in D.C.?"

Mercedes is digging for her cap now. "Yeah, I live here."

"But you commuted to Baltimore for school?"

"I owned a place here. I couldn't afford to rent something else in Baltimore. So yeah, I did the reverse-commute thing. It was...well... It was awful, if I'm being honest." She finally secures her cap to her head. Even in the nondescript commencement attire, she is stunning. The black gown brings out the multitude of colors in her eyes.

"Okay, so now that I feel super awkward, what's next?" She has the prettiest blush I've ever seen but I want to put her at ease.

I take out my phone. "Now, you walk."

A rendition of "Pomp and Circumstance" I just downloaded blares from the phone. My role is that of the audience so I stand off to the side. For a moment, Mercedes doesn't move. Her eyes are wide. Her beautiful pink lips are slightly parted and she seems rooted to the ground, so I cheer her on from the invisible audience.

"There she is! There she is! *Mercedes*, over here!" I wave frantically as if I'm in a crowd trying to get her attention during a graduation procession. She looks at me and blinks. It seems to jolt her out of her temporary paralysis. She starts moving towards me, walking along the long deck.

"Whewww, that's our girl. Mercedes! Way to go, Mercedes! Whewwwwww."

Most people don't know this about me, but I was in the high school drama club and I was good. Before high school, I was in several commercials as a child. My mother claims she knew I could act from the time I was just a year old. According to Sophia Rait, I once pretended to be asleep when she came to get me out of the bed because I preferred my father. That sealed the deal in her mind. Plus, she was hoping to be a pageant mom and wound up with two boys and a mandatory hysterectomy. She made the most of the situation by dragging us both into acting and modeling as soon and as often as she could. When we reached puberty and rebelled, Sophia, never one to be bested, up and adopted our little sister, Ashley. The lone daughter made far worse pageant material than Conner and I, but my parents were head-over-heels in love with the child, so it didn't matter.

Standing here on this breezy May evening, I draw on all my acting skills to give Mercedes the Lochlan graduation experience, which I'd just created. She seems to be picking up on the program because she smiles. The smile is hesitant, but it's there. Pointing towards a chair for Mercedes to sit in, I pick up a hoodie from the deck, my signal that I'm changing characters. I give a commencement address.

"This is not the end but the beginning."

Mercedes rolls her lips inward and presses them together, suppressing her laughter. Dimples, otherwise hidden, stand out in her cheeks from her expression. That stutter in my chest is back.

"Blah, blah, blah, the future belongs to you, blah blah blah, you now have everything you need to succeed, blah blah... We will now award the degrees for Bachelors of Science." I glance at Mercedes for confirmation. Her whole body is shaking with silent laughter, but she nods in agreement. "Yes, as I was saying, the degrees for Bachelors of Science in Nursing." I reach for the closest object that can function as a degree; it's a banana in the nearby fruit basket.

"Mercedes..." I don't even know her last name.

She is gasping for breath through giggles and barely gets out her last name. "It's James," she finally manages.

"Mercedes James."

She walks toward me. I jump to the side and yank off the sweater so I can double as the cheering crowd now. When Mercedes gets to where I am, I quickly jump back and put the sweater back on so I can hand her the banana slash degree. Now, I'm laughing too because this is ridiculous. Mercedes can barely stand because she's laughing so hard. When I reach out to hand her the banana, she starts waving her hands in front of her.

"No more! Oh my God, no more! You are crazy!"

4

MERCEDES

There are tears in my eyes. I haven't laughed this hard in... *forever*. If you have never had a professional basketball player pretend to be a graduation speaker, the conferrer of the degrees, and the cheering crowd all at once, you haven't really lived.

Lochlan tries to remain serious while extending the banana degree to me, but not even he can manage that feat. He is shaking with what I imagine are repressed guffaws. I hold on to his arm for support and double over at the waist. And then it happens. Everything I've pent up behind a tenuous emotional dam burst through, and I ugly cry. I blubber and wail and lose my shit right in front of this perfect specimen of a man who also happens to be kind of a stranger. I don't know how he reacts, but I feel him lift me into his arms. I'm a tangle of my polyester robe, hurt, anger and mortarboard.

"Shh, shhh, it's all right now."

He's beautiful and a liar. Nothing has been all right for me in a very long time.

"I'm so sorry." I bury my head in his chest while apologizing. I'm embarrassed and I don't want him to see my face, but I also feel safe wrapped in his arms. He smells clean and spicy and like refuge. He murmurs words of comfort in my ear. Strong fingers stroke through my hair rubbing my scalp, soothing. Somewhere in my meltdown I became cradled in his lap on one of the deck chairs.

It's a second. A butterfly wing flutter measure of time and everything is different. The intensity of my grief transforms and what is left is equal in intensity but altogether different in focus. I'm aware of the muscles underneath my head, the feel of the skin on Lochlan's arms and his lips. Yes, his lips because he's showering kisses on my head and my eyes. I tilt my head up slowly until I'm looking at him. And it's there: stark, raw desire, and a question, a silent plea for permission. He cups my face in his hands. His expression doesn't waver. I lean closer until our lips brush.

I started it, but Lochlan finishes it. The kiss is sweet and then soothing and then something else.

The robe comes off, my dress, his shirt, jeans, shoes, boxer briefs, and the special lace under garments I never thought anyone would see.

I don't expect to enjoy sex. My experience with the act has not been about pleasure. It was always about utility, a means to an end. Shedding my clothes tonight isn't propelled by an eagerness to engage in the act that follows. The only thing I'm thinking about is comfort and escape. I'm caught off guard by the tingle that runs down my spine and between my legs when Lochlan traces one finger across my collar bone. His touch isn't the only thing that opens the door to the thought of pleasure. It's his eyes. Lochlan's eyes track the movement of his fingers across my skin and it feels like another touch. I've always felt like a receptacle during sex, somewhere for a man to deposit his lust and fulfill his needs. This is not that.

Lochlan is studying me. When his hands move and my back arches, he responds. More pressure, the rubbing pad of thumbs and a twist of fingers that dances on the line between pleasure and pain. My moan is guttural, new even to my own ears. He notices and his lips meet mine. He's drinking in my sounds like some rare wine he doesn't want to waste. He's impatient with the limitations of his hands and eyes. When his mouth follows their path, I squeeze my eyes shut.

"Look at me." His voice is rough, unyielding even. It's not a request.

My eyes open immediately. Every part of me opens at his command.

"You are here with me, Mercy. Nothing else matters. And you're going to look now so that when you do close your eyes, this image of me over you and under you is what you see."

I've never had an orgasm with a man. I thought women who said it was possible were telling indulgent lies. But for the first time, I think maybe there's truth in the rumors of pleasure. The pulsing between my thighs escalates to a throb and even though my eyes are now dry, that part of me weeps shamelessly. Lochlan takes it all, fingers plunging, mouth stroking. When it's too much, my body gives up all the tension and sadness, everything just uncoils and explodes outward. The scream comes from me, but I don't know this sound. This is my first encounter with it.

Lochlan growls in his throat and rises to his feet. I haven't known him for 24 hours, but I recognize the look of his control snapping. He must wait because now I drop to my knees. It's my hands that praise, my mouth that worships, and Lochlan and I collide. We merge in the place where time ends. The slick sound of our bodies is a rhythm punctuated by the beat of our fervent voices. I've had dreams, I've lived nightmares, but I never imagined this.

Right there on that deck, we learn each other's secrets and I am bound to him in a way that I don't have the language to understand. Later in the living room, then the bedroom and then the shower, Lochlan possesses and takes. He marks me and I give myself to him over and over again. There is no pain or abandonment here. I am exalted, cared for, and eventually sated.

I know better. I knew better. But I was broken and alone and I just wanted one night of relief, just one night. But it was so good and so deep that when Lochlan looked in my eyes the next morning and told me that one night wasn't enough for him, I agreed with him. I believed him.

MERCEDES

The smell of cinnamon will always remind me of optimism and dread. Cinnamon is the first thing I smell when I walk into my favorite coffee and sweets shop a few minutes from my townhouse. Mr. and Mrs. Edmunds are both behind the counter doing what they do best, arguing.

"You ate my vegetables and turned up the thermostat. Don't bother to lie about it, Anne. I woke up in the middle of the night drenched in sweat and I'm backed up because you ate all the broccoli I bought."

"Franklin, you just look for stuff to complain about. You ate the broccoli last week, I told you to go buy some more. And you were sweating last night because you came to bed in those big gym socks. I keep telling you to take off the socks before you get in bed."

The entire time they talk, Anne and Franklin Edmunds are in constant motion, plating and packaging sweets, filling up the coffee machines and checking orders. I'm the only customer during this off-time but I've never seen either of the two shop owners standing still.

"Well, well, well, Franklin, look who we have here, it's Ms. I'm staying away because I'm not eating carbs." Anne, the short Korean owner who has been contributing to my need to work out for years, teases me about my latest attempt to free myself from the sugar cocaine she and her husband are peddling. When I giggle at the teasing, Anne almost drops the batch of cinnamon rolls she's holding on a cooling pan. Franklin spins around to face me so fast the liquid in the coffee pot he's holding sloshes over the top. For a few seconds, the only sound in the shop is the coffee machine's buzz and a jazz version of *My Favorite Things* playing through the shop speakers.

"Lord Jesus, the rapture is coming." Franklin gently places the coffee pot on the counter that runs the length of the shop as if he doesn't trust his hold on it.

Anne wipes her hands on the apron at her waist. "I don't think it's the rapture, Franklin, I think this young lady is in love."

I feel my jaw fall open. Love? I don't even know what that means. It's been less than an hour since I left Lochlan. The departure was delayed by the slide of his lips against mine and the demand for 'just a little more.'

"Mercy, tell me you don't want more." It's a dare and he knows I can't do it. Even if I tried, a denial would be hollow while my body is spread open before him. His eyes are fixed on the part of me that is liquid for him. Lochlan licks his lips.

"Tell me."

"I want more." The truth falls from my mouth even as my hips surge up to meet his.

Lochlan refused to be appeased by anything less than my promise to see him again and even that wasn't enough. We agreed that he'll come pick me up when he gets back from his road-trip today. He's ambitious enough to think we can find some place to be out in public where he won't be recognized. Maybe we're going to Alaska.

When I looked at myself in the mirror before leaving his suite, I half expected to look different. Hours earlier I was jagged edges and open wounds. I had the sensation of being softer, of having a healed heart that beat with more certainty. I physically walked away from him but the current of him still buzzes through my system making my steps lighter.

While I suffocated on the smell of patchouli oil in the backseat of the taxi on my way home, I reminded myself of reality.

It was one night. Don't be a silly hoe. The only thing worse than a silly hoe is a broke hoe and you'll be both if you're a silly hoe first. Yeah, he wants to spend more time with you, what do you expect after the things you did to him? He's just a guy doing what all guys do. Have some fun but don't twist yourself in knots thinking this is something else or that you're something else.

The lecture broadcast itself in Jules' voice, reminding me to be smart. The Edmunds expectant smiles give me the sense that I'm failing. I'm letting myself get carried away like a dumb teenager. I'm a grown woman now, I know better.

"It's definitely not love. I don't think they still make anything like what the two of you have." I shrug and hope to feel the indifference I portray.

Franklin looks at his wife standing behind the counter a few feet from him. I see that thing they exchange often, without words. On the rare occasions on which Franklin and Anne aren't arguing, the tenderness between them is palpable. It makes me ache with emotion I can't identify. It's just, I don't think anyone will ever look at me like that.

"I'm not so sure, Mercedes." Franklin returns from his moment with Anne with a speculative look pointed in my direction. "I remember when Anne started carrying that look you got in your eyes now. That look is the stuff of dreams. It means anything is possible. So maybe there is still love to be found out there." The older black man has a gentle grandfatherly way about him even though he's often gruff and yelling orders.

Anne walks over to Franklin and places her hand on his arm as he talks. It's as if they share this moment no matter who speaks. "Franklin is right. If someone put that look on your face and made you laugh, it's worth holding on to, maybe forever."

"You guys are the best, that's why I keep coming in here and letting you fatten me up. But the rest of it...I just don't know." Another of Jules' lessons bounces around in my head:

"There's no such thing as love at first sight. There's dick at first sight, but not love. Don't forget that."

Franklin nods but the sympathetic look on his face when he picks up the coffee pot again makes me uncomfortable. Am I missing something? I'm just trying to be smart, for once.

Anne wraps up a cinnamon roll without me asking. She knows why I'm here. "Just remember something, you can't overreact to meeting the one. There's no such thing. Let yourself learn to smile and laugh. You're too young to be so serious all the time." Anne brings the cinnamon roll around the counter and stands in front of me with the bag held out. When I take it, she surprises me by holding my face in her small hands.

"Be happy, Mercedes."

My response is a nod and a smile that feels sad on my face. Even though I think I'm overreacting to my one night with Lochlan, I can't block the part of me that wants what the Edmunds are talking about. The seed of hope has been planted and despite my best effort, it grows by the minute.

5

MERCEDES - 6 MONTHS LATER

My house can't be more than ten minutes from the Ritz Carlton but sitting in my living room six months after my one night with Lochlan Rait, I'm a lifetime away from that night. The me that dared to hope for more than every single thing I've ever known has been shoved back into the closet she had the nerve to pop out of. Hope died somewhere in the silence of the past three months.

The memory of my last day being hopeful is like an old photograph I've been keeping for nostalgia sake.

The mini dress emphasizes the curves that got me this second date. If a man who makes seven-figures wants to take you out, you need to look like a seven-figure date. The full-length mirror in my bedroom says I do. The buzzing of my cell phone on the night-stand ends my self-inspection. It's August and I can only imagine what he's gotten himself into now.

"Hey, August, are you back?"

"Oh thank God you picked up, Mercury. I'm stuck in Portland at the airport. I've been stuck with this family for almost 24 hours. They have five kids, who has five kids in the 21ˢᵗ Century? One of the kids has something wrong with her. I don't think it's medical or anything but the little girl is not right."

As bizarre as it might seem to an outside observer, this is a pretty stan-dard conversation with August. He's in a random location, there are other unexplained people also in the location and he's providing non-medical diagnosis of other folks. Check, check and check, at least I know his phone hasn't been stolen.

"August, I have so very many questions about absolutely everything you just said but I need to do my makeup, I'm going out."

"You're doing what now?" His question is followed by a lot of shuffling noises and someone screaming for crackers so loudly, I have to hold the phone away from my ear for a second.

"I'm going out on kind of a date."

"Kind of a date? You are going out of the house in makeup on kind of a date? Is it fucking Armageddon? I knew I should not have taken that edible yesterday." August's voice ends on a pitch so high that this time, I decide to just turn the volume down on the phone.

"You're the second person to ask me was the world ending today. Calm down, it's not that serious. I just met someone last night and we're hooking up again."

"You haven't been out of the house for anything other than school or work in the past four years unless I drag you out with my crew. Even then you act like you have to be home in time for curfew and since it's already after eleven, you're past your normal bed-time."

"I know, I know but it's not that serious. I'm just celebrating my graduation."

"You're supposed to be celebrating your graduation with me when I get back tomorrow but we can come back to that later. Who are you going out with? First and last name please so I can do a full social media work-up and tell you whether you're dealing with some Craig's List psycho." August pauses before yelling "those are my chips, where are your parents? I do fight kids."

"August he's not a psycho unless that shit is way on the low. It's Lochlan Rait, the basketball player." My announcement is met by the sound of August choking on something.

"Wait, wait, wait, you're going out with Lochlan Rait?"

"Yes, that's what I said."

"But wasn't he just in some terrible car accident?"

"I don't think so. I just saw him some hours ago."

"No, no, Mercury, when I say just in a car accident, I mean like just now. He's trending on Twitter along with hashtag pray for Loch."

"What? What are you talking about?"

"I know you don't use any of your social media accounts but Google him right now. I'm looking, there are tons of news alerts popping up. He was in a serious roll-over accident like two hours ago. He was trapped in his car."

For some reason, I glance over at the half eaten cinnamon roll sitting on my night stand next to my phone charger. It's weird but I feel like the eaten half is all the good that I get. I haven't even looked yet, but the churning dread in my stomach tells me two things. Something bad has happened to Lochlan. Second, I lied to myself about everything. Lochlan isn't just another guy and it definitely is that serious. He was everything I dreamed about in secret and I don't want to lose him before I even have a chance to have him.

That was three months ago. At the time, I wanted to go to the hospital, but it seemed ridiculous. What was I going to say? I spent one night getting my brains banged out by this guy, I may have stupidly fallen in love with him, even though I don't even know what love is and now I need to see him? Seemed inappropriate. But I can't worry about silly things like decorum anymore, I *need* to talk to Lochlan.

The phone number is disconnected.

The emails are all returned as undeliverable.

His Twitter account is shut down and his Facebook privacy settings don't allow incoming messages from non-friends. Like me.

I tried sending a letter to the Ritz. It was returned. He moved out.

He's been out of the hospital for three months, but I have no way of reaching him. Correction. I have no way of reaching him that doesn't involve overt stalking and the risk of arrest, a risk I'm presently unwilling to take.

I finally break down and call in reinforcements—*Jules.* She answers on the fourth ring.

"Mercedes?"

"Hey, Ju, I need a favor." She sighs deeply. She hates it when I call her Ju. That's why I do it. Considering I'm the one who needs a favor, I should probably turn down the petty a notch.

"You know I'm in the D.R. right now?"

"You're where?"

"In the Dominican Republic."

"What the hell are you doing there? You on vacation with what's his face?"

"Mercedes, stop acting like you don't know his name."

I do know his name, but what difference does it make? He won't be around long enough to make learning his name worthwhile. The only reason I even know it is because he's a famous music producer.

"And no, he's not here." Jules says something else, but I can't hear her because she's suddenly whispering.

"Why are you whispering? I can barely hear you." And why am I now whispering? Why is whispering contagious?

Jules raises her voice enough that I can hear her say, "I'm getting some extra fat injected in my ass."

For just a moment, I'm tempted to ask about this. Jules has or rather had a perfect ass. I have no idea why she feels the need to mess with, it but I quickly decide I don't *want* to know. And if I ask, Jules will tell me. I don't have time for what is sure to be a very long, ridiculous explanation.

"Jules, I need a name and phone number."

Jules pauses for a long time. I can sense her shock from thousands of miles away. I never ask her for anything.

"Okaaaaaay, whose name and number do you need?"

I take a deep breath and do what I have to do. "I need the number for Lochlan Rait's manager."

"Lochlan Rait, the basketball player?"

I knew this was coming "Yes."

Jules huffs and I imagine her rolling her eyes. "Mercedes, he's fine, there's no denying that but why now? He's all mangled and shit after that car accident. You don't want someone whose career is going up in smoke. You can do better. Oh, I know! Trent Marx is single, hot, and I hear he really wants to settle down. He's perfect for you."

I breathe deeply. This is why Jules was my last resort. I *so* don't want to deal with Jules' trading-up life doctrine.

"Jules, please, I just need this one thing." I'm desperate and it must show because Jules suddenly relents without listing any more options for me.

"Okay, Mercedes, let me see what I can do."

"Thank you." I can't help how relieved I sound. I am. I know Jules only said she will "try." But Jules *always* gets her man. She'll be able to get me that name and number or the shit doesn't exist.

IT DIDN'T EVEN TAKE Jules 24 hours to find the name and number I was looking for. That turned out to be a blessing and a curse. Deep down inside in a place I would never admit existed, I thought if I could just find a way to reach Lochlan after the accident, we could pick up where we left off. The connection between us seemed so strong and I thought for sure he felt it too. I was wrong. I became the very thing Jules always warned me about.

I talked to his manager. When he figured out who I was and what I wanted, he said he would give Lochlan the message. It took one week for Paul Rutland, III to call me back.

The day before Paul Rutland, IIIcalled, I sat in my living room waiting for August to return from his second ice-cream run. I asked him to get me Ben & Jerry's grasshopper pie ice cream. He came back with Safeco mint chocolate chip. When I burst into tears, he backed away from me like I was scared animal he didn't want to spook. I knew I was being crazy but I really needed that ice cream.

I awkwardly sprawled out on a bunch of pillows we arranged on the living room floor. For some reason, the couch, which I loved up until a month ago, makes my lower back scream in pain. The pillow fort on the floor is the best August and I could come up with. While waiting for my correct ice cream, I turned on entertainment news.

The lead story was about the "gorgeous Lochlan Rait" who is rumored to have reconnected with his hometown high school sweetheart, Rachel Lawton. Lochlan returned home to Texas to recover from his last surgery and Rachel has been by his side for weeks. "A source close to the couple" reports that being away from the limelight and the league has helped Lochlan put things in perspective and he now appreciates what he had with Rachel. Blond, willowy Rachel who looks like she stepped out of a Banana Republic catalogue.

When Paul Rutland, III calls the next day, I'm already numb, his callous words bounce off of my emotionless shell.

Fantasy is a luxury that women like Rachel Lawton get to engage in. I live in the real ass world and that's not something that I'll ever forget again. The nostalgic memories get burned in the fire of my determination to move on. I didn't believe in love and it didn't believe in me either.

6

ASHLEY –2 YEARS LATER

I know I had a bag of cherry Jolly Ranchers somewhere in my desk. I'm rummaging through office supplies and miscellaneous papers, but my cherry heaven eludes me. I really need sugar for what I'm about to do. Who am I kidding? I really need sugar for everything.

I wasn't there when my brothers were little. They are six and eight years older than I am, but I saw their baby pictures and pictures from when they were little boys. The face staring up at me from the photograph attached to the application file, it could be my brother. The little boy is wearing a white polo shirt and khaki shorts. By pure coincidence, Mama has a picture of my brothers in identical outfits.

It's not just the picture. I met the adorable little boy today during site interviews. Even at one and a half, he looks exactly like a cute baby version of my big brother.

I don't know what to do so I snap a picture of the picture, text it and wait.

My phone rings. "Hi, Mama."

"Hi, baby girl. How is your job at the school going and where did you find that picture of your brother?"

I knew it. Now, what do I do?

7

LOCHLAN

I had a favorite pair of basketball shoes in college. They got soft and creased. That might make a pair of shoes more comfortable to a non-athlete, but for an athlete, it's the kiss of death. The shoes don't support agility and movement, and they increase the risk of injury. When shoes are that broken in, it's time to get rid of them. That's my relationship with Rachel. I know it and she knows I know it. We've had "the talk" and then we had "the talk" about "the talk." Apparently, there aren't words in the English language sufficient to express "it's over."

Obligation. That's a word we all understand. It's what happens when a woman stands by your side after your leg is shattered. You can't just walk away from that woman, not literally or figuratively.

Post-accident, faithful Rachel was sainted in my mind and in the minds of my family members. Post-accident Rachel was consistent and committed. Post-accident Rachel let me go through my mood swings and didn't complain. Post-accident Rachel was okay with the prospect that I would not return to the NBA. But Post-post-accident Rachel? I think she understands obligation more than she gets credit for.

This is a new thought. I first tasted it when Rachel seemed unable to accept the talk. It was just a hint of something. But now, it's sprin-kled on everything. I'm rapidly developing an aversion to it.

"Loch, don't you think the party is going to be fun?"

Rachel's voice brings me back to the present. "My bank account says it better be fun."

"You're so cute." Hair toss. Giggle. Soft and creased. I can't move in this. And I've always hated her calling me cute.

Rachel gives me a contemplating look. "Listen I know you weren't planning on going to the party with me. I get it. But your family expects us to be there together. And I don't want to disappoint them."

Wide hazel eyes full of innocence look at me expectantly. Obliga-tion. I used to think it was a coincidence. Now, I suspect it's a tool. Not a hammer. It's more like a lock pick. It's small and subtle but effective. Rachel might be a thief.

"Let's go in." I shove the suspicion aside and ignore what I now see as possible manipulation. I open Rachel's door. She's quick to link her arm with mine for the family, you know. We walk into the club together. The party is some sort of bubble theme, I think. I don't know, but there are a lot of bubbles in here. Rachel is talking. I tune her out and scan the upbeat partyers for my sister.

My eyes pass over the crowd. My brain doesn't register anything but my body must. My heart speeds up. Everything else slows down.

If this were a movie, this part would play in slow motion. There would be a song. It would be the teen vampire movie song about a thousand years. Ashley had the flu. I took care of her. She made me watch that movie about a thousand times. So, yes, I know that song and it should definitely be playing right now. But this isn't a movie. It's real life and there's no dramatic cinematographic preamble. I just look up and to the left and there she is.

Her hair is longer than I remember and darker. Her body is wrapped in a fitted black one-piece with a deep V in between her breasts. I'm envious of the fabric. I remember everything instantly, and I ache in a place that didn't even exist until right now. The taste of her, the scent. I remember her flesh heating while I watched the moisture I would lap up with lazy strokes of my tongue. She writhed, she begged, and I took my time. She made me desperate to own her and I punished her for inflicting that kind of want on me. I punished her until she shook and moaned my name over and over.

And now, two years later, here she is just like that. She's holding a drink and smiling at the two men in front her.

Mercy.

MERCEDES

'They need you more than you need them.' *Julesism Number12.*

Pathetic. I'm out of the house at an actual social event. I'm wearing an outfit that I chose for myself and it doesn't include yoga pants or gym shoes. This is my chance to mix it up with some people who were born in the same decade as me. But I'm so out of practice, I've fallen back on a list of Jules' rules. It's like a nervous tic.

When Ashley invited me to this party, I had an automatic response: "uh, yeah, no." It originated from a long list of reasons why I'm mostly a hermit these days. Hermitting is underrated. But, Ashley is persuasive and maybe also a little hard of hearing. And for the first time in my life, I want to make a friend. So, here I am.

A tangle of jet black curls and an apple-shaped ass. That was my first impression of Ashley. She was bent over a bag in the intellectual enhancement center. That's what rich people call classrooms. It's possible rich people make money just by being wordy. When Ashley popped up from the bag, I really thought she would come out with buried treasure. At the minimum, I had expected a Chanel bag. Instead, she rose triumphantly clutching a Tootsie Pop. She gave a victorious grunt and I knew I liked her. Any chick who works that hard for a sugar fix is my kind of woman.

Ashley finally notices Liam and I standing in the doorway when Liam exclaims "Lolli!" Then he points at the sucker in her hand. Ashley narrows her eyes at my precious baby. She looks like she's ready to fight for that sucker. I don't know what I should feel. I never know what the appropriate parenting response is. But to me, this is hilarious. Liam agrees, he clutches his tummy and starts laughing. Ashley joins in.

"Oh my God, I need to get some help."

"What like rehab?" I gasp between ripples of laughter "Why? Just because you want to fight a one-year-old for a sucker."

"Lolli," Liam happily corrects me.

"Yes. Yes. This is exactly why people seek professional help. Me, I am people and I need help," she says, pointing at herself

We pull ourselves together. "I'm Ms. Ashley, are you Ms. Dean?"

I nod in the affirmative and point at my son. "Yes and this is Liam Dean."

Ashley puts on her glasses and gets down on Liam's level to greet him. A weird thing happens. She looks shocked for a moment. If this were a Life-time movie, this would be the moment someone recognizes the kidnapped child. Twenty-three hours of labor says this is not a Sunday-afternoon flick. This kid is 100 percent mine.

"Well, Liam, it's so nice to meet you." She seems to recover.

"Nice lolli." Liam gives a pretty standard 18-month-old greeting and grins enthusiastically.

It turns out, Ashley has a sugar addiction. I have a sugar addiction. The relationship was destined to bloom. Maybe Liam felt it too. I think he's the most extraordinary child in the universe, but he's mine. I don't know what explains the instant bond between Ashley and Liam. During the ridiculous pre-K intellectual capacity assessment, they spoke in their own language to one another. Ashley administered the test, but her interaction with Liam was familiar and warm. Liam responded in kind.

I have learned that my son is an excellent judge of character. For that reason, anyone who Liam loves, I love. So, when I did follow up second round interviews with Ashley, the conversation flowed easily.

Eventually, she invited me to her birthday party. So, here I am at Ashley Jenner's shindig.

Here's the funny thing, after years of pretending to be older, I find it difficult to act like a normal 24-year-old. I'd had all the life experiences of someone this age a decade ago and now I'm a single mother. I can barely remember the lean-in-to-giggle rotation and I really want to call August and check on Liam. But life is more than just potty training and working and it's time for me to live again. I have goals now. I will go somewhere frequented by adults at least every other week and if the opportunity presents itself, I'm going on a damn date. I'm 24, not 54. I've had a bad run of it, but it's time to give life a chance again.

This seems like a safe space to reintroduce myself to life. And the two guys I'm talking to, with their solicitous smiles and friendly conversation, are good space fillers. Chuck and Jason are their names. I can't remember which one is which. But maybe I don't need to remember. Both are extremely good-looking and either would fit in my single-mom-life starter kit.

"So, I wind up running down the street buck-naked with my ice cream cone in my hand." Chuck or Jason finishes what was a truly a hilarious story about the summer he slept with his boss' daughter when he was a young intern. It seems like my effortless laughs belong exclusively to my son, but I still find something that can pass for a laugh.

"What about you, Mercedes?" Chuck or Jason turns sparkling, dark eyes on me. He really is handsome. He reminds me of Ashton Kutcher. "Do you have any naked ice cream stories?"

"Damn, I wish I did. I feel like I haven't even lived now."

"Stick with me. We'll make sure you have stories to tell random strangers at parties." His conspiratorial party whisper is perfect. I would bet good money he always gets his girl.

The other Chuck slash Jason looks slightly annoyed that he is being quickly edged out of the running for whatever they think they're competing for. "Let's start out with something less challenging. How about a bubble dance?" He gestures to the dance floor, which is starting to fill up.

I stall. I haven't danced with anyone in public for a long time and I don't have good memories of the last time I did. "You go for it. I'm going to find the birthday girl before the night goes off the rails. I'll find you on the dance floor later."

"Okay, but hurry back. These party stories don't write themselves. We gotta make memories."

If I'm capable of pulling off a fun and casual dating version of myself, the Ashton look-alike is where I could see myself starting.

LOCHLAN

Mercedes is here and she's laughing. She's laughing with someone who isn't me.

"Loch!" Rachel raises her voice slightly, which is my first clue that she's been trying to get my attention. "Who is that?" Rachel gestures towards Mercy who is glowing like the sun. Rachel aims for nonchalance. Her tone lands between whiny and petulant.

"Who is who?" Deflect. Deny.

"The woman who you have been staring at for like ten minutes." The tone meter ticks precariously closer to petulant. Ashley walks over with a drink in her hand interrupting the beginning of my second deflection. It works. The only thing better than a deflection is an actual distraction.

"Happy birthday, little sister."

Ashley beams at me. She's 23 years old, but she will always be my baby sister.

"Thank you, thank you, thank you," Ashley nearly sings the words. She's known to do that. "Don't you love the party?" she asks, sweeping her arm out over the elaborate setup.

The popular waterfront club is draped in white lights. Servers weave through throngs of people with champagne and hors d'oeurves. A live band is playing now, but a famous deejay will take over to end the night. No expense has been spared. I know that because I'm the one who did not spare the expense.

"The party is worthy of you." I smile at her, but my eyes are no longer complying with my plans. They wander right back to the spot where I saw Mercy.

Ashley and Rachel are speaking to each other. I don't hear them. Everything in my mind and my body is locked on Mercedes and it's like I just woke up. I was in a coma for eight days. I remember the first time I blinked my eyes open and the memory of that does not compare to this. All of my senses come alive. I can see better and hear better. The drink in my cup has a more distinct flavor. I can feel my clothes on my skin. It sounds crazy, but it's like I just woke up again but for real this time.

"Loch?"

Rachel and Ashley are looking at me. I use all of my strength to force my head to turn towards my sister and Rachel, and away from Mercedes. Rachel is bordering on extremely pissed. That barely registers. But the look on Ashley's face is incomprehensible. It's somewhere between fright, shock, and awe. Ashley suddenly grabs my elbow and starts leading me towards a hallway. She quickly asks Rachel to give us a minute, but she doesn't even stop to see if Rachel heard her. Ashley is polite to the guests that talk to her on the way, but she is marching toward the hall with purpose. This is all very unusual behavior for my happy-go-lucky sister. If it weren't for that fact, she would not have been able to budge me from the spot where I had a clear view of Mercy.

We arrive in the dim hallway leading to the swanky restrooms and lounges. Ashley stops abruptly and turns to face me. "Do you know her?"

"Do I know who?" I speak slowly. I know exactly who she's talking about.

"That whole deflect-deter thing or whatever it is you and Connor do, is not going to work on me, so save it for Rachel." My older brother taught me the deflection game. I should've known Ashley knew it too. "Do you know Mercedes Dean?"

"Who?" I hold up my hands when Ashley looks like she might actually haul off and hit me. "I know who Mercedes is, but I didn't know her last name was Dean."

Ashley takes a step back from me. She looks like I just hit her and I have no idea why.

"Ashley, how do you know Mercedes? And are you on another sugar fast? You're acting like the sugarless version of yourself and it freaks everyone out."

She ignores my question. "Why didn't you even know her last name?"

"Why do you care and why are you looking at me like something you accidentally stepped in and can't wipe off your shoe?" What's going on? What am I missing here?

We are interrupted by a chorus of voices, the loudest of which screams dramatically, "Ashley, oh my God, there you are. They brought out the flaming cupcakes and champagne and the deejay is cued up. Come on, girl! The party is starting." Ashley's best friend, Rob is leading a pack of rowdy men and women. They are ready to move the party along.

Ashley gives me another totally confusing look and whispers in an urgent tone, "We have to talk about her Loch. Soon."

"Okay, Ash, I don't know what this is about, but I always have time to talk to you," I concede. She nods quickly and walks off with her friends. I lean back against the wall and look up at the ceiling. Ashley is off sugar. Rachel is on her usual BS. I see a headache in my future. Partygoers come in and out of the hallway in search of the bathrooms. Their laughter and excitement narrows my focus to my own isolation. I've been surrounded by people for the past two years, but the majority of that time, I've felt alone. Maybe alone isn't the right word to describe it. Maybe there is no one word. Without Mercy, that's how I've felt.

Well, the answer isn't on the ceiling. My hands in my pockets, armor re-engaged, I turn to re-enter the party and she's there, 20 feet away from me. Plump lips and kaleidoscope gray eyes are two of her many features that mesmerize me. She looks like she stopped in midstride. She has one foot in front of the other and her body is angled as if she was preparing to take another step when she just stopped.

My eyes are hungry things in my face. They are all over her, taking in her red toenails, toned legs, flared hips, and tight waist. Her full breasts that I left my fingerprints on, her neck where my bite marks found a home, and her mouth that did everything that still haunts my sleeping hours are permanent in my memory.

But it's always been her face. God, she is beautiful. Her skin is the color of light honey, high cheekbones, almond-shaped eyes, thick eyelashes, and a lush mouth. She's my dream girl and she's very real. Her expression is inscrutable. I want to say something, but as much as my eyes won't quit, my mouth won't seem to start. Her chest rises and falls. People come and go. We're locked in this moment, neither one of us can seem to break away.

"Mercy." It's a prayer, a chant, a creed. I don't own it and I can't stop it from slipping from my lips.

The emotional glass around us shatters.

Mercedes jolts backward, stumbling a little in her heels. There's a hurricane raging in her eyes and it's headed right for me.

MERCEDES

"Don't you call me that! Don't you dare call me that," I spit the words out like they taste bad. They do taste bad.

This cannot be happening. It just can't be. It is statistically impossible that I could run into Lochlan Rait on my first full day of project "you too can be a normal woman." The universe fucking hates me. And I hate that bitch right back. I'm sick of her vindictiveness.

Two things threaten to steal my ability to stand. First, I'm looking at the face of the person I love the most in the body of the person that I hate the most. I have no idea what to do with this. My son is his father's child. I already knew this from looking at photos. But no picture could've prepared me for the real thing. No picture captured how much everything in Lochlan Rait's face looks like my son. On top of everything else, he's a genetic bully.

Second, my body doesn't care about my emotions. It is immune to my hurt, unaffected by my anger. I am physically drawn to this man like a magnetic force. I step backward to avoid the pull. It doesn't help. The deepest yearning steps out of the corner and grabs me by the neck. Maybe that's why it's hard for me to breath. I try to talk myself down, I'm not listening. I want him more than I want my dignity. And that really pisses me off.

"I… I'm sorry. I didn't mean to offend you." He takes a step toward me. I take another step back. "I'm just so surprised to see you here."

His voice is as deep and smooth as I remember it. I know I just cursed the universe, but I'm now calling on it to help me. This man is too much everything. Send reinforcements please.

"Right. You thought when you ghosted me I would just cease to exist." My laugh sounds bitter and it feels the same. "Nope, the world kept turning and I'm still a part of it. Surprise!" I throw my hands out and roll my eyes in disgust.

"Ghosted you? What are you—" His genuinely confused-sounding words are interrupted by a woman's voice. She's behind me, but I can't make my mutinous body turn away from him.

"Lochlan, there you are. Honey, I've been looking all over for you. Ashley wants you to come out for the birthday dance." The voice becomes a whole person when she walks around me to stand next to him.

His eyes never leave mine.

The blonde woman, who was previously just a voice, looks up at Lochlan. Then she looks at me and back at him again. "Hi, I'm Rachel." She seems to have finally decided on a strategy. She extends a slender tanned hand to me.

I give her offered hand the same regard as I'd give a used tissue I had found on the ground. She puts her other hand on Lochlan's arm. Subtle.

Rachel finally gets the message and withdraws her hand with a frown.

Lochlan asks her, "Can you give me just one minute? I'll be right over." He's still looking at me so he misses the ugly sneer Rachel aims in my direction.

I'm a woman. We can multitask, so I see everything. I take the sneer and raise her a malicious smirk. *Run along, Blondie. You don't want these problems.* She actually looks startled. Ha! I don't imagine she's ready for the havoc of a Southwest D.C. girl who grew up way too fast.

Rachel offers Lochlan a solicitous smile. What a waste. He doesn't even look at her. She walks by me without another word. Rachel is careful not to make physical contact with me as she navigates the hallway. So, she's not as dumb as she looks.

Lochlan was fully a man two and a half years ago, but he seems more mature today. He's got an appealing five o'clock shadow on his strong straight jaw. His hair looks just a little less close cropped than when I last saw him and somehow his lips look fuller. I want to kiss him. What am I saying?

I deflate. I can't fight biology, my sad home life and crazy blondes. This is too much for a Friday. "You didn't have to tell her to go. We have nothing to say to each other. We certainly don't have anything that needs to be said in private." I'm resigned.

"Mercedes, please, I just... Can we talk for a minute?" His rich baritone is pleading and demanding at the same time. I don't know how he does that, but it causes goose bumps to break out on my naked arms. I fold them protectively across my chest. Lochlan's eyes track the movement.

"About what?" My voice sounds weak to my ears, but this is an important question. There is one right answer to this question. Only one.

He takes another step toward, me, but this time I don't move back. He smells spicy and masculine.

"I know it's been a long time, but seeing you here like this..." He rakes his hand through his hair. "I want to talk about us."

No. Wrong answer.

Every time I think I've come to the end of my hopefulness about Lochlan Rait, disappointment reveals how wrong I am. You can't be disappointed when you don't have any expectations. The way I feel right now tells me that against all odds, there was still some thread of belief in that night between us.

"Mercedes, can you just give me a chance to explain? Let's go somewhere and talk."

I shake my head in disbelief "After all this time Lochlan, you're still thinking about some good ass you got? Let it go." My words are my only defense. Underneath the tough-girl veneer, I desperately want him to ask about my pregnancy, ask about our son, prove to me that I wasn't wrong about him.

LOCHLAN

I know it's been a long time since I saw Mercedes and I know that's my fault but I've never thought of her as just good ass. Repeating that in my head is repulsive. Maybe I really did blow my chance with her but I can't just give up.

"I have never thought of you in that way. Ever."

Mercedes crosses her arms over her chest and leans on the wall behind her, the movement takes her further from me in more ways than one.

"I've never experienced anything like the night we had together, not before you and not after you."

"It's just sex, Lochlan and it couldn't have been that earth shattering because I haven't heard from you in over two years."

The bite in her words is the hurt in her voice. I remember the sound of her disappointment from the night of her graduation. I was the guy who said I'd never let her feel that way again and now I can't explain why I did.

"Look, I was just leaving."

"Mercedes, you don't have to leave. My sister invited you, so stay."

"Ashley Blunt is your sister?"

"Yes. She was adopted and chose to take back her birth name as an adult."

"Well, my good luck never runs out." The words are muttered more to herself than spoken to me.

"Lochlan, is there anything else you want to ask me? Anything at all?"

Of course there are hundreds of things I want to ask her and to say to her but this doesn't feel like an invitation to catch up. I get the impression that Mercedes is giving me one shot to accomplish something, but I have no idea what it is.

"I have to go, Lochlan." She turns and walks away. I failed her, again. When Mercedes turns her back on me, the scent of her shampoo fills my nose and it brings back the memory of that day.

~

Lochlan
Two and a half years ago, the day after Mercy

One semi truck. Three Hours. Six firefighters. Eight days. And I have never been the same.

The day after what I considered to be the best day of my life was the worst day of my life. I'm a good teammate and an even better friend. That's why as much as I wanted to stay in bed with Mercedes, I dragged myself into clothes and got on the road to the middle of nowhere Virginia. My best friend was having a "barn" bachelor party. Don't even ask. I just knew I couldn't miss it. Professional athletes are not short on friends. Real friends are a different story. Chastain, of the barn bachelor party, is a real friend.

It was dusk when I lost a battle with a semi-truck on a two-lane highway a few miles from some unknown area of Virginia. I saw the truck approaching as a mundane part of traveling. He had a lane, I had a lane so we should've been fine. At the last minute, the truck swerved into my lane. It happened so fast that I can remember the event, but I can't remember any other conscious thoughts. I just reacted. I automatically jerked the wheel to the left, trying to swing my Range Rover out of the semi's path. My avoidance attempt in coordination with the force of the semi striking the passenger's side of my truck was the perfect combination to send my car hurtling off the road. The semi-truck driver died that day; he'd dozed off at the wheel right before he swerved into my lane.

I struck my head before losing consciousness. I don't know how long I was unconscious, but I remember waking up alone in the dark. I've never been able to describe the pain in my leg. I don't have the vocabulary for that kind of pain. My right leg was somehow pinned underneath the dashboard of my truck. My bone was sticking out of my skin. I assume if someone set my leg on fire and it just burned continuously, that would be the equivalent pain.

I'm aware of other aches and pains. Everything hurts but my leg is a superseding force of misery. My thoughts are scattered. There's no common thread.

I'm alone.

It's dark.

I'm never leaving this car.

I will never see Mercy again.

I will never play basketball again.

I need to call for help.

I don't know how much time passes. It seems like hours, days, months.

I learned about prayer in an evangelical mega church in Texas. My Father was a trustee. My Mother was a church administrator. The church wasn't about religion in my mind. It was a lifestyle. It was where our friends and family were. It was the center of our social world. Church was about being a good person, but God was more of an abstract principle.

Growing up, prayer was like the homemade cranberry sauce for the stuffing at Thanksgiving. It was a tradition. You do not eat stuffing without my grandmother's homemade cranberry sauce. It was a ritual that we observed. Excluding it would have changed Thanksgiving, but at the end of the day, it didn't actually mean anything. Since becoming a professional athlete, I've spent Thanksgivings away from my family and without grandma's homemade cranberry sauce. I survived. I thought of the cranberry sauce in passing, but that was it.

That's how I always felt about prayer until that spring night on that dark road. Prayer was an important tradition that I observed at the appropriate times. But it had been years since I engaged and it hadn't seemed to make all that big of a difference.

Sitting in my truck staring out of the shattered windshield and trapped under the dashboard, a memory parachutes to me and lands in my lap. It's a Sunday school class from my pre-teen years. It was the time right before church really became my parent's thing, the time before I mostly tuned it all out. I had a teacher who told us that prayer was a direct line of communication to God. And since God is all powerful, we have direct access to basically anything in the universe. It seemed a bit farfetched at the time. But I wasn't pinned under a dashboard unable to reach my phone and call for help back then. Now, prayer seems just as likely to work as anything else.

And so I do it. I pray. I start with the Lord's Prayer I had learned as a kid because hell, I don't know. It seems like a better option than the "now I lay me down to sleep," the traditional nighttime prayer. The last thing I want to do is pray a prayer about going to sleep.

Our Father who art in heaven, hallowed be thy name...

First off, I have no clue what that means. Maybe God doesn't either. I get through the whole prayer. Nothing happens. I take a different tact. If I'm going to die out here, I may as well strip it down and get honest.

God, I think you're real. A lot of crazy shit happens in the world, but I'm pretty sure You're still doing good. I'm not the best person, but I'm not the worst either. I haven't paid that much attention to You, but I do believe in You. I heard that You can do anything. I believe that. And maybe I don't deserve to ask, but I'm gonna do it anyway. I need Your help. I'm trapped out here in the middle of BFE Virginia. I don't know how long I have, but it's probably less time than it will take for someone to find me in this ditch. So, I need You to send help.

Nothing happens. Maybe I lose consciousness. Time passes. The fire in my leg roars. I become alert to blood congealing on my fore-head and mosquitoes, a lot of damn mosquitoes. I try again with more desperation.

I know that You're my only hope. That's okay; you're a good hope. But I really need help now.

I bargain

If you let me stay, I'll dedicate myself to You. I'll make You the center of my life and I'll share my story. Think of all the people who could be changed if You do this miracle, God. Are You there? Can you hear me? I need help. I don't want to die.

Darkness.

"I'm here. I heard you. I will help you. You're not going to die."

Those are the exact words I hear. They are spoken by an odd-looking man with a pot belly. He has black hair with a white streak. It's like a bolt of lightning shooting through his round head. His skin is tanned, the texture reminds me of a rancher who spends a lot of time in the sun. He has a light spot on his right cheek, a birthmark, I think. He has on a red T-Shirt. Gray letters written across the front declare "God is Dope." I blink. He's leaning over me. I think I must have misheard him, but he speaks again.

"I'm here. I heard you. I will help you. You're not going to die." Those exact words, again and then I am being pulled out of my truck.

I wake up 8 days later in one of the best hospitals in the country. My brother Connor is the first person I see.

"You look terrible." A coughing fit prevents me from asking my brother why he looks like he hasn't slept in a year. When Connor jumps up in excitement and starts pushing buttons at my bed side and calling for people to come into the room, I finally notice that I'm in a hospital room. It's a large room with a sofa bed that it looks like my brother has been sleeping on.

"Loch, just take it easy bro. Mom and dad went back to my house to grab some showers and food but they're on their way back. You've had a hard time, just, just take it easy."

The water the nurse or other person gives me to slowly sip helps me to form more words. For the first time I'm aware of an ominous pain in my leg. It seems to be saying something about how my life is going to change forever. I try to ignore it for now.

"There was a man who helped to save me. Has anyone found him? I want to thank him."

"Brother there were about 20 people who pulled you out of your smashed up truck. We've thanked all of them."

I take a few more sips of water. The memory of my accident trickles back into my awareness piece by piece and maybe recalling is taking up all of my energy. I suddenly feel very tired. "It was before they got there. There was a man there before all the other people got there."

"I'm not sure but one of the paramedics has checked up on you a few times since you've been in the hospital, maybe you can ask him." The way my big brother hovers over my bed tells me I'm in worse shape than I know. Connor is not the hovering type.

"What about Mercy?"

Connor tilts his head to the side in thought. "I was going to ask you about that when you felt better. I don't know what to make of it but for the last eight days you've been calling out for mercy? Is that like a prayer? What does that mean?"

"It's a person. Mercedes. I met her right before my accident."

"Well damn, she must have been some woman if the memory of her survived your accident, a prolonged state of unconsciousness and now is one of the first things you ask about while awake."

I smile even though the motion makes my face feel like it might crack. We don't get to finish our short discussion. The medical team wants to run tests and do other medical things. My parents show up with Ashley and my cousin Paul and my energy finally gives out.

Over the next week, I get a chance to ask about the man who showed up at the scene of my accident before the paramedics. Everyone is confused. The rescue crew was well documented. My accident and extraction was a big story. There is no one matching the description I gave who was at the scene of the accident.

I am told by the paramedic who had stopped by just to check on me that the man I'm describing sounds exactly like Jeb Sanderson.

But that's impossible because Jeb died eight years ago. I have no explanation for why I searched for a dead man. I mean, if he's dead, he can't be the person who saved me, right? Despite this pretty clear logic, the first thing I do when I get my phone back is find a Google image of Jeb Sanderson. He had won the butter-churning contest at the state fair five years in a row. That's a record. There's a picture of him with his fifth trophy and his lightning bolt hair; same birth mark on his cheek, same pot belly.

The man who spoke to me was definitely Jeb Sanderson and he's definitely been dead for eight years.

8

MERCEDES

"Bad dirt!" Liam screams at my backyard garden. I laugh and give him a confused look. "Why is the dirt bad, baby?"

My roommate and long-time friend, August, rolls his eyes and sips his iced tea. The iced tea that I made for myself for my garden work. This fool is drinking my iced tea. What the hell?

"He probably thinks you're angry at the dirt because you're beating it like it stole something."

Liam giggles.

"I am not beating the dirt," I retort as Liam loses interest in my real attempt at gardening and goes back to his play gardening set. "I am rotating the dirt per chapter 3 of *Gardening for Dummies*."

"Um, no, ma'am. You're beating the dirt per chapter 2 of *Signs You Need to Get Laid*."

"That's not even a book," I mumble as I go back to *rotating* the soil in my garden.

August takes off his straw hat and large sunglasses dramatically so I can appreciate his imperious look. August is in his mid-to-late 40s. His assigned gender identity at birth was female, but he has or is transitioning. After knowing him for several years, I'm still somewhat unclear. When he told me he'd been born a biological female, I was completely confused, because not only is August now a self-identified male, but he's a gay male with more female tendencies than I have. I once asked him if he's just offended by vaginas. He said yes, slammed the door in my face, and didn't speak to me for five days. Apparently, that was not an appropriate question to ask a transgender man. I've learned better trans etiquette since then, I think.

August became the basement tenant when Jules left for L.A. almost a decade ago. He is Vietnamese and Black. It's a shame. He has all that genetic material to work with and neither side appreciates or respects his gender identity. He's been on his own since he was 17. August made his way in the world, in part, because of his exceptional home improvement and maintenance skills. He's a gay man with ample feminine characteristics who is also an expert at home renovations and fixing almost anything that can go wrong in a house. He's a transgender millennium man.

My grandmother hired him to be the full-time caretaker of our home right before I turned 15. I can't prove it, but I think she knew she was getting sick. She owned the house outright, but it was old, and she and I couldn't care for it. August had almost singlehandedly renovated the entire kitchen and sitting room for our next-door neighbors. When Grandma saw his work, she made him an offer he couldn't refuse. It eventually involved free room and board. August is good at his work, but he is anti-working to live. Moving into our basement apartment allowed him the flexibility to work only when he felt like it. He only felt like it when new handbags, shoes, and clothing items were involved.

Together, August and I have gutted and re-done about 70 percent of grandma's house. Today, I'm attacking the backyard landscaping with righteous indignation and fervor. When the father of your child is interested in you but not his own flesh and blood, you either pound dirt or you pound his sorry ass.

August sits up in his lawn chair. This is a lawn chair which he produced today from God only knows where. I've never seen it before. He dramatically places his non-stolen, iced tea-holding hand on his chest and says, "Are you going to tell me what is wrong with you or are you actually digging a trench we can bury your weird-ass attitude in when it's complete?"

I drop my small shovel in exasperation and sit back on my haunches in the dirt. "I saw him, August."

There is only a brief moment of confusion before August realizes who *him* must be. "You saw *him*?"

"Yes"

"Where? When? How?" August is sputtering questions at me. His eyes have gotten comic-book large.

"Liam, are you trying to eat the flowers, sweetie?" I yell at my child who I see in my peripheral vision attempting to put items in his mouth.

"No, Mommy." He laughs like I asked a ridiculous question.

"Well, are you trying to eat the dirt?"

"Yes, Mommy, Mommy."

I think he was watching some Diego or Dora the Explorer episode where the characters say everything twice to make things happen. Now, he randomly repeats things and he's laughing at me like I'm the one asking dumb questions.

"Okay, well, don't eat the dirt. I have cookies in the house." Liam keeps giggling but also appears to stop trying to sneak bites of dirt.

"Mercury, would you please leave that child alone about the dirt. You're going to feed him those vegan cookies, but he can't eat a little dirt? Girl, please, he's better off with the soil. Now, stop stalling and tell me how you ran into Liam's dad?"

"You know I hate it when you call me Mercury." I scowl at August.

He sings songs back to me, "And you know I don't care."

I do know.

"Stop stalling, Mercury. Now, tell me what happened."

"You know I went to that birthday party of the really nice girl who works at Liam's new school?"

"Right. Yes, and...?" August waves his hand. Patience is not his strong suit.

"Well, thanks to Google, I pretty easily discovered that she is the sister of Lochlan Rait. I guess she just doesn't use her last name."

August holds up his hand. "Hold the phone. You finally make a friend and that friend is the aunt of your child?" His voice gets louder with every word.

"Yes, August. Do you want to yell it a bit louder? I don't think they heard you on Mars."

"Excuse me for being shocked at how bad your luck is. But who randomly and totally on accident becomes friends with their child's aunt when she hasn't even told the baby daddy about the baby."

"Shut it, August. You know I told him about his child."

"Honey, you told his lawyer or PR person or whoever. You never actually spoke to him."

"That's dirty, August. You know I stalked him every way I could imagine and I'm pretty damn creative. Getting to his lawyer required me to actually pull a rabbit out of a hat." I lower my voice to a whisper and say, "I had to call Jules." For some reason, we whisper when talking about Jules. It's as if she might hear us and magically appear if we're too loud.

August has the decency to look both shocked and repentant. "Oh dear God, you had to call in Satan?" August refers to Jules by her nickname. He's actually not the only person to call her that behind her back.

"Yes, I had to call her and she connected me to Loch's lawyer slash agent. And by the way, August, the guy is his first cousin. It wasn't like I was talking to some distant stranger."

"And you told him you were pregnant and who you were?"

"No, August, I told him I wanted Lochlan to sign my basketball sneakers," I retort sarcastically. "Of course, I told him I was pregnant. I explained how Lochlan and I met so that he could verify my story. He checked in with Lochlan and came back and offered me money to "take care of it." When I made it clear that wasn't going to happen, they offered me even more money, a lot more, in exchange for a NDA and an agreement not to seek child support. They were so concerned about keeping me quiet that they never considered anything else."

"I hear you, Mercury. But are you sure this is what Lochlan wanted?"

"I specifically asked that question. Cousin Paul told me that Lochlan would meet with me in-person, but I needed to sign the NDA first and agree to all of their terms. Oh, did I mention the paternity test I would need to take as well?"

"I'm sure you responded with class and dignity to all of this," August quips deadpans.

"I sure did. I told Cousin Paul that he and the whole family could get fucked with a rusty razor blade and that I wasn't signing anything less than an exclusive deal to tell my story to People magazine."

"Oh dear." August pretends to be aghast.

I know he's pretending because this is the same person who showed up to his lover's office on K Street with a spatula, pink wig, bikini, and stilettos after he found out his lover was "happily" married. My antics have nothing on August's proven record of pure fuckery. And just what was the spatula for?

Liam wanders back over with his little bucket and shovel. I assume, based on his appearance, he's decided to wear the dirt when I told him he couldn't eat it. Of course, he wants to give me dirt kisses. I let him. There is no such thing as a clean mommy who doesn't employ a fulltime nanny. I revel in Liam's dirt kisses and inquire as to whether he found any worms.

"Ahem, I hate to disrupt your maternal bonding, but can we please refocus our attention to you know who with whom you have you know who."

I pick Liam up, sit him on my hip, and head into the back sliding doors of the house. August is right on my heels.

"What is there to say? I saw you know who and he didn't even ask about you know who."

"What do you mean he didn't ask? He didn't even want to know whether you had him?"

I put Liam down in his high chair to restrain him while I get a bath ready for him.

"I don't know if he wanted to know. He didn't ask. That's my point. After all this time, there was clearly still an attraction between us. He cared about that, but he didn't seem to care about what that attraction had already produced."

"So, what are you going to do?" August asks this while he helps himself to more of my iced tea.

"I'm going to kick your ass-cot if you don't stay out of my iced tea."

We change the end of curse words to protect Liam's baby ears. But I think he'll just grow up to use really odd curse words. We might be creating a more awkward situation for him.

August waves off my beverage aggression. "Now, what are you going to do about Lochlan?"

"LaLan LaLan LaLan." Liam sings the baby version of his father's name with toddler enthusiasm. Of course, he would repeat that. I press my hand to my forehead. I feel a headache coming on.

"I'm going to continue living my life as I have been living my life. What else can I do?"

"Maybe you should try to talk to him again?"

I just glare. August is getting on my damn nerves.

"Save your death glare, sis. I'm suggesting to you that it is odd that you know who didn't even ask about you know who. You didn't describe him as a cold-hearted sociopath. None of the news coverage of him or what he's done since his accident would lead one to believe that he's the deadbeat type. Don't tell me this hasn't even occurred to you?"

I don't answer August because the answer scares me too much to verbalize. It has occurred to me that I'm jumping to the wrong conclusions. August is right. Lochlan is not the type who wouldn't even ask about the possibility that he has a child. When I calmed down and really thought about it, the reality that he truly doesn't know about Liam or my pregnancy sprouted in my head like one of those weeds in the backyard. If I'm being honest, I don't know what to do with that. If Lochlan doesn't know, then maybe I didn't do enough to inform him. That is a scenario that I'm just not prepared to deal with. At this point, how do I justify not swallowing my pride and trying again for my son's sake? Even if the chance of Lochlan not knowing of Liam's existence is minuscule, how do I not do something while there is still a chance?

LOCHLAN

I walk into the new offices for my physical rehabilitation app company, *Rebound*. I still can't believe that I'm a successful business owner with employees, offices, and a very healthy bank account. After my accident, I couldn't go back to playing basketball. To be frank, I'm blessed to be able to walk.

There was a brief moment in time in which depression and self-pity seemed to be reasonable options for daily life. I mean I went from standing at the apex of the universe to being actually crippled in an instant. Before I could latch on to the sadness that was reaching for me, I remembered that I'm still here. If my leg was missing, I would still have my life. And my leg isn't missing. It just can't run and leap like it did when I was in the NBA. So no, I don't feel bad about what I lost. I feel fantastic about what I didn't lose.

My older brother, Connor, is the brains behind our app. Before my accident, he was already working with me on technology that would allow athletes to track their progress along certain metrics. The unique aspect of our app was going to be that it contained development resources for professional athletes. After my accident, Connor and I reworked the app so that it is geared towards those with physical rehabilitation goals. Instead of connecting to a broad group of professionals, the app connects to elite physical rehabilitation professionals all over the country. Services can be provided via the app's broadcast functions or in-person via the app's live scheduling features. The app includes wearable accessories that track certain athletic functionality in real time. The results are reported to connected professionals who can tweak rehab programs based on the results.

We signed the lease on this office space after we solidified a sponsorship relationship with Ath-Elite. The company is the leading producer of athletic equipment and apparel. They are also the reason why I'm in the office today. This is the big contract-signing day. We will formalize the multimillion-dollar deal with Ath-Elite. If I were any sane person, this would be my mind's sole focus. But apparently, I'm not sane. All I can think about today is Mercedes and the huge mistake I made two years ago.

"Lochlan."

I hear my name called over the office intercom. It took me two months to get my executive assistant to stop calling me Mr. Rait. He can't be more than three to five years older than me and the "Mr. Rait" thing was just too strange for me.

"Yes, Phillip?" I respond to the voice suspended in the air. "Connor and Mr. Rutland are here to see you."

"Send them in, Phillip."

I face the glass wall of my office and gesture to my brother and cousin to come in. My wall is glass, so we can all see each other. I pointed this out to Phillip. He will not give up the formality of announcing my appointments even if one of them is the co-owner of the company who has his own office suite right down the hall. I got the first-name concession. Phillip is an excellent assistant. I will not try to push him further beyond the bounds of his sense of decorum.

Connor and my cousin slash attorney Paul walk through my office door so that we can start our pre-contract meeting. After about 30 minutes of discussion, Connor holds up his hand and points at me.

"You, what is going on with you?"

I pretend not to know what he means.

"Bro, don't play dumb with me. I know you. You've been laser focused on this deal, but today you seem like you wouldn't notice if an actual spaceship landed in this office, little aliens jumped out, and started doing the electric slide." Only Connor can create that kind of imagery.

"Is this some more Rachel drama? I thought you were going to learn sign language and sign that it's over since she doesn't understand any spoken language."

My cousin looks up from the deal documents he was studying and glances at Connor and me. He seems to finally tune in to the discussion going on in front of him. "Wait, you broke it off with Rachel? Why would you do that? She's perfect for you."

Paul squints at me. Where Connor and I are tall and fair, Paul is a cousin on my mother's side. He inherited the darker features of that side of the family, including the green eyes that now look confused.

I ignore Paul for the moment. "I saw Mercedes this weekend."

Paul's eyes get slightly wider. Connor looks momentarily confused before recognition encroaches on his features. My big brother is generally thoughtful. I want to hear his opinion about this unexpected turn of events, but it's Paul that speaks first.

"Why would this be a source of distraction for you?" Paul is using his lawyer voice on me. It's annoying as all hell but he continues. "You went down this road and you decided to get off of it two years ago. When Mercedes got in contact with me while you were in the hospital, you made your choice and it was a good one. The fact that she disappeared without another word, not even to check on your condition is proof that you made the right choice. So, what's the issue now?" Paul leans back in his chair as if he's resting his case.

Now that I've seen Mercedes again, it's difficult to remember why I was so convinced I was making the right choice back then.

I have waited impatiently for this day for over three months. You would think that the most important thing on my mind would be my physical recovery and you'd only be half right. I've wanted to get my strength back, rebuild my leg and start walking again but mostly so that I can pick up where I left off with Mercedes. I've endured three months of some of the most intense physical therapy and two reconstructive surgeries. When the pain medication wasn't enough, the memory of her face, her voice, her laugh has been a sanctuary for me. My life as I knew it has crumbled. There's no more NBA for me. I have to figure out who I am, now and I plan to do that with Mercedes.

I'm finally being discharged from the hospital and the only thing I want to do is find Mercy.

My cousin Paul walks into the room while I'm doing some of the strengthening exercises I learned in PT. As usual, Paul is dressed in a suit, he's not good at relaxing.

"How's the recovery going?" Paul greets me as I continue my leg exercises.

"It's going great. I'm coming along faster than any of the doctors expected. But enough about that, tell me what you found. I've been waiting to hear about Mercedes for months."

Instead of answering right away, Paul gives me a thoughtful look. "Lochlan, you remember how you talked about re-committing yourself to your faith?"

I'm not sure where he's going with this. I end my exercises and sit in one of the two reclining chairs in the room. Paul is perched on the edge of another one waiting for me to answer.

"Of course I remember that. I want to be more focused now on things that matter in the long-term. Seeing how fast my NBA life crumbled has helped me to understand that all of that stuff was temporary. That's why I wanted to find Mercedes. I want to start-over and I'm hoping to do it with her."

"That's the thing, Lochlan, I don't think this is the girl you want to start over with."

This feels like a trap I'm walking into but I don't have any choice. I wipe the sweat from my workout with a small hand towel on the arm of the chair. My next question is one I want to stall as long as possible.

"Did you find her?"

"I found her. She's looking for you too."

"Spit it out Paul. If you found her and she's looking for me too, what's the problem?" *I know that letting my temper loose is not helpful but Paul's dramatic build up is starting to unnerve me.*

"Mercedes *is like the women you said you don't want to deal with anymore. And she might even be a little worse.*" *Paul pulls his phone out of his pocket and begins scrolling through it looking for something.*

A lump of foreboding forms in my throat, I can't seem to swallow past it. Wanting to be with this woman has propelled me through some of the darkest days and now I get the sense that my motivation is about to be stolen from me.

"Here it is. *I need you to see this. And let me just say, I'm sorry man. I know how important finding Mercedes has been to you but I'm here to look out for your best interest. This woman, she can't be it.*"

When I take the phone from him, only the slight tremor in my hand betrays my fear about what I'll find. Whatever I thought I'd see, this is so much worse that my brain can barely process the images. My Mercedes high crashes so fast and suddenly, even my stomach drops like I just hit a steep decline on a roller coaster ride. I wish I hadn't seen this but even more I wish it didn't exist.

"Is the woman you see there the woman you want to start a new journey of faith with? That's the question you have to ask yourself."

The memory of that day fades into the present and back to Paul's current question, what's my issue now? I kind of want to punch my cousin, mostly because he has a point.

"It wasn't really the right time to be making significant decisions," Connor speaks.

I look at my older brother who has stood and is leaning on the glass wall. Our height, hair, and coloring make us very similar in appearance. But Connor's eyes are ice-blue and they get even frostier when he is deep in thought or angry.

"You were lying in that hospital all mangled and shit. That had to have had an impact on your thought process."

"That's not necessarily a bad thing," Paul responds to Connor. Paul is between Connor and me in age and there's always been a little tension between the two. I have no idea where that comes from. It's not the kind of thing guys sit down and chat about.

"Trauma can give you a perspective you didn't have before and it can be a necessary one. Mercedes is a certain type of woman who is used to being with a certain type of man. You didn't want to be that type of man and so you chose not to be."

Connor tilts his head to the side and looks at Paul. "What are you even talking about right now? Do you know this woman? I was under the impression that she's a total stranger to you. That would make you full of shit as usual." Connor employs the same bored tone he uses whenever Paul is annoying him.

"Actually, to protect your brother's interest and the family's, I conducted a background check. So, I know more about Mercedes than either of you."

Connor smirks and puts his hands in his pockets, "I doubt you know more about her than Loch."

"I know that she's from a rough part of D.C. and has no parents to speak of. There isn't even a name listed under "father" on her birth certificate. She was raised by her grandmother until she was 16. Her grandmother died and she was basically left on her own. It looks like she learned to survive by being kept by rich athletes. One paid her way through the remainder of an elite private high school and two more paid for college at John's Hopkins." Paul finishes with a smug look.

Connor is unimpressed. "She sounds resourceful to me." He shrugs.

Paul snorts. "She's resourceful all right. There is digital proof of how resourceful and flexible she is."

"Let it go, Paul." My voice is quiet. I feel the old basketball rage starting to percolate. It's a heat just under the surface of my skin. It would break out before violence followed close on its heels. It's been a while, but I still recognize the feeling. I don't care what happened between Mercedes and me, the sound of someone talking about her this way is not going to fly with me.

Connor comes off the wall. "What digital proof? What are you talking about?"

"There is a footage of Mercedes "earning" her tuition."

"I said drop it, Paul." I take a threatening step toward him. Paul and I have fought before; we all have. We grew up together. We're more like brothers than cousins. We're a pretty even physical match most of the time. But I'm not sure how Paul would match up against my level of pent-up aggression. We're all cut from the same cloth though, so neither of us is going to back down.

"You're telling me there's some kind of... What? Is it some Pornhub-type shit of her? And you've seen it? And you told my brother about it when, while he was in the hospital? What the fuck?"

"Get off your high horse, Connor. Or at least recognize that you wouldn't own that horse if it weren't for the work I do to protect the family's interest."

"Funny you should say that. Aren't you the one always telling us that all good things come from the Lord above?"

"I stand by that statement. That doesn't mean that humans can't and don't facilitate the will of God on earth."

Connor rolls his eyes at Paul's statement. Paul has remained devoted to our evangelical upbringing. Connor left the church behind when he left Texas to attend college at the age of 18.

"I've heard it all. There's an actual corporate lawyer sitting here telling us about the will of the good Lord."

Paul tries to speak, but Connor holds up his hand in his direction while looking at me.

"So, what? You decided you couldn't even pick up the phone and call this woman back because of some rumors about her sexual history? You were in the NBA, bro. There is not enough communion this side of heaven to make your shit not stink. And now look at you? We're supposed to be signing a multimillion-dollar contract and you can't drag your mind from two years ago to the present." Connor ends on a disgusted note.

"Did you not hear that the girl is an actual porn star?"

"Enough, Paul. No one has even seen that footage. It's not in the public domain. It is in someone's private home collection. You only know about it because of a friend of a friend of a friend or something," I explain.

"You didn't give the girl a chance over the rumor of her being on some racy footage? You haven't even seen it?" Connor's eyebrows creep closer to his scalp.

"I saw a snippet. Paul's friend three times removed sent me a clip. It's definitely her with two football players." I turn to look fully at Connor. "So yeah, I did make certain assumptions about what kind of person she was and I didn't believe her reasons for tracking me down were sincere. But after seeing her this weekend, I'm pretty sure I messed up badly."

Paul spins around in his chair to face me. "You saw her for what? 30 seconds? And now you think everything you knew about her is something else? Come on."

"What I'm saying is that if she was some slutty gold digger, why did she react to me like I had the plague? Nobody who was just in it for the money would have that kind of reaction to a missed meal ticket. She was hurt, which means I didn't imagine that she had some real feelings for me."

"In one night? You're saying she had real feelings for you after one night? Again I say, come on. Even if that's true, doesn't that strike you as being odd? I mean who falls madly in love with someone after one night?"

I think I did. I definitely don't tell Paul that. But Connor knows me better. I don't have to tell him.

"She just wanted to talk. What would it have hurt for me to call her back?"

"You don't know what she really wanted."

"What does that mean? You told me she wanted to talk to me. Did she want something else? Did she call you up asking for money? I mean what are we talking about here?"

Paul's face shutters and I wonder if he knows something I don't. Maybe there was some better reason to keep Mercedes away from me. "Well, what about Rachel? What are you going to do about that?"

"Why are we talking about her? I'm not going to do anything. She went back home to Texas and she needs to stay there. There's nothing between us."

"So, what are you going to do about Mercedes then that doesn't involve wasting more of my time and money?"

Connor's annoyed by the timing, but I can tell he's sympathetic to my situation.

"I'm not sure yet." That feels like the right answer, but in my heart, I know that I will go to the ends of the earth to track Mercedes down. It turns out the ends of the earth aren't as far as they sound. I start with Ashley.

9

MERCEDES

I don't know why I'm here. I thought about cancelling. I probably should have cancelled. I tap my foot on the floor of one of the most exclusive restaurants in Washington D.C. Tapping, rocking, and general fidgeting are my long-time discomfort signs. I shouldn't be uncomfortable. I've known Greg for a couple of years and this isn't the first time I've had a meal with him. And yet, here I am tonight feeling like I want to peel off my own skin and walk away from it like an outfit that didn't work.

This is the Lochlan effect. I spend a few minutes in his presence and like magic, I'm drowning in self-doubt. I'm right back to feeling like a pretty package that gets discarded after it's unwrapped.

The restaurant, Azul, is located in the recently gentrified south-west waterfront area. The interior of the restaurant is arranged to give the impression that you are dining inside of an aquarium. The walls are lined with exotic fish floating in blue water and encased in glass. The seafood is said to be the best in this part of the states. I'm sure Maryland would like a word about that.

For the past six days, my mind has been wrapped around every memory of Lochlan that until recently had been kept under mental lock and key. I think August is right. I have to at least try to have a conversation with Lochlan about Liam. That thought is the beginning and the end of my plan of action. Right now, I need to drag my mind into the present. I owe it to Greg to not be thinking about some one-night stand from my past. Ugh, I wish I really thought of Lochlan as just some one-night stand. I should.

A hand on the small of my back refocuses my attention to the present. Greg has arrived.

"Hi, beautiful. Am I late? I thought I would beat you here." Greg smiles down at me.

"No, you're not late. I actually got here early."

"You should've let me pick you up. You didn't need to drive."

"No, it's fine. I had to make a stop before I got here, so it worked out and you didn't have to go out of your way."

Greg looks like he wants to say something else about my mode of transportation, but the hostess approaches us and addresses him.

"Mr. Klein, it's good to see you again. Your table is ready." Of course, Greg would be known in a place like this. This is where you would find all of D.C.'s elite on any given night. Greg is definitely one of them.

"You look stunning as usual, Mercedes."

Greg leans back in his chair after we have been seated. His eyes roam all over my outfit. The dress was made for this kind of attention. It comes down to about mid-thigh and is red with black tiger stripes. It has a wide tie at the waist made from the same material as the dress. It is the plunging neckline that is the real show stopper. It dips all the way to the waist line. My breasts are suspended in the dress by prayer and some well-placed dress tape. My hair is bone-straight, parted down the middle and pushed behind my ears so as not to obstruct the view of my dramatic smoky makeup. Nobody can ever say that I don't play my part with vigor and authenticity.

I smile at Greg's compliment. He bought the entire outfit, including my shoes and accessories. I guess it turned out the way he had imagined it would. A server arrives with our drinks. Greg orders our meals. I let him.

Greg is 45 years old, a widower, and one of the younger NBA

coaches. His wife died of ovarian cancer six years ago when he first retired from playing in the league. He's been a successful head coach for the past three years. He never remarried.

I met Greg right after I had Liam. I had just come off of maternity leave and was returning to work at the pediatric hospital. Greg volunteers there with some of the guys from his team every few months. I ran into him when I was leaving work. When I say I ran into him, I mean physically. I was distracted, thinking about Liam at home with August and I wasn't looking where I was going. When I looked up, Greg was holding me by my arms and asking me if I was okay. I was so shocked by the sight of him. He probably thought I was having a stroke.

Greg is strikingly handsome. He's 6'4" with an olive complexion that denotes his partial Portuguese heritage. His face is chiseled like it was sculpted and his eyes are an unusual shade of hazel with green flecks. His mostly-black hair is thick and wavy and always neatly pushed back. He has just enough gray mixed into the hair on his head and face to make him look formidable and distinguished. Even though Greg is old enough to be my father, his athletic body that he obsessively keeps in shape does not put me in a paternal frame of mind.

Despite his unusual good looks, I don't have romantic feelings for Greg. No, this is something else. The first time I met him, I noticed him. You would have to be blind not to notice a man like him. But besides apologizing for not looking where I was going, I dusted myself off and kept it moving. The very last thing I wanted in my life at that time was an aggressively attractive man. As fate and her messed-up sense of humor would have it, almost a month later, I hit Greg's Escalade when I was leaving the hospital. I was really distracted back then. I was still getting the mom thing down and my child was a nocturnal creature. He was trying to hang out all night like we were at the club when I desperately wanted to go to sleep.

When I saw I had hit an Escalade I had only one thought: *Fuuuu-uuuuuck*. Most people in D.C drive Maximas and Sentras. Why couldn't I have hit one of those? I dug my insurance information out of the glove compartment and walked out of the car like I was surrendering to police custody after committing a double homicide. I had a distinct memory of my reaction when Greg walked around the truck and I saw it was him.

"Oh my God, why do I keep literally running into you?" Totally inappropriate.

Greg only briefly glanced at the damage to his passenger's side before giving me a thoughtful look. I wished I'd been better dressed. I was wearing my hospital scrub bottoms with the Georgetown Medicine T-Shirt a lot of the nurses wear. My hair had grown seriously long while I was pregnant and I hadn't done anything with it except put it up in a ponytail. I had on no makeup. My few natural freckles were the only thing on my face that day. At least I had put on a little Chapstick. It didn't really seem like enough for the way the good-looking stranger was looking at me.

"I'll tell you what. You buy me dinner and we'll call it even." Greg spoke while glancing between his passenger's side bumper and me.

I was tempted to say no.

Greg smirked at me and crossed those big arms over his chest like he knew what I was thinking. "It's up to you, but I would take door number two over what your insurance company will do to your premiums when you report this claim."

Dammit, he's right.

So, I took Greg to dinner, allegedly, because he wound up paying the bill.

Greg is much more serious and reserved than any guy I had ever been around. He listens more than he talks. He is thoughtful and actually gives good advice. The very first time I went out with him, he gave me investment advice and set me up with an advisor. It was a very weird experience. I had just turned 23. I was used to guys talking about all their stats and all the stuff they had. Lochlan was the only man I'd ever been with outside that general mode and that had been different. Greg was a different kind of different. He seemed to be beyond the flashy portion of the life of a professional athlete. He's more settled and subtle.

Over time, I came to kind of look up to Greg. It's hard to explain.

August frowns on the entire situation even though he's only met Greg once. According to August, Greg isn't dating me, he's adopting me. Whatever. August didn't complain when Greg sent us on a trip to the Maldives for my birthday and he definitely doesn't complain when he's driving the Range Rover Greg bought me. However, I do have to deal with his snarky "sugar-daddy" comments.

Greg and I don't profess our love to one another. By some unspoken agreement, we don't even see each other more than every few months. He's never told me what he wants in a relationship, but I'm not dumb. I can see that Greg withholds most of himself. He once told me that he found his one true love, his wife. He wasn't looking for another one and he didn't think there could be one. That didn't bother me at all. I would never consciously admit it, but on some level I feel the same way about Lochlan. I convinced myself that this type of distant relationship is enough. Ironically, it was meeting Ashley that made me want something different. Ashley is so young and carefree. She has a fun aura about her. I felt dull being in her presence. It made me wonder if just maybe I could be young and carefree and normal. And yet, here I am with Greg. There is a pause in our easy-flowing conversation between the ahi tuna tartare appetizers and dinner.

"Do you know Lochlan Rait?" The words just come blasting out of my mouth before I can stop them. I hope they don't sound as thirsty as they are. *What is wrong with me?*

Greg gives me a curious look before answering, "Yes, I know who he is. I played against him when he was a rookie. He wasn't doing much actual playing back then, but I remember him. Why do you ask?"

"I ran into him the other day." I try to sound nonchalant.

Greg raises one eyebrow at me. "You ran into Lochlan Rait?"

"Yeah, funny story. It turns out that his sister is on the admissions panel at Liam's school. We kind of hit it off during the interviews. We're girl crushes."

"Girl crushes? Is that a new thing?"

"Yes, I think it is. It should be."

Greg laughs. "We have to spend more time exploring that later, but please continue."

"Well, as I was saying, my girl crush invited me to her birthday party and I ran into Lochlan there."

Greg snaps his fingers "That's right. He's back now. He had that bad accident and now he and his brother have started a company that's headquartered here. Hm, I hear he became kind of a Bible thumper after his accident. He doesn't run in any of his old NBA circles, but he does a lot of community work with one of those big Texas churches. Now that I think of it, one of my cousins goes to the church. She told me that Lochlan was kind of the face for the church's next-generation pitch. She was surprised that he decided to return to D.C. Apparently, he is or was a really prominent part of the church. Hey, speaking of the school, how are things going with the application process for your son?"

I feel like taking a deep breath and sagging in my seat in relief. I have never been so glad in my whole life for a change of topic. I mean Lochlan is some religious fanatic now? What the hell? He didn't seem like he had Jesus on his mind when I ran into him in that hallway. To the contrary, he looked like he wanted to do things to me that would send me straight to hell, and I would have let him. *What? No. Absolutely not. Focus.*

I gather myself and return to the topic of Liam's school application. That is much safer ground than his father. "Everything went well. He got in." I can't help the pride in my voice.

Greg beams a bright white smile back at me. "Well, there was never any question. You are his mother, so I'm sure he's brilliant."

Greg compliments me all the time, but it still makes heat creep up my neck and into my cheeks. If I was such a great mother, would I be here with self-doubt and shame, my old persistent friends?

"It's the Notre Dame Day School Prep, right?"

"That's the one. Don't act like you don't know," I tease him.

Greg gives me a fake wide-eyed expression, feigning innocence. "What?"

"I know you pulled some strings, Greg. The waiting list is two years long. I would have had to put Liam on it the day I conceived him, and I didn't. I know you had something to do with him getting an interview."

Greg leans across the table. The low lighting creates shadows that only emphasize his handsome features. This is one of the most exclusive restaurants on the D.C. waterfront, but the ambience has nothing on Greg.

"It is important to you, Mercedes. It was a two-minute phone call for me. It was worth it."

I raise my eyebrows at him. "A two-minute phone call? That's all, huh?"

All wealthy and powerful men have some degree of arrogance. Greg is not an exception even though he's not obnoxious about it. Now is one of the rare times I even notice it. He knows damn well he did more than make a two-minute phone call. Liam's entire tuition has been paid in advance for the whole pre-kindergarten program. Apparently, you get a discount if you pay all three years at once. I really wonder why rich people like giving rich people discounts? If you can afford to pay the $37,000 per year tuition, three years in advance, you don't need a discount. It's the people who are on month-to-month prayers, bottle-return, and donated-plasma plans who need the discounts. Greg is good at letting me know he is not one of those people. The nearly six-figure payment is a rounding error in his bank account.

It's also the reason why I'm sitting here tonight. I want to be a better person emotionally. Jules used to tell me that only basic bitches beg men for stuff.

"Rich men expect to pay and they expect you to be grateful, that's it." I hear Jules' voice in my head and my ahi tuna turns a little in my stomach. I don't think I'm *that* person.

I take Greg's hand in mine. "Thank you. I really appreciate everything that you've done."

"You're welcome and it's my pleasure, I'm happy to do it. I wish you could come out to the shore this weekend with me and relax for a couple of days."

The tuna churns a little more in my stomach. Greg has a beautiful place along the Maryland Shore. I've been there with him a few times. I always have a good time, but it's also the only place where he and I have slept together. I don't think he means anything by it, but when he mentions it in conjunction with his gift, it reignites the feeling of discomfort I felt when I arrived. *Because you knew it would come to this.*

I try to shake off the uncertainty. The bottom line is that Greg has been really good to me, and he's never asked me for anything. I sleep with him because I want to. I tell myself that same thing like I have been for a while. It used to be enough to quiet my doubts. But I know at some point, I'm going to have to confront myself and the truth might look very different from the cover stories I've been spinning.

LOCHLAN

I sincerely wish Ashley would hurry up. I knew it was a bad idea to bring her to her favorite sweet shop in D.C. This had been my idea to butter her up, but now she's suffering from some sort of sensory overload. She's been at the counter ordering for several minutes. She is up to two cupcakes, a piece of pie, a very large cookie, and some sort of sorbet. The girl needs help. She is extremely fortunate to be blessed with a supercharged metabolism and a love for outdoor sports. If not for both, she would definitely be starring in an episode of that 600-pound show.

I walk up to the counter that looks like it came from a 50s fountain shop and drag my sister back to our booth while juggling about 5000 calories worth of treats. Ashley gives me the stink eye while she bites into the giant cookie.

"Why did you bring me here if you were just going to interfere with my blessings?"

I notice her Southern accent is stronger than normal. It does that when she's annoyed or excited.

"I only let myself have this cookie once a year. This is a big deal, Lochlan. This is like if I charged in the middle of one of your playoff games and stole the ball and ran off with it."

No. This situation definitely is not analogous, but she's on a roll so I don't try to stop her.

"This is a Mars bar cookie with marshmallow. It is possibly the best cookie on the planet." She points an accusatory and sticky finger in my direction. "And you have no respect. You do not rush this kind of greatness."

I hold up my hands in surrender. "Okay, are you finished?"

"I am not."

"Well, what else?"

"Now, I'm finished."

I love my sister and I know her well. None of her behavior is surprising or even off-putting. This is who she is.

"Good, let's get down to business. Tell me everything you know about Mercedes."

Ashley drops the cookie so fast, it almost seems like she forgot she was still holding it when her hand opened on reflex.

"Lochlan, there is something about Mercedes you need to know but it's not my place to tell you."

"Like what? Is she married? Does she have a terminal illness? What is it?"

"You need to talk to her for yourself." The entire time Ashley speaks her cookie is forgotten so I know this is serious.

"I don't want to get in your business but did you have a sexual relationship with Mercedes?"

My sister has never asked me a question like that about anyone. She usually acts as if she's allergic to information about my sex life. "Why would you ask me something like that?"

She still doesn't pick up any of her sweets and my alarm level notches up higher. "Mercedes has a lot going on. If you're looking for a return trip down groupie lane where you used to live, leave her out of that."

"Gee, Ash, thanks for the vote confidence."

"I'm sorry, I'm just trying to figure out where your head is at because you need to talk to her but it doesn't need to be about you rewinding some sexual fantasy. This is serious."

"Why is me wanting to reconnect with an old friend so serious? What aren't you telling me?"

"I'm going to give you Mercedes' contact information, you ask her all of your questions and you guys figure it out."

"How did you meet Mercedes?"

"I met her at work. What's the deal with you and Rachel? You're here asking me about Mercedes but you were literally just with Rachel."

I ignore Ashley's pivot. "Does Mercedes work with you?"

"No. She's actually a nurse. And rude! I see what you just did there. Anyway, Mercedes was at the school..."

I gesture for Ashley to continue. Unbelievably, she finally remembers her sweets and takes this moment, mid-sentence, to sample one of her cupcakes.

Ashley rolls her eyes back in her head before she continues. "Loch, this is butter cream frosting." She waits for my reaction. When I just stare at her, she becomes exasperated. "I'm not adopted. You and Connor are adopted. Our parents appreciate brilliant desserts."

I pinch the bridge of my nose. Connor and I are the spitting image of our Irish father. Ashley is Samoan. Are we really going to have a discussion about who is adopted? Mind you, this is a long-running actual debate. Ashley is convinced she is the genetic child of our parents and that Connor and I are imposters. She's crazy. I love her, but she's actually crazy.

"What was I saying? Oh yeah, Mercedes is a nurse, but we worked on a project together for the school." Ashley's face does this little subtle twitch. I know that twitch, I grew up with it. It means that Ashley is holding something back. Interesting.

"We had a lot in common and we kind of hit it off. She's different. She's really serious and mature. I wouldn't have thought that she's just a year older than me. Mercedes has this world weary way about her. Underneath it though, she's got a really genuine personality and a great sense of humor. Wait. You never told me how you know her."

"It's complicated."

"I bet it is."

I ignore my sister's knowing sarcasm.

\ "I'm going to reach out to her." I pause to get Ashley's reaction.

"I trust that you will do that, Lochlan. I really do. Something about the way you talk about her and look at her makes me think she's important to you and that's important to me. I'm kind of confused though. Are you still the chief ambassador for the millennial Christians or has the cross-shaped stick been removed from your ass?"

Ashley still indulges our mother and attends church faithfully when home. Privately, she wholly rejects the idea of organized religion and embraces a more liberal spirituality. I think it's a cop-out and a way to avoid accountability. That's an argument that has been thoroughly played out.

"I'm going to ignore you because I need your help."

"That seems wise. I'm just trying to say that Mercedes doesn't strike me as being the religious type. I mean she is as far from Rachel as butter crème is from cooked liver. And *hellooo*, you were at the party with Rachel."

"I wasn't with her."

"Pretty sure you were."

"I mean I was with her, but we're not together."

"Say no more. I don't want to do a deep dive into your Christian-mingle dysfunction. I just don't want any of that having a negative impact on Mercedes or..."

"Mercedes or what?"

Ashley doesn't respond. She just shakes her head.

"Come on, Ash! What were you going to say?"

"Loch, I just want you to have your head on straight before you connect with Mercedes."

"My head is on straight for the first time in a long time."

"It might not be what you're expecting."

"I haven't even decided what to expect yet so I'm not sure that's a possibility."

Ashley nods thoughtfully. It's strange to see her so protective of someone she doesn't know all that well and also vested in our meeting. I brought Ashley here to bribe her into giving me the information I wanted, I didn't think she also wanted me to find Mercedes.

MERCEDES

"Mercury, Liam and I are going on our walk. I think I'm going to stop at the Safeway. Do you want me to pick up that seasoning you wanted for your shrimp salad?"

I swear that August waits until I go into the bathroom to start asking me questions. It never fails. Between August and Liam, I never get to use the bathroom in peace. I quickly finish washing my hands and run down the stairs to find August standing at the bottom.

"Why are you whisper-yelling at me?"

"Liam is sleeping!"

"How did you get him to take a nap before you started walking?"

"No, ma'am. I will not be sharing my secrets. If you know this stuff, you may stop needing me."

"If you keep interrupting me while I'm trying to use the bathroom, I may stop caring that I need you."

"Girl, please. Do you want this seasoning? What was it? Ocean Bay? Back Bay? Down River? I need to start back taking my Echinacea because I can't remember shit."

"Instead of taking herbs, maybe stop smoking so many. And, it's Old Bay, August. I'll text you because I know you won't remember by the time you get to the store. What are you still doing here? I thought you left 10 minutes ago?" Hence my plan to use the bathroom.

"No I couldn't go. I couldn't find my lip stuff. You know how I feel about being in public with dry lips!"

I roll my eyes at August, who is still loud-whispering, and checking on Liam in his stroller. He is nice and comfy and sleeping soundly. I can tell he's in a good sleep because he's holding on to his stuffed puppy like he does when he really settles in. My heart brims with love and adoration. He is so beautiful with his little blond curls. Leaning over, I kiss his chubby cheek because I just can't help myself.

"Mercedes, if you wake him up, he is staying here with you."

"Don't you loud-whisper threaten me, August! If you don't get me this seasoning, I'm not making your shrimp salad and I'm not texting you the name of it until you leave. So, buh-bye." I give August a little finger wiggle wave and spin back towards the kitchen.

August opens the door to leave, still muttering something about how he better get his shrimp salad.

Stepping into the kitchen, I actually sigh. After a full week of internal mental drama over what to do about Lochlan and three 12-hour shifts, the kitchen is a welcome distraction. I always take a minute and observe the renovation work that August and I did. Well, mostly August, but I did help. The floors are a light walnut with darker brown stains. The cabinets I selected are a dark teal with gold accent handles. We put in a large country basin sink that faces the back yard and two windows. My favorite thing is the huge island in the center of the kitchen. It's big enough to have four stools fit along the length of it. The quartz top is easy to maintain and gives me space to prepare food while Liam is parked in his high chair eating snacks, or often doing other things that have nothing to do with eating, mostly food art.

I open the over-sized stainless steel refrigerator and take our the vegetables I need to add to the seafood salad. It takes five extra minutes to locate my favorite cutting knife because August was using it to cut the tags off some new clothes he bought. If August wasn't wonderful in every other way, I'd evict him because he's the worst roommate and it's not even close. Speaking of August, I stop to text him the ingredients I need him to purchase because he will not remember. I'm not all that surprised when I hear his phone ding. It's sitting on the table in our breakfast nook along with August's keys. You know you've got a problem when you can't get reminders because you forget the device on which you need to receive the reminders. I roll my eyes, shake my head and turn up my 'Saturday vibes' playlist.

"Baby Boy" by Beyoncé and Sean Paul blasts out of my portable Bluetooth speaker that's set up on the counter, and I'm full-on dancing when I hear the doorbell ring. I set down the vegetables I was cutting up and head back to the front door. I know it's August. I'm going to buy him some vitamins my damn self.

I march to the door and open it with a flourish. The teasing I had planned dies in my throat because it's not August standing at my front door. Not even close.

It's Lochlan Rait.

He's wearing black slacks and a black polo shirt that makes both his tan and his gray eyes pop. Whatever that spicy scent is that it is always on his skin invades my senses as I inhale sharply. I feel as if someone just pushed me off of a cliff and I'm trying to process all of my final thoughts before I meet a concrete death. Like a drum or still the beat of the song, my heart pounds in my chest. Maybe it's from the dancing; but probably not.

"Mercedes, can I come in?"

LOCHLAN

"Mercedes, can I come in?" Okay. Not exactly how I had planned to start.

Mercedes is mid-laugh when she answers the door. She looks like she was getting ready to say something until she sees me. It makes me wonder who she was expecting. And that makes me feel rapidly and unreasonably jealous. Hungrily, I drink her in the same way I had done at the party. She is everything my eyes ever hope to see. Mercedes' face is makeup free. I remember now that she has a few tiny freckles sprinkled on both of her cheeks. Her wide eyes are the same kaleidoscope gray from so many of my thoughts and dreams. Her hair is up, but it is more textured than I have ever seen it. It reminds me of when Ashley misses her weekly blowout appointment. I love this look on Mercedes. She appears more carefree than I've ever seen her.

Before I can remind myself that it's totally inappropriate, my eyes roam down her body. She's wearing a white crop tank top and high-waist yoga capris, tie-dyed in pink and white. Her feet are bare, with cotton-candy pink toenails. Her body... God, help me. My heart stutters, slows, and then starts trying to climb right out of my chest. What was I thinking? How could I ever have wanted to be apart from her?

I had to circle the block a few times, looking for a place to park. I had plenty of time to go over what I want to say to her. But seeing her again, words scatter from my brain. My plan is to explain to her what happened with my accident and get her to understand the reasons for my choices. But when I look at her, I'm not sure the justification for my not calling after I recovered makes much sense. Part of the problem is that I'm not even clear on the answer. Two years later, my reasons for not doing anything don't seem as credible as they did back then.

I probably should just leave her alone. I mean, if I were her, I'd want nothing to do with me. But here I am anyway. Because I can't not try, that's the only way I can explain it.

Now seeing her, the rest of the world just stops. Logically, I know there are still people walking by, birds chirping, dogs barking, and other daily life activities. But everything inside of me is completely focused on her. Nothing else registers.

"I-I... um... I... How did you find me? How did you know I live here?" Mercedes licks her lips nervously and crosses her arms in front of her defensively.

The actions have the opposite effect of what I guess she intended. The result is that my focus is drawn to her plump lips and her breasts, which are now pushed up even higher by her crossed arms. Here's the thing about being a person of faith. You never really know how much you have until it is tested. Today, I find out that I don't have as much as I thought. I already took a step back from my church ambassadorship, but now I can't even recall who that guy is. Standing here right now, I'm just a regular man who wants absolutely nothing more than to bury himself inside this woman.

"Ashley told me your last name at the party. I looked you up." My voice sounds husky even to me.

"I'm not listed."

"Yes, I know, but I have my ways."

Mercedes rolls her eyes at my statement. It doesn't take away from her beauty one bit. I like fiery Mercedes as much as I like wide-eyed, innocent Mercedes. I like all of her.

"Please. Can I just come in for a minute? It took me 30 minutes to find a parking space out here. I'm just asking for a minute. Please."

MERCEDES

It wouldn't be unreasonable for someone in my position to faint in shock at the sight of her long lost baby daddy standing on her porch. But I'm not actually that surprised to see him. Deep down inside, I knew when I walked out of that hallway that he would find me, it was only a matter of time. This is my life. The bad shit always comes knocking.

Even if I wanted to be shocked by Lochlan's appearance, I can't think when he's looking at me like this. He looks like he wants to devour me. God, help me. I would *never* admit this, but when he spoke, I felt my body turning to liquid—*literally*. My nipples are poking through my thin tank top like flashing indicators of how desperate I am to be touched by him. I might as well have a huge sign above my head, reading "Thirsty." Greg is the only person I've been with, and it's been several months since I got some. *Embarrassing*.

Lochlan has this way of not begging. He's asking me to come in, but my body registers it as a demand. My body responds before my sluggish brain can catch up. I back away from the door and let it swing wide so he can walk in. We don't have much of a hallway. The front door leads right into the formal sitting area. If this had happened two weeks ago, there would have been framed pictures of

August, Liam, and I all over the walls. August is going to paint the sitting room so I took all the pictures down and covered them with canvas.

Lochlan looks around my space. I remind myself not to fidget.

"I can see you're still doing work in here, but I have to hand it to you, this place looks amazing for what you've already done. Are you doing this work or did you hire someone?"

I don't bother to answer. There is only one thing we need to discuss and that is Liam.

"Listen, Lochlan, I'm glad you're here. I want to talk to you."

"You do?"

Even though the sitting room is an open space with plenty of room, Lochlan is crowding me and making it hard for me to think. He towers over me and all I want to do is rub myself all over him. I take a step back. He takes a step forward. I step back again.

"Do not come any closer."

He holds up his hands "I'll stay right here. I just like the way you smell."

Oh hell no. This situation is going left. Tell him and get him out of your house.

"Why are you acting like this? If you're so into me and it's so easy for you to find me, why didn't you pick up a phone and call me at any point over the past two years?"

Amazingly, even a sheepish look is sexy on him. "You're right. That's part of what I wanted to explain to you."

I hear the sound of the sliding back door opening followed by August's voice.

"Mercury! Oh shittlesby!" August does the thing we do when we curse around Liam on accident. "There's my phone *and* my keys, Liam Lime. Mercury! Where are you. I left my daggone phone."

I look at Lochlan. His eyebrows are raised in a curious way. He's looking towards the opening to the kitchen where August can still be heard moving around. August is not big enough to explain all the noise he makes in any given room. He could never become a burglar or anything that required stealth.

Before I can respond to August, he walks into the sitting room.

"Mommy, Mommy, Mommy!" Liam squeals in baby exuberance. And even in these crazy circumstances I still delight in how excited my child gets to see me after any absence. I know that one day, he'll be older and it probably won't be like this. I don't look at Lochlan again. I can't. As Liam hurls his little body at me, I just turn and scoop him up.

"Hi, Mommy's baby. I missed you soooo much! Give me kisses," I coo at Liam and kiss his chubby cheeks the way I always do whenever I've been away from him.

August finally enters the room. His timing is fucked up as usual, but he wouldn't be August if he didn't make an entrance.

"Mercury, you would not believe I... Oh, oh! Yoooou haaaaave commmmmpany." August is talking in a high-pitched voice and drawing out words in a completely unnecessary way. It would be funny at any other time.

I finally look at Lochlan. I can't really describe his facial expression. It's evolving too rapidly, like swiping through photos. Thoughtful, shocked and confused are all mixed together, torturing his handsome features.

"Lochlan, this is my roommate, August. August, Lochlan." I point between the two of them. Neither says anything. They just stare.

Here goes. I break the awkward pause, which threatens to stretch on forever.

"And this handsome fella here is my son, Liam." I point at my son who is clinging to my neck like a heavy spider monkey. I turn to the side so that Liam can see Lochlan, his father.

"Hewwo" Liam hasn't quite gotten that double "L" sound down, but he is as friendly as ever.

Lochlan hesitantly steps closer and really looks at him. I can tell when recognition starts to dawn. He opens his mouth and then closes it. He comes even closer to Liam and me. Liam lays his head on my shoulder but still looks at Lochlan curiously.

August is giving me urgent looks. I can almost hear his thoughts screaming at me. "Oh shit! Oh shit! Oh shit!"

"He looks just like my baby pictures." Lochlan swallows "I have a son don't, I? This is my son."

"Yes, he is." It was a statement and not a question, but I answer it anyway.

Lochlan starts shaking his head like his brain can't accept what his eyes are showing him.

"August, can you take him please?"

August walks over to me and holds his arms out to Liam. He goes to him. Liam must sense the tension in the room. August ordinarily has to bribe him with bananas or other goodies to get him away from me when we haven't been together for a while. August starts to creep toward the kitchen with Liam when Lochlan speaks.

"Stop. Where are you taking my son?"

"Excuse you, Lochlan. August is going to take *my son* to get a snack and out to the backyard so you and I can talk." The fucking audacity. Where was this "my-son" act two years ago when I was alone, pregnant, and terrified? He better calm down immediately.

As soon as August is out the back door with Liam, Lochlan slowly swings his blazing gray gaze back to me. For a minute, his chest just goes up and down. I can tell he's struggling to get himself under control.

"How old is he?" The muscle in his jaw is ticking. His teeth are clenched. Okay, time to accept that maybe he didn't know about the pregnancy.

"He's nineteen months." I pause and the silence hangs in the air between us like a living thing. "I called you repeatedly. I used every phone number I could think of. I found your email and I sent you a message. I stalked every social media site I could find for you. I got so desperate I called your agent and your lawyer."

"I know."

"Wait! You know which part of what I just said?"

"I know that you talked to Paul. He told me."

"You actually got my message?"

Lochlan has the decency to look slightly embarrassed. "He told me he talked to you."

"Wait, wait, wait!" I wave my hands in front of me as if I can ward off the tidal wave of truth. "Did you know that he offered me money?"

"I didn't know that part, but I knew you wanted to talk to me."

For the first time, I realize that way deep down inside I really thought Lochlan didn't know. Some part of me always thought maybe he didn't get my message. I feel like I can't breathe but also like I might explode.

"Did you also know that the only way he would allow me to speak to you is if I agreed to sign a NDA?"

"That was my idea."

"Get the *fuck* out of my house!" I point a shaking finger toward the door.

"What? I'm not going anywhere without my son."

"Your son, says who? Not you. Not two years ago when I was pregnant with him. Back then you didn't have shit to say. I didn't hear from you when I was in labor for 27 hours. There was no "my son" when he didn't sleep at night for the first twelve months of his life. I didn't get this kind of energy from you when he needed insurance, diapers, formula, clothes and oh yes, shelter. Didn't hear you saying a motherfuckin' thing back then."

"And that's what matters to women like you, right? Money. Paul was right."

I detonate. "Fuck you *and* Paul. Get. The. Fuck. Out. If you think that's your son, get a lawyer because that's the only way you are getting near him or me."

Sometime during our standoff August popped back into the kitchen. He now has a can of pepper spray and a spatula. Always with the kitchen utensils.

"Mkay, thanks for your visit. Time to go." August is using his psycho sing-song voice. I've only heard it once before and I wound up bailing him out of jail.

Lochlan rakes his fingers through his hair and takes a deep breath. He looks like he's trying to pull it together, get control. Good luck to him. I'm way past that point. He nods his head as if he's responding to some inner thought.

"Fine. I'll leave. But I will be back with an army of lawyers. I hope you're prepared for that. Because there is no way I will ever walk away from my son. Not ever."

Lochlan turns around and stalks out. I'm frozen in place when the sound of the door slamming echoes through the house.

LOCHLAN

"You knew." I'm just barely leashing the old fury when Ashley opens the door to her condo. "You knew and you didn't tell me."

I played out the conversation about Liam with Mercedes in my head a thousand times while I drove to Ashley's house. Standing in her kitchen, I was irrational and that impacts my hearing and comprehension. Now, I'm trying to parse out the discussion and understand it in reverse. But I keep coming back to this one thing: she didn't tell me about my son. Who calls and says they want to talk instead of "I'm pregnant." It didn't occur to her to share that tidbit, but I was supposed to figure it out by osmosis and offer paternal support? Nothing about this makes sense and I have this feeling that I'm missing something. But I was mad as hell at that time. That only ends one way with me. I lash out.

Ashley takes a deep breath, turns, and walks away from the door.

"Come in. I have to get my muffins out of the oven."

"Ashley, to hell with your muffins! How could you not have told me that Mercedes is the mother of my child?" Grabbing her shoulder, I spin her around to face me. To tell me to *my face*.

Ashley puts out her hands and starts backing towards the kitchen.

"Loch, you know I have anxiety issues. I can't have this conversation without sugar. Just let me get my muffins or a piece of candy or something."

I don't say anything else. It is too much to debate with Ashley over her mood issues and addictions right now. I'm barely holding it together. Maybe I'm not holding it together at all.

I take out my phone and text Paul that I need a referral to a family law attorney. He texts back three question marks. I put the phone away when Ashley returns to the living area with a muffin wrapped in a paper towel.

"First of all, I didn't know."

"Bullshit."

"Oh, oh, oh, the ambassador for Christ is cussin' now? Hmph. You hate to see it."

"Ashley, I do not have time for your anti-organized religion crusades. Anyone who sees my son and sees me would know he's my son. He looks exactly like me."

Ashley nervously takes a bite out of the muffin she was blowing on and swipes at some crumbs on her mouth.

"Okay fine. I had a strong suspicion. But Loch, she didn't tell me who the father was. I went back and checked her admissions application and there was no father listed. I checked Liam's birth certificate and there is no father on that either. All I had was a suspicion."

"So, why the hell did you invite her to your birthday party? You knew I would be there."

"That's why I invited her. I wanted to see if you knew each other. I figured if the kid was yours, you'd recognize her. But then I was still confused because it seemed like you sort of knew her, but not really. You didn't react to her like a random groupie, though. That was even more confusing."

"I bet it was, because listening to you describe it is confusing me." I can't believe I have a son. He's beautiful.

"If she was just some random groupie, I could see her maybe getting knocked up and not telling you. But you looked at her like... I don't know how to describe it. You were looking at her like the rest of us didn't even exist, which was kinda rude since it was *my* birthday and all. I've never seen you look like that. You've been with Rachel for years, but you've sure never looked at *her* like that."

I sit down on one of the high-back barstools at Ashley's dining table. My legs don't feel like they're going to hold me much longer.

"So, I was confused. If there was something between you two, why didn't you know about Liam? You're a good guy and she seems like a good person. I just thought she would've told you. Then I convinced myself that I made the whole thing up and that I was being dramatic."

"What about when I came to you and asked you to help me find her? Why didn't you say something then? Ash, for crying out loud, do you know what just happened to me? I'm standing there talking to her and my son…" I get kind of choked up on the word. "My son just walks into the room. Ash, he doesn't even know who I am."

"I'm sorry, Loch. I messed up. I wanted you to know, but I didn't want to get in the middle of it so I tried to let you find out on your own. I'm sorry because you're right. I could've said 'Hey, by the way, she has a kid!' or something. I just… I'm sorry. It seems really stupid in retrospect."

"She brought him to your school, didn't she?" The pieces start to click together.

"Yes. She applied for a spot in the pre-K program. I was the one who administered his admissions test." Ashley hangs her head.

Great. Now, I feel bad. There isn't much my sister could do to make me stop feeling protective of her. I'm still pissed, but this is my mess, not hers.

"What is he like?"

Ashley looks at me with misty eyes. "Oh, Loch, he is absolutely the most amazing little boy I have ever met in my whole life. He's so smart. He blew the little assessment out of the water. And he's clever, you know? Not just smart. He's not even two yet and he has an honest-to-God sense of humor. I'm glad he's yours because that means he's all of ours. Mom and Dad are going to spoil him so rotten that he won't be fit for life in the outside world."

Telling my parents about my illegitimate child? I can't even think about that right now.

"Hang on...how do you—" Ashley's sentence is interrupted by the sound of the front door opening.

"Ash, do you have my muffins?"

It's Connor. He rounds the corner from the hallway and stops when he sees me sitting at the table.

"Oh, hey, Loch, I thought you were tied up today? You should have told me you were free. We could have gone for a ride. I still need to because if these muffins are as good as they smell, I'm going to eat way too many. Wait. What are you two discussing? The vibe in here is weird as hell."

"I have a son," I say it because I still can't believe it. It's like I have to keep saying it to make it real.

Connor squints at me and shakes his head a little. "You have a what now? What's in these muffins, Ash? What are you talking about, Loch?" Connor looks at Ash and me like we've lost our minds.

"I went to go see Mercedes. She has a 19-month-old son and I'm his father. I have a son."

"Whoa, whoa, whoa! How do you know it's your son?"

"Trust me, brother, he looks like I cloned myself. He's definitely mine."

Ashley snaps her fingers and picks up her phone from the sofa and starts scrolling through. She thrusts her phone at Connor. "Here. Look."

I walk over to Connor and we look at the phone at the same time. There he is, the chubby, tanned version of me smiling at us from Ashley's phone.

"Holy shit! He looks just like you. Holy shit!" Connor's mouth hangs open momentarily. "You knocked her up? And you didn't know?"

Ashley and Connor are both looking at me expectantly.

"Of course, I didn't know. Do you think if I had known I would've left my kid?"

Connor is thoughtful as he gestures up and down at me. "This

Lochlan wouldn't leave his kid, no. But Bible-belt Lochlan..." Connor shrugs his shoulder.

"Oh, would you two come off of it? I'm not a different person because I dedicated myself to the church."

"Oh, I agree you don't have to be, but you choose to be."

"And what, Connor? You think this alternate version of me would walk away from my child?"

"I don't know what that other person would do. That's my point."

"Well, surprise, I still go to church." I turn to Ashley "I'm still involved in the 'organized religion thing.' And I would not leave my child. I can't believe you two."

Connor just shrugs again. "I'm not going to apologize. I've treated you how you've behaved."

I get ready to say something, but Connor puts up his hand, "I'm sorry, but can we all just re-focus here? Where is this child? When are we meeting him?"

I blow out a long breath. "That's going to be an issue."

Ashley returns from the kitchen with the whole pan of pumpkin muffins. "I think we are going to need these." She has barely set the pan down before Connor is digging in.

Ashley faces me. "Okay, Loch. What did you do?"

10

MERCEDES

Yesterday was the king of epic trash. Today is trying to steal yesterday's crown. After Lochlan left, my mental state was devastated. I couldn't hang on to any one negative thought because they were all bombarding me at the same time.

Not good enough....Sloppy leftovers... Just a baby mama... Not good enough... Not good enough...

What was I thinking? All this time I've been holding on to the fantasy that I'm the woman who falls madly in love with the handsome hero, who also happens to be sensitive, funny, and talented. For just a minute, when Lochlan showed up at my door, I really thought there was a chance for this to become a whirlwind romance story. I could feel Lochlan in my heart, my body, my mind, everywhere. I was surrounded by a glass house of hope. But I've thrown my share of rocks. Karma don't forget shit.

His words replay over and over in my head: "Women like you." I take a big gulp of my homemade margarita and lean back on the sofa. "Women like me..." I laugh. You don't even know the half of it, Lochlan. Who was I kidding anyway? I'm not some fairytale princess. Truthfully, I wouldn't even be cast as a stepsister.

The Fugees' version of "No Woman, No Cry" wails quietly from my portable speaker. I don't know if the melancholy is me or the song. To make matters worse, Liam was extremely fussy after Lochlan left yesterday. He simply would not settle down. Kids know things. They experience energy in a way that we don't. I think the residue of the fight between his parents has messed up Liam's whole mood. Today, it seems like he's getting a little bug. He barely slept last night and barely ate today. His nose is running, he's coughing, and he continues to be uncharacteristically cranky.

I finally sent August away. He was worried about me. He was worried about Liam and he was stressing me the fuck out. He needed to leave the house or he was going to suffer an unfortunate accident. Besides, he already had a date planned and had the nerve to try to cancel. I strongly insisted that he go for both of our sakes.

Now, I'm in the house by myself. Liam is sleeping and I feel like I'm drowning in bullshit. What if Lochlan does get a lawyer? What the hell am I going to do? I already called Jules. I don't really have anyone else in the world besides August. Jules is a bobble head at life, but that chick has nine lives, and she always lands on her feet with men. Her advice is unsettling, but I know she's right.

"Call Greg."

"Jules, I don't want to tell him about this. I don't want him to know about Lochlan."

"Mercedes do you know how much lawyers cost?"

"No. How much?"

"How the hell would I know? I've never hired a lawyer that a man didn't pay for. I also don't know what my mortgage costs, the taxes, my car payment—"

"Okay, okay, I get it. You can't count." I was taking my frustration at Jules' advice out on her.

"Oh no, bitch, I can count. One, that is the number that matters, because one rich man equals zero problems."

She's wrong about that part. I take a sip of my margarita. I've known a lot of guys with money. They all came with problems. But she's still right. If I need a lawyer, I will have to call Greg. I can't afford to hire anyone who could face off against a lawyer that Lochlan could afford. *Shit.*

It's not yet 9pm. The sun is just starting to set when I hear Liam crying on the baby monitor. I take a deep breath. It looks like it's going to be another long night. I should've slammed my margarita when I had the chance. Now, I'm going to have to deal with this on the four sips I got.

I walk up the stairs and into Liam's room. He's sitting up in his crib. His little cheeks are flaming red and he's wailing.

"Mommy's here, my little cookie monster. What's da matter with Mommy's baby?"

I pick Liam up from his crib. He's burning up. I unzip his pajamas to cool him off. His chest is warm. I notice for the first time ever, he's kind of wheezing. I gently rock him on my hip. He lays his head on me and stops crying, but he's still burning up, and his breathing is wheezy. I get the infant thermometer and take his temperature. *Shit*! It's 106 degrees. Babies can have higher temperatures than adults, but that's too damn high. I check Liam's other vitals. His heart rate is accelerated. I give him some infant Tylenol and sit him in his little baby chair so I can pack his bag. We're making a trip to the Emergency Room.

LOCHLAN

I'm pounding down the hallway in the hospital, frantically searching for the room number Mercedes gave me.

"Sir, sir, you can't go back there without a pass." I was getting ready to run past the circular desk at the end of the hallway when the receptionist or whoever she is, stops me with a monotone voice. I glance down the hallway and think about making a run for it.

"Please, sir, it takes less than a minute to get a pass. Don't do anything ridiculous. We've had enough of that tonight, I swear."

I relent and back pedal to the desk. After what feels like an eternity of checking my ID and entering my information into some computer system, the woman at the desk asks me what room I'm visiting. When I tell her, she says, "Hold on one moment and let me call back because you're not on the visitors list."

She can take that visitors list and stick it— I lose my train of thought when Mercedes comes walking down the hall. If I'm being honest, she still looks gorgeous, but stressed. She's wearing a plain gray sweat suit. Her hair is still the mix of curls and waves I saw for the first time yesterday, but it somehow looks bigger and messier. She's twisting the rings around the finger on one of her hands.

Mercedes walks right up to me. The impulse to hug her or to

touch her in some way is strong, but I get the impression that would not be well received.

"Hey, sorry if I worried you. I didn't mean to be all hysterical."

"No, don't apologize. It's fine. How is he?"

"He's fine. He just got a breathing treatment and fell asleep. I want to get back. I just was coming out to add you to the visitors list. I forgot when we first got admitted."

"Mercedes?" Bored receptionist appears to know Mercedes by name.

Mercedes turns to face her. "Hi, Gayle."

"Hey, hun. I thought that was you. Is your baby in here?"

"Yes, and don't worry, Gayle. He's fine. He's back in 38B. I just came to get this guy." She points at me. "I forgot to put him on the visitors list."

Gayle finally looks like something interesting is happening. Her bushy eyebrows creep toward her graying hairline, but she doesn't comment. She just reaches to the printer and pulls off my pass. After fastening a snap to the top, the badge is slid across the desk towards me.

"Thanks, Gayle."

"You're welcome, sweetie. Give that precious baby boy a kiss for me."

"I will give him lots of kisses." Mercedes smiles and inclines her head toward the hall, indicating that I should follow her.

"They think he has asthma."

"Okay, well, his grandmother has asthma."

Mercedes looks at me over her shoulder but doesn't say anything. When we walk into the hospital room, I see Liam in the little crib bed. Immediately, I notice that he is cuddled on his side holding some kind of stuffed animal. He even sleeps like me. Mercedes stops to talk to the nurse who is entering information into the computer at the end of the bed. I walk right up to my son.

When Mercedes called me tonight, I was sitting outside, breathing fresh air and trying to clear my head. I really didn't want to involve lawyers in the situation with Mercedes and my son. I had prayed about it. Also, I was not going to be away from my child. I had prayed about that too. I had texted Mercedes earlier in the afternoon to find out if we could sit down and talk. She hadn't responded. I don't know if I'd thought an answer would magically appear at dusk or what, but I'd been staring up at the vanishing daylight when my phone rang.

"*Mercedes. I didn't think you would call.*"

"*I wasn't going to. Trust me on that.*"

"*We need to talk.*"

"*Later, Lochlan. Right now, I'm at the hospital with Liam. Don't freak out, but he had a fever and his breathing was kind of labored. I thought it might be best to get him to a doctor.*"

I was already up and out of my seat. "*Where are you?*"

"*I'm at the Georgetown Pediatric Hospital. Liam is being admitted.*"

"*I'm on my way.*"

"*Listen, Lochlan. Liam is okay. They are running tests, but he's okay. I just...*"

"*You don't have to explain. He's my son. I'm on my way.*"

I threw a sweatshirt over my head, picked up my baseball cap and keys, and rushed out. This is the closest I've been to my little guy. His eyes are closed and his little blond curls are all over his head. He has little round cheeks and he still has some of his baby fat. My mom always said I was chubby until I was three and then I turned into a rail. I rub his hand and he clutches my finger in his sleep. I have a son.

It's gotten quiet in the room. I look up and Mercedes is staring at me. Her eyes brim with unshed tears. I messed this up so bad. God, I hope I can fix it.

MERCEDES

"I'm not going to try to keep you away from him," I say it because it's true. I hate how Lochlan made me feel about myself, but I can't take it out on Liam. I won't. I can clearly see that Lochlan is going to love Liam. He looks at him like he's a miracle. That's how I look at him. I wish to God I had known my father and I'm not going to deny my son the opportunity.

"I'm sorry. I'm sorry for what I said, how I said it, and when I said it. I'm just sorry for all of it."

"It's fine, Lochlan. This isn't about us. This is about..." I pause and gather all my strength and will. It was time to face facts. "This is about *our* son." There. I said it.

Lochlan's face softens. He visibly relaxes his shoulders. "What are the doctors saying?"

"They think he had an asthma attack that was triggered by an upper respiratory infection. His pulse ox dropped to about 94 percent at one point so he needed to be admitted." I'm a medical professional. When I saw the pulse ox reading, I knew I didn't overreact by bringing him to the hospital.

"I have so many questions. I want to know everything about him.

I've already started thinking about decorating his bedroom and setting up a playroom. Oh, I ordered a foosball table too."

"Well, Lochlan, he's not even two yet and can't quite reach a foosball table so..." I talk very slowly and let my words trail off. Huh. So, is this what fathers are like?

Lochlan laughs. He's standing there in a black hoodie and gray gym shorts. His facial scruff looks like it definitely didn't get cut today. That laugh still makes him the most compelling man I've ever met. I must be staring because he stops laughing abruptly and stares back at me.

"I'm sorry."

"You said that."

Lochlan looks down at Liam again. "I just... Why didn't you tell me about him?"

Before I can respond, the curtain is drawn back and Dr. Shine walks in. I've known Dr. Shine since he transferred to Georgetown Peds a year ago. He's one of the younger doctors, probably in his late 30s. He doesn't do the whole superior doctor-insignificant nurse act so he's cool with me. If I see him in the cafeteria, I sometimes have lunch or a cup of coffee with him.

"Dr. Shine, what are you doing here? And in scrubs no less?" Most people don't know this, but doctors don't work after business hours. If you see a medical professional outside the ER after 5pm, it's a nurse or maybe a physician's assistant. In other words, the majority of care is performed by nurses. You're welcome.

"I picked up a rotation in the ER. All three of the ER ped docs have the flu, so I'm trying to help out. I must have missed you when you came in. - There was a three-car accident and three kids in one of the cars, so I was tied up, but I heard you were up here with Liam." People also don't realize how fast gossip travels in a hospital. HIPAA be damned. Everybody knows everything. "I wanted to come check on Liam myself. But I didn't know you weren't alone. Is this a bad time?"

I glance over at Lochlan. He's looking at Dr. Shine's hand, which he placed on my arm in a comforting gesture. His eyes lift to look at

Dr. Shine's face and raises one eyebrow. I didn't know he could do that. It's sexy as hell. Dr. Shine drops his hand and I struggle not to roll my eyes. *Really, Lochlan?* I like Dr. Shine, but there's nothing there and I'm pretty sure he feels the same way about me. He's a good-looking doctor with lots of options. Plus, I heard he had a fiancée who's a lawyer or something else big-time. I doubt he's thinking about some nurse.

"No, it's not a bad time. Liam's father and I will probably be here for a while." I get stuck on the F-word word every time. The doctor does a double take before asking, "Aren't you Lochlan Rait? You used to play for the Wizards? I remember you. You were really good."

Lochlan nods but doesn't seem overly impressed by the recognition. His response is brief. "Yup, that's me."

"And this is Liam's father?" Dr. Shine addresses me and I'm sort of at a loss.

Am I supposed to double check now? I mean I just said it was his father. Luckily, Lochlan steps in.

"Yes, I'm his father. Are you here to examine my son or..." I'm not sure what belongs at the end of that sentence, but it kind of sounds like the other option is get the hell out.

"Actually, Lochlan, I work with Dr. Shine. He's probably not on Liam's rotation yet."

An idea comes, though. "But, could you take a quick peek at his chart? I don't want to disturb him with an exam, but I trust you and I'd like your opinion."

"Anything for you, Mercedes. Of course, I'll look."

Lochlan looks like he might put hands on the doctor when he squeezes my arm before walking over to the computer to pull up Liam's chart. I look at Lochlan behind his back, and give him a gesture meant to ask what the hell he was doing and warn him to knock it off at the same time. Lochlan lazily rolls his eyes. It doesn't inspire confidence that he's going to get his act together.

"I see. Okay, it looks like he has a preliminary case of asthma. I would agree based on the results of the early testing. But his lungs look good and his pulse ox is back within normal range. The fever responded immediately to Tylenol, but we need to keep an eye on that." Dr. Shine rattles off information in that list fashion that doctors employ. I wonder if they learn that in medical school. "If he remains stable overnight, I'm guessing he'll be discharged tomorrow with something to keep the inflammation in the lungs to a minimum. Then we pray that he doesn't have seasonal allergies. Did you have allergies as a child?"

"No, I didn't."

"What about you, Mr. Rait? Do you have any seasonal allergies in your family?"

"No, just my sister, but she's adopted."

"That bodes well for your little guy. He should be fine."

Dr. Shine shuts down the computer and moves back to the curtain. He lingers for a second.

"Thank you so much for stopping by, seriously. I'm buying the coffee next time," I say and I mean it.

Dr. Shine smiles at me. He really is handsome in a very different way than Lochlan. He's got a butter-caramel complexion and dark brown eyes. He's a little over 6 feet tall and usually sports a low fade. He also has more of a runner's build than that of a NBA player. But if you take all that and combine it with the M.D. behind his name, he's a 9 if not a 10. He's not for me, but I appreciate his fiancée's luck.

"I think it's my turn to get the coffee, but you can get the next lunch." We both turn at the sound of Lochlan. - Was that a grunt?

"Goodnight, Doc. Thanks for stopping by." Lochlan gives him a chin lift clearly meant as a dismissal. Dr. Shine takes the hint and retreats, swishing the curtain closed behind him.

When I face Lochlan again, I don't say anything for a few seconds. He finally says with a shrug, "What?"

"You know what. What the hell was that?"

"How do you know him?"

"Lochlan." I take a deep breath. He is all over the place and seriously, he's been in the picture five minutes and he's pulling this shit? I don't even know what this is right now.

"I work here, in case you didn't notice. I know most of the people who work here. That was me having a conversation with one of my colleagues. Why am I explaining this to you?" I throw up my hands in frustration and walk around the little crib bed so I can sit in the chair next to my sleeping child. He must be so tired. He hasn't moved except to snuggle closer to his stuffed puppy.

Lochlan is standing on the other side of the bed looking at me thoughtfully. I roll my eyes at him because I'm super mature.

"So, you really don't see that guy was flirting with you in our child's hospital room?"

I hate how calm he sounds. It makes me question if I'm missing something. The way he tilts his head at me like he's genuinely confused is triggering all my defenses.

"He has a fiancée. He was not flirting with me. Trust me. He would not want someone like me."

"What the hell does that mean?" The force of his reaction to my comment throws me off a little bit.

"I don't know, Lochlan. *You* tell *me* what you meant by "women like me." I didn't get the impression it was positive."

He visibly flinches at that. "Mercedes, I didn't—"

"You did and it's fine. I don't even care. I just need to get through tonight and get my child home tomorrow."

"*Our* child." His response is immediate.

I can see he won't be letting that go *ever*. "Whatever, Lochlan. I already told you I'm not going to keep him from you." I recline my chair and close my eyes. "I'm just going to try to get some sleep."

Lochlan sits down in the other reclining chair. "Fine, get some sleep. We can talk in the morning."

"You're staying?"

He just looks at me as if to say "duh." I barely even have the parenting thing down. Now, it looks like I'm going to have to master co-parenting too.

11

LOCHLAN

"**C**an I just say how glad I am that I did not have to hit you with that spatula?"

Mercedes' eccentric roommate calls out from the kitchen while I play with Liam in the den. The den must belong to the little guy because there are toys, books, arts and crafts, and kiddie furniture everywhere. I can tell exactly where he was last playing, because one corner of the room looks like a bomb went off in it. The room is decorated in navy blue, gray, and white. Bright color photos of classic trains, planes, and automobiles adorn the walls. A large model antique airplane hangs from the ceiling. It's a perfect play-room for my son. The thought apparent in every detail shows me how much his mother cares about him. But the best part of it all is my busy little boy, who is currently dragging out another truck for me to play with.

We were discharged from the hospital late this morning and Liam has since made a full recovery. August showed up as we were leaving the hospital. That was a scene. He had on a Fedora and wide-legged pants, simultaneously threatening to faint and also to kick my ass if I was causing problems. Somehow, we made it back to the house in one piece. August seems to take his cues as to how to respond to me from Mercedes. She's investing all her energy into Liam and is pretty quiet when it comes to me. This appears to calm August down. Well, at least he's no longer threatening me with violence.

"Truthfully, I hadn't thought about what you'd planned to do with that spatula."

"Well, it's water under the bridge." August peeks his head around the corner and gives me a severe, appraising look. "For now, anyway."

I've been vroom-vrooming and choo-chooing for about 30 minutes straight while Mercedes takes a shower. Liam seems like he could keep going for much longer when August steps fully into the room.

"I put some lunch together for him. Do you want to bring him in the kitchen? You got all psycho-diva the last time I tried to remove him from a room where you were."

I ignore August. "Hey, bud, you wanna go get some lunch?" I stoop down on my son's level so I can talk to him.

He laughs like I said something hilarious and screams right in my face, "Nanas!"

I wipe his baby spit off my face and lift him up, and follow August into the kitchen.

After we get him all set up at his high chair with an assortment of finger food selected by August, he zeroes in on me.

"So, what is your deal? What do you want with Mercedes and Liam?"

"Well, August, I'm Liam's father, so I plan to be that."

"And what about Mercedes?"

"What about her?"

"Look, she's already been through a lot. I know it's hard to see it because she acts tough, but she's... Well, she is tough, but she's also very human and can definitely be hurt. She's been hurt. I couldn't always protect her, but I can now." August starts wagging his finger aggressively. "I'm not just going to stand by and let anything happen to her. Think of me like her very young, attractive dad who will still fucksickle you up." He glances at Liam who is partially eating his lunch and partially smearing it on his high chair table. Liam giggles at us like he knows he's been busted. "So, yeah, I need to know what your intentions are."

What do *I intend?*

"I know she's been hurt. I know that."

August put his hands on his narrow hips. "How would you know anything about Mercedes' past?"

"Not that it's your business, but she told me."

"Let me get this straight. August points at me and waves his finger up and down. "Mercedes James Dean told you about her past?"

"Mercedes' full name is Mercedes *James* Dean?"

"Oh, oh, I thought you kneeeew Mercedes?"

"We spent less than 24 hours together, so I'm sure there are things I don't know, but yeah, she told me some things. So, I do know she's been hurt and I know she overcame a lot to get where she is. I have a lot of respect for her for that. But I didn't know the last half of her name is James Dean."

"First, Mercedes had a young mother who was and still is, an idiot. She wanted a Mercedes and she thought James Dean was hot. That's the whole story of her name. Second, Mercedes doesn't tell anybody about her past. I mean *nobody*. The only reason I know the things I know is because I was there for things. She does *not* talk about that stuff *ever*. I don't know why she trusted you, but she did. Then you completely shitted on her. This is why I need my spatula at all times."

"You need to calm down with the spatula talk. Look, here's where I am right now. I already love my son more than anything else on this planet and I plan to spend every minute of the rest of my life making up for the first 19 months. When it comes to Mercedes, I just don't know. I don't understand why Mercedes didn't tell me about him and I'm trying to work through that."

"Now, wait a damn minute, Mr. Sexy Passionate Speeches! She *tried* to tell you and your little attack-dog lawyer told her to get an abortion and then told her that you wouldn't talk to her without a NDA, which, she comes to find out was all *your* idea! So, you can climb your fine self right down off your high horse."

"What the hell are you talking about?" Liam looks startled at the sound of me yelling. He drops his spoon and his mouth forms a comical oh. "Uh oh." My son knows his stuff because this is definitely turning into an uh-oh situation.

"I admit to the NDA, but I never would have said anything about an abortion. I don't even believe in abortion and neither does Paul!"

"He didn't actually use the word abortion."

"Mommy." Liam reaches out to Mercedes when she walks into the kitchen. She is out of the shower and smells like something I want to eat. I have to physically restrain myself from rubbing my nose on her skin when she walks by me to take Liam out of the high chair.

"He just offered me money for the problem." It sounds obscene when she says it while holding our child on her hip. Our child who is bending towards the floor trying to get away.

"I get the train, Mommy."

"Okay go get the train." Mercedes puts Liam down and he runs toward his playroom with August following behind him.

"Now, listen here, little boy, you are not gon' be running over my pedicure with that train. Not today."

"Mercedes, listen, Paul wasn't offering you money for an abortion."

"Okay, I'll play along. What was the money for?"

"He thought you were some groupie who was looking for a payday. That's why I suggested the NDA. It had nothing to do with you being pregnant. We didn't even know about your pregnancy."

"Paul knew."

"No way."

"Lochlan, I told Paul Rutland III that I was pregnant with your child."

"No. No. He would've told me."

"So, now you're telling me you didn't know?"

"What? Of course, I didn't know. I mean why wouldn't Paul tell me that? Even if he thought you weren't serious, I..." I can't even find words right now. This isn't possible, is it? "Wait a minute. The other day when you kicked me out, you thought I knew? I mean you thought I knew you were pregnant?"

"Well, yeah." She shrugs.

"This is so fucked up." My use of the F-word seems appropriate in these circumstances. God will forgive me. "I can't believe you thought I knew. God, no wonder you hate me." I put my hands on her shoulders and stare into her eyes, trying to press the truth of my words into her consciousness by sheer will. "I promise you I never heard it said or even implied that you were pregnant. I had no idea you had a child until he walked in the door two days ago."

She's quiet. I can't read her expression and I hate that she backs away from my touch.

"I don't hate you." The only sound for what seems like eternity is Liam screaming and August also screaming about Liam running over his feet.

"Well, maybe you should. Maybe you should hate me. I'm not feeling too good about me right now."

Mercedes nods her head thoughtfully. "Maybe. But it seems silly to hate someone for something you thought they did that they didn't actually do once you know the person didn't actually do it."

"Mercedes, I need to go."

"O-kay." She looks confused by my sudden declaration.

"Do you think we can start over again?"

She sighs deeply. "If you mean start over figuring out our co-parenting, absolutely."

That is only part of what I meant. But I don't tell her that.

"Let me just tell my little guy bye and I'll be back. Should I get anything while I'm out like diapers or baby food or I don't know?"

"No, we're fine. Are you coming back?" I love the way she wrinkles her face in confusion.

"Is it okay if I do? I don't want to be away from him for too long."

"Okay, but Lochlan, we need to figure this out. I have a life, you have a life, so we need a schedule or something."

I nod, but there's not going to be any schedule. I'm here now and this is my family.

MERCEDES

I'm cleaning as if I can calm my inner thoughts with vigorous swiffer-ing. If I can get this house spotless, maybe I can wipe the bullshit grime off my brain. Liam is down for the night. I hope. August is in his quarters, as he has named his living area, listening to music and doing his beauty treatments. He's alternating between rap and early 90s rock. I don't know who the hell can set any kind of mood with that wide of a selection. One minute I hear "fuck bitches, get money," and the next George Michael is singing about things he doesn't want to learn. It is the playlist of someone with a split personality.

I have reorganized the den, disinfected all the hard toys, and cleaned every surface when I hear the doorbell. Lochlan and I are going to definitely have the talk that all parents have with their child-less friends: don't ring the fucking doorbell *ever*. I run to the door before he can ring it again. But it isn't him.

Jules is standing at the door with her finger poised at the buzzer like she doesn't mind if she loses that digit tonight. Damn, I'm really bad at guessing who's on my front stoop. Of course, it's Jules. Wher-ever shit is completely out of hand, she appears. My life being in shambles is like a beacon for Jules to show up and make shit worse.

"Well, hello to you too, Mercedes." She brushes past me in a cloud of Gucci Bamboo fragrance and struts into the house that she spent years partially residing in. "Why are you just standing there looking like you just found out your new Louis bag is a knockoff? Aren't you happy to see me?"

Happy is not the word I would have used. Yes, I call Jules when I need emergency advice, especially about men. And no, I really can't be that picky about who I count as my support network since there's not much to it. But Jules' and my relationship is complicated.

I last saw Jules when Liam was born. She popped in, supposedly to check on me. But I knew she was seeing some new guy who lived in the area. I figured that was the real reason she fell from the sky. Jules has never liked babies or children. Her maternal instinct is pretty much nonexistent. So, I seriously doubt she was dying to see Liam. When I finally told her I was pregnant, I was already eight months along. Her exact words were: "Mercedes, ew, why?"

"Jules what are you doing here?"

"Hel-lo, you called me about your baby daddy drama. I wanted to see if you needed a little muscle." She huffs in indignation. It's well practiced but probably insincere. Jules is too shameless to ever really get indignant. She just don't give enough of a fuck for all that.

"Are you the muscle?"

"Um, no Mercedes, but you know I can always find some. Where's the kid?"

"He's not hiding behind one of my potted plants, Jules, so you can stop looking at them like he might jump out at you. I will also thank you to stop referring to my son as 'the kid.' His name is Liam, and he's sleeping. It's 7pm, that's baby midnight around here. Do you want something to eat or drink?" I lead and Jules follows me into the kitchen.

"Wow! You've really fixed this shithole up."

"Mkay, thanks?" I search the refrigerator for some leftovers we can snack on while Jules makes herself comfortable at the breakfast nook.

"You had that beautiful place near U Street with Clay and you chose to come back to this place before the waterfront was, uh, *the waterfront.*"

The refrigerator slams harder than I intend it to. I spin around to glare at her. The fucking nerve.

Jules had introduced me to Clay nine years ago after my grandma finally worked herself into an early grave and I still remember the night with clarity.

"Baby girl, you fine as shit."

We were at an exclusive lounge in Adams Morgan in an even more exclusive VIP section. My almost C and a half cups were popping out of the sparkly gold dress that barely stretched to my mid-thigh. I wore my hair, which had grown out some from the short bob, pinned back on one side to make the side part look even more dramatic. Since my first foray into night life, I'd learned a lot about hair, makeup, and attire. Jules, my constant mentor, sat on the lap of Clay's teammate. His hand was under her short dress, and Jules giggled at something he murmured to her. She must've sensed me looking, because she glanced at me and sort of subtly tilted her head at Clay encouragingly.

I laughed on cue. "Thanks, Clay. I picked this outfit out for you. Jules told me your favorite color is gold."

"She didn't lie." For the rest of the night Clay kept me close to him, touching me and whispering in my ear. Later, in the mirrors of the bathroom, Jules squealed at me in delight.

"I can't believe it! He actually likes you! Do you know how much his contract is worth?" Of course, I had no idea. "Thirty-three million, Mercedes! Thirty. Three. He's one of the highest paid quarterbacks in the league. If you can reel him in, all of our problems are solved."

Not so sure about that plan. Men like Clay clearly thought being a gentleman was out of fashion. "I don't know, Jules. He's kind of a jerk. All he talks about is what he wants to do to me and his hands are everywhere all the time like a fucking octopus."

Jules backed me up against the wall and put her hand on each side of my head, caging me in. She spoke slowly, as if to a child. I was a child, really. "Listen to me, sweetie. You need money to get a lawyer and get your-

self emancipated so you don't wind up in foster care now that your grand-mother is gone."

"Jules, you're old enough so why don't you just stay with me?" We had been over this twelve times since grandma had died two months before. I already knew the answer, but I couldn't stop myself from trying again. I was terrified about the idea of being left all alone, and the social worker was all up in my business. I had to figure it out soon. Jules wasn't much, but at least an adult and not a complete stranger.

Jules rolled her eyes dramatically and turned back towards the mirror, reapplying her lipstick. She smacked her lips, posing. "Look, I'm not telling you to do anything that I'm not doing. I'm not working at some dead-end job so I wind up dead before my 60th birthday." That stings because I know she's talking about my grandmother. "We don't have to sit in that shitty house in southwest scraping by. I was gone in a few months, tops, anyway. Now, you don't have to stay there either. You can have all the best shit. Don't you get that? Clay Fucking Farrell has been stalking you all night. How is this even up for discussion?"

I guess she's right, I remember thinking. My grandma had worked so much between the factory job and being an overnight caregiver, she was exhausted for two years straight. I barely even got to see her. I knew she did it all so that I could stay in my good school and have a better life than she'd had. Didn't I owe it to her to at least try to maintain what she had started for me? And what other options did I really have?

"Here's my suggestion," Jules preaches, readjusting her breasts in the mirror. "Let him hit it from the back. Make sure to throw it back so he can see that jiggle. Guys love that. Do the hip swivel I taught you, and I swear we won't have to worry about anything for a long time." Jules looked at me like she had this all figured out and was certain of her plan.

So, that's what I did. Within a month, Clay had moved me into a place he was using in the U Street area. He bought me absolutely anything a girl could want, and most importantly, paid my high school tuition in full. He even gave me an allowance to pay the upkeep and taxes on grandma's house and all my legal fees so I didn't lose it or myself to foster care. I told him that I was 18 and had been held back for two years. He never asked me any questions.

Everything was fine until I came home from school early one day near the end of my senior year. That's the part of the story Jules doesn't seem to recall but I damn sure remember.

I fucked up. I got so wrapped up in my AP chemistry final that I forgot to take my birth control a couple of times. I was so close to being free from Clay and this bullshit now that I'm 18 but two lines shredded my plans for my future. I have enough scholarships to pay for my tuition, I only needed cash for some of the other stuf,f but the other stuff didn't include daycare and diapers. My steps are slowed by my anxiety over the future. When I unlock the heavy wood door to the condo I live in with Clay, it feels like a door closing instead of opening.

I drop my keys on the table in the entryway and sit my backpack down next to it. For a minute I think Clay must have left the TV on. I'm early because I didn't feel like going to my AP chemistry study group. I texted Clay to tell him and he told me he was working out with some of his team-mates. The noise gets louder when I round the corner that leads from our entryway to the sunken living area.

"Bounce that ass up and down."

"Like that? Is that how you like it?"

"Fuck yeah, ride that dick just like that."

I know those two voices, Clay and Jules. The way the sitting room is set up, Clay's back is to me but I can clearly see Jules bouncing up and down and winding her hips, just the way she taught me to do. She looks at me, just right at me but the winding of her body never stops or slows. She plays with her nipples and licks her lips as I watch.

I don't feel anything but tired. I've seen Jules perform this act enough times that I'm not effected by her vulgarity. I'm just exhausted and confused. I didn't even know she was in town. That's what I think to myself as I walk to the kitchen to get a bottle of water. I know Clay's sounds; they've got awhile to go before he's done. I may as well grab a snack. Pregnancy makes me feel like I'm starving all the time. The kitchen is off to the side of the living room so Clay still can't see me. I'm glad. If I had to watch him pretend to be sorry, I'd vomit and it wouldn't have anything to do with the baby.

I did everything Jules told me I needed to do to be free and I'm still in this fucked up world with these fucked up people. I take my water out of the refrigerator and get a box of teddy grahams for the road. I don't even pay attention to Clay talking about how good Jules' pussy is. We could trade places and Clay wouldn't know or care. It's just a warm hole to him. I need to go upstairs, pack a bag and grab the rest of my school stuff. I'm leaving and I'm not coming back.

Remembering that day makes Jules' statement seem even more outlandish than the usual shit she says. "Well, Jules, if I hadn't come home to you riding Clay's dick, maybe I would've stayed on U Street."

Jules doesn't even look embarrassed. She just rolls her eyes and waves my comment off. "Those professional athletes are for everybody. How many times do I have to tell you that? They don't belong to any one woman; they belong to the streets. I set you up with him so that you would be taken care of, not so you would fall in love with him."

"I wasn't in love with him. You. Fucking. Sociopath."

"Ohh, big words from a little girl. Keep that energy when it comes to your baby daddy. It's lost on me. My point is that me fucking Clay had nothing to do with your situation with him. Do you think I would ever let some thirsty hoe stop my bag? No, there's no way."

"Huh, so you finally admit to being a thirsty hoe?"

"Watch it, Mercedes. I still carry my razor."

I practice controlling my breathing while I make a salad. Jules might still carry a razor but she knows I got these hands and I don't care anything about a razor that she'd have to get to before she could use it. I don't throat punch my here today, gone tomorrow fake friend, because Jules is technically right, I didn't love Clay or even like him all that much and nobody knew that better than her. Clay was good-looking, rich, and a complete asshole.

I had finally resigned myself to life with someone who I didn't love and didn't even really like. But I couldn't bring myself to fuck my kid up with all this drama. My child winding up like me was an outcome I just intuitively rejected. So, I packed my shit and went back to my grandmother's house. I really was 18 by then and I owned it outright.

It ended up not mattering. I lost the baby a few weeks later. I never even told Jules about the pregnancy. She probably would've just told me to thank her for helping me dodge that bullet. On second thought, she definitely would've said that.

"Aw, hell no, who left the damn gate open?"

August's voice snaps me out of my fucked-up trip down memory lane. Let the eye rolling and name calling commence.

Jules greets him with her usual charm. "August, I see you're still lingering like a bad yeast infection."

"Satan." August nods towards Jules. "You would certainly know a bad yeast infection."

"Don't start with me boy-girl-boy."

I reach out and grab August before he can get to my kitchen utensils. "Absolutely not, Aug, no spatulas tonight."

"Mercury, let me just give her a light tap."

"No. My nerves can't take anymore tonight and if you guys wake Liam up, everybody is getting fucked up!" My hand sweeps across the room so that they know I'm talking to both of them. Jules isn't even paying attention anymore. She's texting someone at a rapid pace.

"I got that lawyer for you, Mercedes."

"What lawyer? And I know you're not taking help from Lucifer?" August looks less than impressed. He's winding up, I can tell. God, he hates Jules.

"August..." Hopefully the pleading warning tone I'm taking will get him to back down.

"No, Mercedes. You always call her when shit goes left. She shows up and you know what happens? The shit goes even more left! You still don't get that?" The undertone of sympathy in August's tone is the worst part. It's like he's saying, "Poor Mercedes still doesn't get that she's all alone?" That's how his words feel to me.

I'm actually grateful when my phone starts buzzing on the counter. Anything to get a break from dealing with the clusterfuck that is Jules and August in the same room at the same time. I glance down at the phone and see that it's Lochlan. My heart stupidly swells in my chest. Lochlan doesn't need the don't-ring-the-doorbell speech.

He's texting to let me know he's around the corner. This is what I remember from my brief time with him, the feeling that I don't need to tell him things because he just knows what I need.

August and Jules have returned to arguing, verging on an all-out war. I'm clear on Lochlan wanting to be in his son's life; but who's going to want to deal with me and all my baggage?

12

LOCHLAN

I t takes me about 30 minutes to travel from Mercedes' house to my cousin's house in Arlington. The whole time I'm driving too fast and remembering every detail of that night two years ago.

I know I'm being a creep, but I can't stop staring at her, Mercy. She's sitting up in the bed watching some old sitcom on TV. Her naked body is barely covered by the sheet draped across her waist. Mercedes' hair looks exactly how you'd expect it to look after someone's hands were buried in it. She's gorgeous in the soft light of the room. I've learned that any light agrees with her. When she sees me standing in the bathroom doorway with a towel wrapped around my waist, she looks embarrassed.

"I didn't know you were there? Why didn't you say something? This show is so crazy. I was using my alone laugh."

I walk over to the bed and drop the towel before I get in next to her. Once I pull her so that her softness is touching my hardness, I'm content for the moment.

"What is an alone laugh?"

"You know you have a people laugh, and then your psycho laugh that other people will judge you for?"

"No, I can't say that I've ever heard of that." I punctuate my words with

a kiss to her neck. I've been buried inside of her twice already and I can tell it's not going to be enough to hold me much longer.

"Why are you alone on your graduation day?"

She takes a long time to answer. I think she's deciding if she wants to tell me.

"I don't really have any family. I've never met my father and I don't even know who he is. My mother had me when she was really young. She basically couldn't handle the responsibility and just left me with my grandmother."

"Where is your grandmother?"

"She died when I was 16. I got myself emancipated and I've pretty much been on my own since then. I have August. He's a good family friend who lives in my basement apartment and helps me take care of the house."

"Where is he?" My weird and severe jealousy over the mention of this August character is both new and strange.

"It's hard to explain August. He's a complete drama magnet. He went to the islands to visit this guy he met on one of the dating apps. Somehow, he got detained at customs when he tried to re-enter the country. It's a long story, but he couldn't make it back in time for the ceremony. He should be back in a couple of days, though."

The only thing I really take from that story is that August is probably gay. I'm feeling better already.

"What about aunts or uncles? Anybody?"

"My mother was an only child. My grandma had her young and some-thing went wrong during labor and delivery. She couldn't have any more kids. I don't know my grandfather, but I heard he was a drug dealer who was gunned down when my mother was a toddler. My grandmother has a brother. I talk to him sometimes, but he stays on a mission trip in South America. There isn't really anybody else."

"What about your mother? I know she was young when she had you, but she's got to be older now? Why didn't she come?"

Mercedes shifts next to me. Maybe I'm probing too much.

"I don't... It's hard to explain. We don't have a mother-daughter rela-tionship. I think of her more as a surrogate for my grandmother. I wouldn't pick up the phone and call her for something like this. She wouldn't care

and as much as I would want to be unbothered by her not caring, it would bother me. It's best to just leave her in whatever hole she's in."

"Tell me about your family. Talking about myself is depressing as hell."

"I'm from Texas. My folks are back there. I've got an older brother and a younger sister. We're all very close." I default to the safe story.

"I've always wondered what it would've been like to be normal, you know; to just have a mom and dad and siblings, what I wouldn't give..." The quiet longing in her voice prompts me to be more forthright.

"Every story has its flaw, Mercy." I wrap my arms around her a little tighter. "I grew up in a very religious environment. The church was at the center of everything. My parents weren't in charge. The church was in charge. Our entire lives were dictated by what the church believed was good. My parents are amazing people, they really are. But I don't think they love anything more than the church. We were there seven days a week, three days for various services, and four others for meetings and social events."

"It sounds kind of cultish."

"It wasn't really like that." My defense is automatic, but there's something about that characterization that rings true with me. "We could come and go as we pleased, but my parents just chose to be involved in everything."

"Well, you still managed to become an NBA player so maybe it wasn't all bad."

"Huh, funny you should mention that. My career is not something the church approves of. I kind of separated from the church and sort of from my parents too when I started really training. If it wasn't for my uncle who is a college basketball coach, I don't think I would've even gotten the training and exposure to be here. Thanks to him, I've been training and playing since I was eight. My parents didn't attend one of my games until I was in high school. By that time, I was a local star and not even that seemed like all that big of a deal to them. They were always more concerned about me missing church than playing basketball. It was the weirdest thing. Everybody else only wanted to talk to me about basketball. But my parents? I got nothing more than a very vague affirmation from them. I would mention that I'd scored 20 points and got 8 rebounds in the last game. Their response *would be very robotic and brief, not heartfelt or congratulatory and then they'd change the subject."*

I have no idea why I'm telling her all of this. I never talk about this. I try not to even think about it.

Mercedes twists her body to look at me. "Well, how did you get around? How did you go to all the camps and shit kids go to?"

"It was my uncle at first. He knew I was gifted and he invested in getting me around. The more I played and got exposure, my uncle was able to find sponsors for me. I'm not even sure my parents know everything my uncle did to make sure I got where I am today."

I briefly lose my train of thought. Mercedes keeps moving and the more her body rubs against me, the more I need to wrap up the conversation portion of the night.

"I don't get it. Why wouldn't your parents be happy to have such a talented son?"

I understand why Mercedes asks this question. I used to ask it all the time. I couldn't understand how something that was so important to me and I was so good at was just ignored by my otherwise loving parents.

"The church viewed athletics as being too secular. The time I spent at camps and practices was the time I wasn't in the church and that just wasn't acceptable. Most parents didn't let their children participate in any extracurricular activities. Church was our extracurricular activity. I..." My voice trails off.

"You, what?"

"I don't know why I'm talking about this. I've never even really thought about it like this before. But I think on some level, I kind of resent my parents' lack of support."

"Is that why you have a bad temper?"

"What? What do you know about my temper?"

"I know you're called the golden boy with the red streak. And the red is not for your pleasant disposition. I know you've been teched up more often than most players of your vintage. You fight and you talk a lot of shit. The only reason why you get away with it is because you're really good and the ladies love you, which means you're good for business."

"Well, damn! I thought you weren't into basketball!"

"I'm not, but I'm also not deaf and blind. I've seen and read the many headlines about you."

"Basketball is an aggressive sport," I deflect.

"Maybe, but it ain't hockey."

That's funny. One of my coaches had actually said that to me once. 'Loch, if you want to fight, you need to hit the rink and stay off my court. I don't got time for your bullshit.'

"Okay, so, what does this have to do with my parents?"

"Everyone wants their parents to be proud of them and support them. I mean look at me. I broke down and cried like an idiot in front of a gorgeous stranger because I had no mommy and daddy cheering me on for this big accomplishment in my life. I don't even know my dad and his lack of support still feels huge and painful. I can't speak for you, Lochlan, but in my life that pain has translated into a lot of bad shit. Maybe your bad shit is anger."

Is she right? All this time I've thought of my temper as the curse of the Irish. Maybe there's something more to it. I don't say any of that, though. I need more time with these new thoughts.

"Wouldn't I be justified in having negative feelings about being unsupported?"

"Hmmm..."

Mercedes' eyes are fixed on my face. Her hair falls to one side, following the thoughtful tilt of her head. I kiss her lips softly. "What? What are you thinking?"

"I... Never mind. It's not my place."

"I'm making it your place. Tell me what you're thinking."

"I just... I get what you're saying but I kind of think your parents struck a compromise."

"How so?"

"Well, your parents could have been like all the other parents and kept you from playing basketball, but they didn't. Do you think your uncle could have taken an eight-year-old to basketball training and camps if his parents didn't allow it? I doubt it. Maybe your parents couldn't tear themselves away from the church, but they gave you the opportunity to become who you are now. That's support in a different kind of way."

Life changes in single moments. It might seem like change takes a long time, but that time is composed of moments stacked on top of one another. We don't usually perceive the moments, but sometimes we do. This is one of those times. I feel the truth in Mercedes' words and I know it will affect everything from this point forward.

"I'm not trying to get in your business. Seriously, I'm the last person to know anything about healthy parenting. It's just that I spent all this time being angry at my grandmother after she died. I felt like she was always at work and left me kind of on my own in the world. It took time to realize that she was compromising being there for me to give me the education that would get me to where I am today. And yeah, it's different with your parents, but I'm guessing they thought their participation in the church was a good thing that would somehow benefit their kids."

"Yeah, they definitely did."

We stare at each other in a kind of awe until Mercedes climbs on top of me straddling my hips. And then the time for talking is over.

There was only one person I had ever been completely honest with before I met Mercedes: my brother, Connor. But Connor and I are brothers. We aren't exactly paragons of introspection and emotional openness. I followed Mercedes because I couldn't help myself. I was drawn to her. But two years later, she's still in my head and my heart because she heard my story, she didn't judge me, and she helped me to see it more clearly. That's way more than I'd done for her.

Andrew's door is open. I knew it would be. It's fantasy football night, the door is always open for about an hour to allow the fellas to show up. I'm usually one of the fellas, but tonight, I'm looking for Andrew's brother. I find Connor in the kitchen piling food on a tray. Connor is usually in close proximity to the food and is ordinarily the one to keep the group stocked with snacks while we hang out in the sunroom in the back of the house.

"Hey, bro, I'm surprised to see you here. I thought you were going to stay with your son for the rest of the day. How is he? When can I meet my nephew?"

Connor finally seems to notice my expression. He puts the tray down. "What's up, Loch? Is something wrong with the baby? You look like you rode in here on a storm cloud."

"Everything is good with Liam. He's back at home. I have so much to tell you about him. You're not even going to believe it. He's exactly like me."

Connor frowns "Okay, that's all good news, which just makes your facial expression less understandable."

"I need to talk to Paul."

"You're still going to get a family law attorney? Did something happen with Mercedes?"

"No, this isn't about getting a lawyer."

"Okay, well, help me carry this food out back. He's in the sunroom with the rest of the guys."

"I'd rather not see the rest of the guys right now."

My brother looks at me for a long moment. I know this facial expression. He's trying to decide what to do. I guess he decides because he picks up the tray and walks towards the sunroom.

Paul walks into the kitchen not even a minute later. My brother knows me well enough that he follows Paul into the kitchen.

"Mercedes told you she was pregnant."

"The fuck?" Connor sounds like he almost choked on the words before he got them out. He steps around Paul and stands diagonal to me facing Paul. I note that he's managed to strategically place himself between me and my dear cousin.

"Come on, dude. I got calls like that from women back then. It was my job to screen them for you and that's what I did."

"What are you talking about? You know I never had unprotected sex. Who the hell was claiming that I knocked them up?"

Connor rakes his hand through his hair and interjects. "Loch, he's not lying about that part. I used to get messages sometimes on social media. I knew it wasn't true, but I didn't bother to tell you about every false alarm."

Okay, I'm shocked. I never knew this was happening.

Paul's words drag me back from this revelation. "The fact that you never had unprotected sex is the reason I didn't take Mercedes seriously when she called. I reasonably figured she wouldn't be the one time you decided to go bare back." He's wrong about that.

"Then why did you offer her money?"

Paul holds up his hands like he's trying to slow me down. "I knew you slept with her. She was the first thing you talked about when you woke up in the hospital. I could see she had some kind of hold over you. If she was making up pregnancies, I thought she could become a problem."

"Hang on. You knew she wasn't just some random groupie. I *told* you that. It was me who asked you to find her. I only suggested that you offer her the NDA because you were behaving as if she could do something to harm my reputation."

"That's exactly what I'm telling you."

"But you never told me what that something was. You never said that she was claiming to be pregnant. After everything I told you about my feelings for her, how the hell did you not mention that?"

My cousin Andrew, Paul's older brother, walks into the kitchen. "What is going on? Loch, I didn't even know you were here, but we can hear you yelling all the way in back." Andrew stands next to Connor and looks at all of us like he's waiting for an explanation. Well, he's going to have to just keep waiting.

"Loch, you have to see it from my perspective. You were with the girl for one night and it had been months. I thought you were all messed up in the head from your accident. I just didn't think you had really fallen in love with her and I definitely didn't think you knocked her up after one night."

Andrew looks at me with a frown. "Wait. What? You got some-body pregnant?"

"I'll explain later, Drew. Just let them hash it out." Connor is the voice of reason as usual.

"I wanted to get more information about the person who was claiming to carry your child. I had our firm investigator do some digging and it didn't take much to learn that she was the type to bounce around between professional athletes."

I take a step towards Paul. Connor and Andrew tense up and

move to form more of a physical barricade between us. The old anger is becoming almost too much to contain. "I'm going to say this to you only once so listen to me very carefully. Do not *ever* again talk about Mercedes that way. Not ever."

"I don't understand how I'm the bad guy. I literally brought you video evidence."

"But you did it without context. The context being 'Oh and also by the way, she says she's pregnant.' That context!"

"Would it have even mattered? You were the one who decided you didn't want her."

I lunge for Paul. Connor holds me back, Andrew blocks Paul.

"This isn't about her. This is about my son. I missed almost two years of his life because you decided his mother wasn't good enough for me."

"I love you, Loch and I'm sorry you missed that time with your son, but you're wrong, brother."

Connor lets me go and stands in front of me facing me. "Paul didn't decide Mercedes wasn't good enough for you. He gave you certain information about her. As far as we know, all of the information was true. It was you who made the decision that she wasn't good enough for you. It was you who wouldn't take any of her calls or messages. That was you, not Paul."

There it is, the thing that I really didn't want to face. I want to blame someone else for the time I missed with Liam, but Connor is right. I had choices to make and I made them. Now, I don't like the consequences and I want badly for it to be someone else's fault.

Paul takes over with a quiet explanation. "I didn't really think much about Mercedes after you moved back to Texas. I thought that if she really had something on you, she would've filed a lawsuit or something. I thought, and I'm not saying this now, I'm just explaining what I thought back then, I thought she was out for money. If she were really pregnant and looking for a payday, there's no way she would've just let it drop. But she did."

Everyone looks like they're suffering from an identical loss of words in the silence that follows.

"I promise I didn't know anything about you having a son until Connor told me a few minutes ago. You were determined to make this renewed commitment to God and the church. I thought I was helping you by showing you what kind of person I thought she was. I know I can't get you back two years of time, but I'm sorry. I really am. I just had no idea."

I could've disregarded Paul's information. I could've chosen to believe the best about Mercedes and I didn't do that. It was almost two years and I never tried to reach out to her. I didn't even try.

"I'm sorry, Loch." Connor puts a sympathetic hand on my shoulder. "You still have the rest of his life. That will have to be enough."

I nod, acknowledging the truth in Connor's words. I just need to know one more thing.

"Paul, where exactly did you get that video from?"

"I'm not sure anymore, but if memory serves me right, the investigator had a contact who had another contact, a music producer, I think? And then the music producer knew somebody who knew somebody who had the footage. Or something like that." I can see that Paul is trying his best to remember, but that's not good enough.

"Paul, there is something you can do to help. I need you to find the original of that footage."

AFTER THE SITUATION with Paul is somewhat sorted out, Connor walks me out to my car.

"Just help me understand something. If your feelings for her were and are this strong, why did you let her go two years ago?"

I know he's been thinking this the whole time. I don't answer right away. I don't really want to. "I knew you would ask me this." I did. I know this would be the thing Connor would not just let go. He is quiet until I'm about to get in my truck, when he puts his hand out to stop me, insistent.

"Do you know what the answer is?"

The deep breath I've been holding finally puffs out along with my answer. "You remember how I was trapped in that car for a while before anyone came to help me?"

"Of course, I remember. I'll never forget that."

"Well, what you don't know is that I prayed. For the first time in my life, I prayed really hard. I didn't want to die and in that moment, I knew that if God didn't intervene, it was over."

Connor leans against the truck and crosses his arms over his chest. "Yeah, Loch, that makes sense to me. I woulda prayed too."

"Okay, well here's where things get weird. So, just... Just try to stay with me." I wait for him to nod in acknowledgment before I go on. "I'm pretty sure an angel appeared to me that day. Not a person acting as an angel, but like an actual angel." Connor is squinting at me with a mildly disbelieving look on his face. "Listen, I know this sounds crazy, but I have a very specific memory of what happened that day. A man came to help me in the car. He repeated back to me the exact words that I had prayed. I remember what he looks like and what he was wearing."

"Okay, Loch, I hear you, but that could have just been a volunteer who was on the scene." Connor is talking slowly and seems to be measuring his words carefully.

"I know, Conn, I've thought of that. But I had such a detailed memory of this guy I was able to describe him to someone else who was on the scene. He told me it sounded like I was describing this man who had been dead for several years. I Googled the person and I swear on my actual life, it was the man who came to help me out of the wreck that day."

Connor probably doesn't even realize that he's slowly shaking his head.

"I know, man, it's hard to believe, but I'm telling you it happened. Even when I tried to convince myself it was just a normal person who looked like and was dressed exactly like the dead guy from the photo, there was still one thing I couldn't explain away. How the hell did the person recite the exact words from my prayer?" I throw up my hands helplessly. "You know I'm not a hysterical dude and I'm definitely not superstitious, but something happened out there that I can't explain."

"Okay, okay, let's just assume it was an angel for the sake of argument. What does that have to do with Mercedes?"

Here comes the hard part. "It just seemed to me that if God had sent an actual angel to save me, I owed Him. I promised God that if he gave me another chance, I would do better. He kept up His end of the bargain and I thought I should do my part."

"But why couldn't that include Mercedes? I never would have believed in love at first sight for you. No offense, but you were no..." Connor pauses and searches for the right word. "You were no angel in your NBA days. I would've thought love was the furthest thing from a possibility for you. But when you woke up in that hospital and started telling me about Mercedes, I was pretty sure you loved her. And then the next thing I knew you wouldn't even speak to her and you were running back to Texas."

"After Paul told me all that stuff about her and showed me that video, I didn't think I could keep my commitment to God with someone like her by my side."

"Wow. That's fucked up."

"Gee, thanks, Conn."

"I'm sorry, but it is. This is why I still believe in God, but not the church. It's not God that made you make a choice like that. It's the church that teaches us to be judgmental."

"That's not completely fair. Part of the job of the church is to help people lead lives that are suited to a relationship with God. That means being wise about what company you keep. That's even in the Bible."

"Save it, Loch. I could run circles around you with the Bible. While you were playing basketball, I was actually in all the youth indoctrination programs. Let me tell you something you seem to have missed. God doesn't view people through the lens of every mistake we've ever made. If God could forgive you and accept you after everything you did, why the hell couldn't you have given Mercedes the same chance? What puts you or any of those church assholes above the judgment of God?"

I deflate and explode at the same time.

"For fuck's sake, Connor, don't you think I know this now? Why do you think I came back? Why do you think I gave up on my mission to be the perfect church member? I see it *now*; I get it *now*. Isn't it enough that I paid for my mistakes by missing almost two years of my son's life and maybe the only chance at love that I'll get in this life?"

I interlace my fingers behind my head and walk a few steps away from my brother to calm my breathing. This truth has been the one clawing at the edge of my consciousness since the day I saw Mercedes at Ashley's party. The reality that I needlessly tried to prove my worth to God by proving my worth to people is a tough pill to swallow.

"I'm sorry, Loch. I'm not being fair to you. I'm taking out all my church shit on you and that isn't fair. You tried to do what you thought was right and you're still doing that. My problems with the church are not yours. You don't have to answer for an entire institution." I know he means that so I just nod at him and decide to let it go.

"What should I do now? And I'm not talking about my son. I know what to do about Liam. What do I do about Mercedes?"

"What do you want to do?"

"I want to be with her. I want us to make a family together."

"Wow! I mean, that's where I thought this was headed, but it's still crazy to hear you say the words."

"I know. I'm as shocked as you are. I still haven't spent a complete week with her yet and I'm sure I want to spend the rest of my life with her."

"Loch, the video still exists. How are you going to deal with that?"

"I'm going to find it and get rid of it."

"Okay, but that's not what I'm talking about. How are you going to deal with being with someone who was in that position?" He pauses. "No pun intended. But what's different now?"

I know the answer to this, but I have no desire to get into the details so I put it in the simplest terms possible.

"I'm different now."

MERCEDES

I try my best to get Jules out of my house before Lochlan gets back. I have no specific reason for doing so, just pure instinct. Lochlan is coming, so Jules needs to go. But he must have been closer than I thought. I haven't even succeeded in breaking up the never-ending argument between August and Jules when Lochlan texts me that he's outside. *Shit.*

"Stop it, you two. Stop it right now." I'm reduced to hissing because what I know about these two is that yelling is like flipping a turn-up switch on them. If you increase your volume around them, they do the same.

"Mercedes, this is ridiculous. I haven't seen you in almost two years. Call your angry Chihuahua off so we can at least catch up."

I take it by Jules gesturing to the corner of the kitchen to which I banished August under the threat of serious bodily harm that she is talking about him.

"Oh, I got your Chihuahua you, snaggletooth demon."

Why me? Why me? Why me? Jules is not even snaggletooth. In fact, I swear she's aging in reverse. She is at least 39, probably 40, but her skin is flawless and wrinkle-free. Her body is tight. Nothing is slouching or sagging. We honestly look like we're the same age. I guess we always have. That doesn't matter right now. All that matters is my need not to let Lochlan know about all the crazy shit that is constantly swirling around me. I don't want Lochlan to think this is the environment in which I'm raising his son.

Yeah, Mercedes, that's it. Your panic at the thought of him being around Jules is out of concern for your son.

Oh, shut up, inner voice! I don't have time for self-analysis right now.

"I have to go open the door for Lochlan."

"Wait! Baby daddy is here? I thought he was threatening to take Liam from you? Why is he here?"

Breathe Mercedes, breathe. "I'll catch you up, Jules. I promise. But things have changed and I have a strong desire to keep the peace. So, please, *please*, at least try not to fuck that up."

"So, you're asking her not to be herself?"

I turn on August and jab a finger at him. "You, do not antagonize her. Just put a lid on it for tonight."

August rolls his eyes but doesn't say anything.

When I finally open the door for Lochlan, I've convinced myself that the people in the kitchen are going to act like adults and control themselves even though that would absolutely be a first.

Lochlan looks just as sexy as the last time I saw him. I wonder if that feeling like someone just knocked the air out of my lungs will stop popping up every time I see him. He's just so handsome and he vibrates this energy that I instantly respond to. I move back so he can walk in.

"Hey, I'm sorry you came all the way back. Liam's been down for a little over an hour. He's probably out until tomorrow." These are the safest words I can find. I throw them out like bricks that can build a wall between us. I don't think it's working.

"Hey, Mercy." My brain short circuits at the name only he calls me. He says it like a challenge. I should be angry, I should object. Instead, the air just sizzles and crackles all around us. Something is different about him. He left one person, and came back as the more compelling version of himself from two years ago. I back up. My goal is to escape whatever influence he's exerting over me. He just steps closer to me, crowding my space until my back hits a wall.

I'm not a scary chick. A lot of shit has come my way, and I've managed to make my way out of most of it, but there's no point trying to convince myself that I'm not completely shook right now. I want him so much that it feels biological or hell, spiritual, I don't know. There's all this unresolved business crowding in around us, and it doesn't matter one bit. He must know it too. I look up at Lochlan's arm, which is on one side of my head, so that I'm half caged in. He just looks in my eyes and waits. It's like he's giving me an escape route and daring me to use it.

"I'm here for you, Mercy." His lips follow his words. He doesn't crash into me. Lochlan is slow and deliberate. The dare is still there: run if you want to. When our lips finally meet, I want to cry for some reason. It's like I inhaled two years ago and never let the breath out. I've just been holding everything and trying to hold on. I feel myself letting go, and I can't find the guilt that I thought would come from doing this inevitable thing with the person who threw me away. It's not there. I only feel relief, and unadulterated lust. The kiss becomes more intense when Lochlan presses his hard body against mine. I moan and my hips start moving without any specific permission. My body just knows.

"Well, call me a pickled hippopotamus." August's voice jars me back into reality.

I gasp and break the kiss to see August and Jules standing behind Lochlan. I look between the two of them in embarrassment. Who does that? Who just starts making out with someone and forgets there are other people in the house or on the planet? Jules has her arms crossed over her chest and the look on her face is a cross between disgust and confusion. Lochlan doesn't move for what seems like a really long time, but probably isn't. I can read the message in his eyes quite clearly. He doesn't care what anyone else thinks of this. I step around him and he shocks me again by putting his hand on the small of my back. It feels like he's supporting me.

I had planned to say something. Nothing comes out.

"So, this must be Baby Daddy."

"Jules, this is Lochlan, *not* baby daddy. But yes, this is Liam's father."

"And you are?" Lochlan's tone is not what I would call friendly. It's somewhere between hostility and curiosity.

"I'm the person she called to help her get a lawyer and keep you away from the... Liam."

"You's a messy bitch. I told you, Mercedes. I told you." August is on the verge of starting up again, but Lochlan has the cure.

"She won't be needing that lawyer now."

"Ha!" August is triumphant. "So, you can return to your lair now, Satan."

Jules just rolls her eyes and flicks her wrist like she's trying to shoo August away. "Actually, my ride's here, so I'm out." She turns to me before opening the door. "I'll be at my usual spot, Mercedes. Call me tomorrow." The door is closing before I can even respond. She didn't even ask to peek in on Liam. Whatever, she's never going to change. I need to find some new people to surround myself with.

"I'm going to retire to my quarters for the evening, Mercury. Please open some windows or light some sage, so that all Jules' horrific energy can be dispersed the hell up out of here."

I feel Lochlan looking at me. "August, she's not that bad. She barely even said anything."

"Okay, Mercury. Tell yourself whatever you need to so that you can be in the presence of her supreme evilness." August says all of this while departing with a flourish. He doesn't feel like he's left a room unless his departure is dramatic.

I turn to Lochlan and blow out a breath. "I'm sorry about all that."

"So, that's your friend from years ago? Jules?"

"It's a long story. Friend is not the right word to describe her."

"Well, what is? She doesn't make a great first impression."

"Really?"

"Why do you sound so surprised? You haven't noticed that she's kind of a witch?"

"She's not that bad. She hasn't heard very many positive things about you. I mean we haven't been in a great place for several years, so it isn't like I told her what a great guy you are." This is a first. I don't usually or ever have to defend Jules to men. They take one look at her and nothing else matters. And also, why am I defending her?

"I get it, but she didn't even seem all that friendly towards you. And as much as I hate to agree with August, who is constantly threatening me with kitchen utensils, he's right. She's got a bad energy around her. Maybe we should open the windows. I don't want any of that getting on our son."

My stupid heart does a stupid flip when he says "our son." You would've thought he just proposed marriage. I'm not even sure what else he said. All I heard was the end. Reality looms over me, though. We haven't worked out anything, and there is nothing to work out. Nothing changes the fact that he didn't try to find me for two years. I need to stop acting all goofy and weak.

"You're over thinking it." Lochlan gently lifts my head up with his hand under my chin. "It's happening so just let it."

"No. It's not happening, Lochlan. And I'm not over thinking it so don't gaslight me. I've already told you I'm on board for co-parenting, but us making out in the hallway and acting like no time has passed, I am not up for that." As I talk I back away from him, trying to escape that sizzling bond between us. It doesn't break; it stretches. I wonder how far I would have to go to get away from it and I'm scared of the answer.

"Liam is out for the night so you should go. I'm sure you have work tomorrow."

"I own the company. I work when I say I work."

"Congratulations. That must be nice." My tone is purposely dry.

"I'm sorry. What I meant to say was that I will make time to see Liam tomorrow and every day. I would like for you both to come to my place tomorrow. I have a surprise for Liam and I can make us something to eat."

He knows I took off work this week just to monitor Liam, so I can't even use that as an excuse.

"Can you come around 4? I'll go into the office early and leave early, so I have time to spend with you guys."

"I will bring him, Lochlan. But you need to remember this is not a package deal. At some point, we have to start talking about you having your own time with Liam." When I don't feel like my words are having any effect on him, I provide further clarification. "That means time without me."

"I will give you whatever time you need." Okay, is he pretending to not understand what I'm saying or does he really not understand?

"Lochlan." I try to make my voice firm, so it comes out sounding like a warning. I'm not sure if I even got close to hitting that mark.

"It's fine, Mercedes. We don't have to work it all out tonight. We've got the rest of our lives."

The rest of our what? Okay, I do need to open the windows because everybody around here is losing their minds. And yes, I'm totally including myself in the everybody.

Holding the door open, I try to speak firmly. "Goodnight, Lochlan."

"Can you do me a favor?"

"I don't know what is it?" *Never trust a guy who needs a favor.* Jule-sism Number 42.

"Facetime me when my big guy wakes up in the morning so I can say good morning to him."

Well damn, I wasn't expecting that. Is this what I have to look forward to for the next 16 years? Is he constantly going to be saying the right things and making me feel like all I want is to be with him? I don't think I'll make it a month.

"Okay, sure. I'll do that." Just leave so I can regain my common damn sense. He looks like he wants to say something else, but he ends up saying goodnight and walks out the door.

I spin around and run to find something to clean like someone is chasing me.

13

MERCEDES

L iam is in love with his father. They are engaged in an endless love fest; that's the only way I can describe it. From the minute we arrived at Lochlan's beautiful townhouse in Woodley Park, Liam was attached to his dad, bodily, for the most part. I'm guessing that while I was in the shower a couple of days ago, Lochlan informed Liam of his status as "Daddy." It has since become his new favorite word. I swear the child woke up this morning and said, "Daddy!" I'm trying not to be annoyed - but dang, "Mommy" went out of style fast.

Lochlan's "surprise" was a brand new, fully furnished bedroom for his son. I have no idea how he got it set up so quick. No, wait, I know exactly how: money. The room is decorated in a style very similar to Liam's playroom at our house. It's gray with a navy-blue accent wall and pictures of all sorts of classic planes and trains. Liam is sold on the room from the minute he steps foot into it. I know I said that Lochlan needs to find time to spend with Liam without me, but seeing that he has already taken steps to make that a reality is somehow off-putting.

Liam fell asleep about 10 minutes ago and I laid him in his new bed. Lochlan said he wanted to discuss our co-parenting, but the looks he's been giving me don't have anything to do with parenting.

"So, you wanted to talk about co-parenting, right?"

"Right."

I'm sitting on the plush couch in his second-floor den. It's close to Liam's new room, which makes me feel more comfortable. Even though he has a baby monitor with a camera on it, I want to be close by if Liam wakes up disoriented in his new environment. Given the current status of our situation, he'd probably just call for his daddy.

This upper-level den is my dream hang-out space. Of course, this townhouse is my dream house. The ceiling is slanted with a skylight. The back wall features French doors, which lead to an outdoor patio. I have serious house envy. The den has a huge sectional sofa with a chaise lounge on one end. The sofa is bright blue and more importantly, it's one of the most comfortable things I've ever sat on. But did I mention it's huge? That's why I'm confused as to why Lochlan is seated so close to me. He sat down right next to me and turned his whole body towards me. It's fucking up all my essential brain functions. I keep getting wrapped in his spicy scent and that penetrating gray gaze. I can't remember anything I wanted to say.

"You need to stop looking at me like that."

"How am I looking at you?"

"You know how you're looking at me."

"I know, but I want to hear you say it."

"Okay, goodnight. I'm leaving." Lochlan grabs my arm when I push off the sofa. "Wait, you don't have to go, I'll try to stop." I try to leave again and Lochlan finds the strength to select better words, "I'll stop. Just please talk to me."

"Lochlan, I don't understand you. I don't know why you're acting like I'm your long lost love. I'm not either of those things. I damn sure haven't been lost. I've been very easy to locate for the past two years. You acting like we were kept apart by circumstances and miraculously reunited by fate is sending me over the edge."

"You don't feel like we were meant to be together?"

Let me try a different tactic. "Why did you disappear?"

Let's cut the bullshit and get down to business.

LOCHLAN

"I didn't disappear."

I knew this moment would come and I still don't know how to explain it. Mercedes pushes her hair back over her shoulder and looks at me like a specimen she's trying to figure out. I sense that I have a very limited window in which to make my case.

"I thought I needed to start over."

"Right. Without me."

"That's not what I meant."

"Okay, what did you mean? Because the last time I was with you before you started over, it was *you* who told *me* that you didn't want us to be a one-night stand. You told me you had never been with anyone like me and that you couldn't even imagine anything better than us together. It was you, Lochlan, who said all of that. So, please explain to me what exactly it is you meant." She turns away from me and crosses her arms over her chest like she's trying to protect herself.

"I didn't mean for us to be a one-night stand. I didn't lie to you when I said the things I said that night. None of it was a lie."

"Let's pretend I believe you. What changed?"

"It's going to sound crazy if I try to explain it, but I'm going to try anyway." I rush out the last part of the sentence because I can see Mercedes getting more agitated.

"Do you remember how I told you all that stuff about how I came from a really religious family?"

"I remember."

"After I had that near-death experience and found myself having to reconsider everything in my life, it's like I reverted back to the things that had been drilled into me. The whole world collapsed all around me and the only thing I was sure of was that there is a God."

Mercedes is quiet, but she doesn't look like she's on the verge of jumping up and leaving. She seems to be trying to understand.

"I grew up with two things, Mercedes: basketball and the church, that's it. When basketball became the center of my world, the church and the things I had learned there became background noise. But it was still a constant, it was still home. Does that make any sense so far?"

Mercedes has this thing she does when she's thinking. She kind of twists her mouth to the side and sucks in her lip. I'm glad to see she's doing it now because it shows she's trying to understand where I'm coming from. "I think I'm with you so far. I know what it's like to live in a kind of small world. I think that's what you're saying."

"Yeah, that's it. Basketball seems like such a big world, but it's not, and the NBA is an even smaller subset of the basketball realm. When my leg was messed up and there was no more basketball, I felt like everything was in free-fall. The church was the only thing left that had always been there that hadn't changed. Plus, because of how my accident happened and how my life was saved, I thought I owed it to God to be a better person. The only way I knew to do that was to return to where I had learned to be a better person."

"And that was in Texas with the skinny blonde chick?" How is it that you can know a question is coming and still be so unprepared to answer it?

"I didn't go to Texas to start a relationship with Rachel. I... It's hard to explain now and I'm not gonna lie, it sounds stupid even to me. But the relationship with Rachel was nothing like you. It was just part of the package. Work in the church, be wholesome, date one of the assistant pastor's daughters. I wasn't thinking about love or happiness. I just wanted to do the right thing, be the right thing."

Mercedes nods slowly. When she stands up it doesn't seem like she's about to storm out. Instead, she gets up slowly and paces back and forth for at least 30 seconds before she responds.

"I'm not part of the perfect guy package. I get it." Her voice sounds stilted and she doesn't get it at all.

"There is no such thing. That's what I'm trying to tell you, Mercy... Mercedes, I was wrong. I was completely wrong. And I lost two years because I misunderstood what it meant to owe God and another year thinking you wouldn't want me back." I don't know if I'm fixing things or making it worse. But all of this is true. I came back to D.C. for one reason: Mercedes. I can't get the words out, but deep down inside I thought she wouldn't want an unemployed, former NBA player.

"How did you know I wouldn't fit your perfect package? I mean we'd just met. What gave it away?" I stand up too. She still doesn't get it.

"It wasn't just about you fitting, Mercedes. It was me too. I did think that you were a certain kind of woman, and I didn't think that woman would want me either."

"Not church material, huh? No, I feel like I'm still missing something like you know something I don't know, but about me. What am I missing?"

I love this about her, and right now I hate it too; she's perceptive as hell. *Just gonna have to tell her.*

"When you contacted Paul while I was still in the hospital, he had an informal background check run on you."

"Okay...well I don't have bad credit, I'm not a felon, I don't have any contagious illnesses, and I didn't lie about anything in my background. So, what? What did you find out that changed your mind about everything that you'd said?"

"I didn't change my mind about everything that I'd said. I just didn't think..." I stop mid-sentence, because I realize that as much as

I'm trying to spin this, the conclusions she's jumping to are right. I'm complicating things more by not admitting to it.

"You're right. I changed everything that I said. The background check didn't bring up anything about you being a criminal or having bad credit, but..."

When I pause too long, Mercedes urges me to continue. "What is it? Please, you're freaking me out."

Deep breath. "There was a video of you."

"What? What video? I've never been in any video. It wasn't me, Lochlan." She dismisses it so quickly that I know she isn't lying.

Mercedes doesn't know about the video, so I say my next words very carefully. "It was definitely you, Mercedes. You have a birthmark on your back. I could see it in the video. And I could see your face."

"What the fuck are you talking about? I seriously have no clue what video of me you think you saw."

"You looked different. You had short hair and it was dyed with blond highlights. Mercedes, are you okay?"

Her eyes are now unfocused and she's shaking her head but in an unnaturally slow way, as if to shake the information out of her head. When she speaks again she's still not looking at me. Mercy's voice, which is usually animated, is completely flat. "What was on the video?"

I falter. I never prepared for the possibility that she didn't know. *Shit.* "It's... it's you with two guys. You were..."

"Fucking, right? I was fucking two guys at the same time." The perfectly flat tone is the most disconcerting thing right now. Mercy has her arms tightly folded, and is staring resolutely forward. I don't answer out loud, but I nod. When I reach out to touch her arm, she finally snaps out of her distant daze and jumps back. "Don't! Do not touch me."

"Mercedes, talk to me. What's going on?"

"I-I... I need some fresh air. Please." I don't hesitate, but immediately open the French doors. When I follow Mercedes out onto the patio she stands staring down at the street. Her arms act as her security blanket and hug her body once again. Even though her eyes are now focused, I have no idea what she's thinking.

I wait. And then I wait some more.

It's probably 10 minutes before either of us speaks.

"Can I get you something? Anything?" She dabs at a tear I just noticed in the corner of her eye and shakes her head.

"I want to see it."

"You want to see what?"

"The video. I want to see it." I feel like it was ages ago when we talked about the video. It's been at least 90 emotional years since I brought it up.

"I don't have it anymore. I would never keep something that showed you like that."

"The guys with me. Could you see their faces?"

"Yeah, I could see them."

"Football players. Right?"

I nod slowly. I recognized both of the guys from the L.A. team. I think one is now in D.C. Not sure where the other is.

"The video has to be 10 years old."

"I know. I know you wouldn't do anything like that now." I was expecting a lot of things but I was not expecting her to laugh.

"What? What's funny?"

"You are, Lochlan! I don't need you to absolve me of my hoeish past or present. I don't give a fuck. Let's just get that straight." Whoa. I didn't see that coming.

"You're right. I'm nowhere near your perfect church girl. So, let's just end this little charade here and now." Mercedes stands up and this time I know she's leaving. "I'm going to get Liam and head home. If you want to see him in the evenings, I'll drop him off for a few hours and I'll find something else to do. We'll have to figure out overnights and weekends."

"Mercedes, wait, I... I want to understand. I don't want you to leave."

"Lochlan, you made your choice and it was the right one. If I were you, I wouldn't want the girl on that video either. There's nothing else to talk about other than our son."

I have the same feeling I had the time I came to school, and all the kids were laughing at me. I couldn't figure out what was so funny. Finally, I realized I'd sat on a bench painted brown. Of course, little kids thought it was hilarious that my whole butt was brown. I have that feeling now, like there's something that Mercedes can see and react to, and I'm missing it. She's walking into the house, probably to go get our son and leave.

What am I missing? What set this whole thing off?

God, help me out here.

MERCEDES

I splash water on my face in Lochlan's hallway bathroom. I'm going to fix my face and get the hell out of here. I just need to get out of here. Maybe if I can leave without losing my shit, I can go back to yesterday, a day on which none of this was real, because I didn't know about it. I just have to get out of here.

"You would have been fifteen." I hear Lochlan's voice as soon as I step out of the bathroom. Oh God. He figured it out. No, no, no, no, no. I don't want to do this. God isn't listening.

"If that video was ten years ago, you were only fifteen." I don't even realize I'm closing my eyes until everything goes blissfully dark. When I open my eyes, Lochlan looks horrified. Join the club. I haven't cried since I was in labor. Before that, I hadn't cried since the night of my college graduation. Now, I feel tears threatening to pour out of the storm cloud rolling in. I hold on for dear life. I think that if this dam breaks, I might drown, be swept away with the floating debris of my life. So, we just stand in the hallway silently. Finally, I sink down to the floor against the wall. My legs weren't going to hold much longer, like they're carrying all of the weight of my suffering.

"I was fifteen." I confirm what math seems to have already

revealed to him. He doesn't say anything. He just sinks down next to me. "It was my first time going to a nightclub. I was scared to stay home by myself so I convinced Jules to take me out with her." I don't know why I keep going, I just do.

"You've known Jules since you were a teenager?"

"Yes. Jules used to live with us off and on. More off than on, but my grandma always let her rent the basement apartment if she was in town." He nods, and I keep traveling along the path to disaster. "We'd had a break-in while my grandma was working the night shift. Some meth head or something like that. He wasn't really doing anything but eating my cereal. Looking back on it, I probably would've scared him more than he scared me. But I was 15 and I was terrified to be in the house after dark by myself after it happened."

"That makes sense to me."

"Jules could be annoying when I was younger. She always acted like I was bothering her. And not by doing anything in particular, it was more like my existence was an issue. Which, okay, but stay ya ass in the basement and it wouldn't be a thing. Anyway, by the time she moved back in that time, I was actually relieved. She got a reduction on rent because she promised my grandmother she would stay with me overnight. My grandmother hated leaving me alone, but she couldn't miss work because I went to this expensive private school with ridiculous tuition. I think she would've let Jules stay for free because she was so grateful for having someone to stay with me. Unfortunately, Jules was nocturnal and also a general bobble head most of the time. She was only supposed to be home for three nights of the week, but she averaged one night."

"She would leave you home alone?" Words seem to be slowly draining my energy, so I just nod. "Did she know about the break-in?"

"I told her. She said I was being childish. The back door and the lock had been replaced and nothing bad actually happened to me. I guess maybe she was right."

"She was not right, Mercy." I turn my head to the side to look at him. His face has a severe expression; it matches the vehemence in his voice. "You need to get that. She was dead-ass wrong." I want to agree, but I don't. In my heart I feel like if I had listened to Jules and stayed home, none of this would have happened. And by none of this, I mean a lot more than just that one night.

"I convinced her to let me go out with her. We made up a whole cover story about me being in college or something ridiculous. It didn't matter. The bouncers at the club didn't care about my cover story. I don't think they noticed anything above my neck."

"What happened?" I don't... can't look at Lochlan as I get lost in the worst memory of my life.

Clubs are different than I thought they'd be. I had this picture in my head of packed dance floors and people laughing as they danced the night away. So far all I've been doing is sitting in some closed off section. The area is bracketed by red ropes and is elevated on a balcony, I guess to let everyone know we're important. The occupants of the important people area are women dressed in even less clothing than I'm wearing and a bunch of big guys who have Jules bubbling with excitement. I guess these are the "pros" we're supposed to be looking out for. I keep tugging at the skirt of my dress but I can't get comfortable. I feel exposed and out of place.

"Hey, pretty girl." A tall caramel colored guy who must be a professional athlete stands over my seat with a friendly smile on his face. It's good to see a friendly smile, it makes me feel less awkward.

"Hey." That was a dumb response Mercedes. Do better before you wind up sitting here alone for the rest of the night.

"I'm headed to the bar. How about if I buy you a drink and you pay me back with a dance."

I'm thrilled at the chance to get out of my seat and do something. Before I can even respond, Jules is there with another guy I assume is a professional athlete.

"We're headed that way too, let's do some shots." I guess the word shots sets off some kind of internal club alarm. When Jules says it, like five different people yell shots in a unified response and the whole group moves in the direction of the private bar located near our section of the club.

After a couple of drinks, things get much less uncomfortable and much

more as I'd pictured. My dancing partner is Dexter Taylor, or Dex. I stay
with him much of the night. I'm not a great dancer but the alcohol helps
and Dex doesn't seem to care. I can do this. I can hang with Jules and not be
at home fighting off meth heads. This could really work.

"Mercedes, come on, we're getting ready to leave." Jules waves her hand
at me. I found my way back to our seated section after losing track of how
many songs I danced to.

"Oh, are we going home? I'm not really feeling that great. I feel like I
need to lay down." My words are a little slurred but I made sure I only had
two drinks. Jules told me club drinks get watered down so I should be okay.

"No, we're not going home yet. Dex and his teammate Brian invited us
to a party downtown. We are not passing that up?"

"Are you sure about this? It's almost one in the morning and I have
school tomorrow?"

Jules tosses her hair over her shoulder and texts on her phone without
looking at me. "Mercedes, I swear to God if you make this hard on me, this
is the last time you're coming anywhere. Just get your ass up and come on."

"Fine, fine, fine, no need to be rude about it. I'm coming." Only because I
have no other real options. I feel less and less stable by the moment. A fog
has descended over my head that I'm having a hard time shaking. If I got
accidentally drunk, I'll be mad at myself. Jules warned me a million times to
watch my alcohol intake so I don't wind up looking washed out in the eyes.
I feel like I blink and we're outside the club. I hear voices around me, people
laughing and talking but it all seems like an echo coming from somewhere
else. I blink again and somehow we're getting out of an Uber on Mass
Avenue.

"That's the last thing I remember about that night. Getting out of
the Uber on Mass Avenue."

"I don't worry about the tear that escapes. It's fine for one to
struggle loose as long as I don't agree to the act of crying, I'll survive
the night.. Lochlan must see the tear because he takes my hand. I
let him.

"I woke up the next morning and I was at home in my bed."
Another tear escapes.

"I knew something was wrong, really wrong. I was a virgin so I'd never... you know. But when I woke up, everything hurt and I could smell people on my skin and in my hair." I will never for as long as I live forget the smell. I don't say it because I can't, but there were fingerprint shaped bruises and hickies in places I had never even been touched by another person. I will not cry. Crying doesn't change anything. It never has, it never will.

"Where the hell was Jules? Did she leave you alone?" I'm surprised this is the question he asks. "She told me that she asked me if I'd be okay if she went to talk with some guy for a minute. Apparently, I told her that I'd be fine. And for whatever reason, she believed me. She said she left me sitting on the couch and I seemed like I'd been drinking, but still I was okay"

Lochlan is shaking his head. "That makes no sense. And isn't that a violation of the girl code or something like that? Who just leaves their friend like that? Their friend who is a teenager, I mean, come on." It's weird that Lochlan is angry at Jules. She specifically told me not to drink from any open container and I did it anyway. That's on me.

"Jules had her own situation. I can't blame her for what happened to me." I don't want to talk about Jules anymore. "I just, I never knew exactly what happened that night and now you're telling me that someone has it on video..."

I can feel it. If I don't get out of here, the crying is coming. "Lochlan, I'm tired. I just want to go home and go to sleep."

"I want you to stay here." Well, that brings me back from the edge. "Um, no, I'm not staying here with you, Lochlan. I'm not that sad 22-year-old girl anymore. I can take care of myself."

He looks at me with so much compassion. It feels like a different kind of breaking approaching. "You haven't just taken care of yourself; you've taken care of my son. Even when I had my head up my own ass, you were taking care of what is most important to me." He doesn't specify that he is talking about Liam. "I have a room for you, right next to Liam's. You can sleep in there. You don't have to worry about getting home and you don't have to wake Liam up. Please, just this once, let me take care of you."

I want to keep arguing. I want to say no but all my fight is gone. All I want to do now is sleep.

So I stay.

14

LOCHLAN

It feels like I've just fallen asleep when my phone starts ringing next to my bed. I check the time before I answer. It's 6:00 a.m. So, I know who it is.

"Good morning, Mom."

"Did I wake you up, Loch? I thought you'd be getting ready for your morning workout by now." She's right. Ordinarily, I would be up and heading for my home gym at this time. But last night I couldn't sleep. First, I was obsessed with checking in on Mercedes. She'd been through so much so I wanted to make sure she was okay. Then, I walked by Liam's room and he was sitting up in his baby bed. He wasn't crying, he was just holding his stuffed dog and looking around. When I went into the room, he got excited and jumped up. I was worried he would wake his mommy up, so I brought him into my room to try to put him back to sleep. I clearly don't know how babies work. Apparently, if you remove them from their bed in the middle of the night, they don't just go back to sleep. Liam bounced on the bed, talked to me for four hours and had me getting him "shnacks" until about 4:00 a.m. When he finally went back to sleep, he had his dog in one hand and a half-eaten Graham cracker in the other. I have a California King bed and I was still worried about smooshing my son. And also, I wasn't completely sure about the rolling abilities of a 19-month-old. I wound up putting him in the middle of the bed and half dozing for a few minutes at a time. Liam appears to not have moved. I probably worried for nothing, but the night is gone.

"I, uh, didn't sleep very well last night, so I'm getting a late start this morning. But don't worry about it, Mom. What's up?"

"I won't keep you long. You really should try some warm milk and those melatonin drops. You need to get your rest." This is my mother: full of well-intentioned but completely unnecessary advice.

"Okay, Mom."

She laughs. "I know you, so I know you're not listening to anything I say. Fine, fine, fine, what do I know? I just spent eighteen hours bringing you into this world." Oh God, it is entirely too early for the labor–and-delivery speech. "Lochlan Theodore Rait, do you know they didn't even give me any drugs? You were nine pounds eight ounces with the same broad shoulders you have now. So un-crease your forehead and drink some warm milk at night." My face, which is involuntarily scrunched up, immediately straightens out.

"Yes, Mother. I will drink warm milk and melanin."

"Loch, it's melatonin."

"Mom, I'll drink monkey-brain juice if you just let me get back to sleep for fifteen minutes."

"Oh, sorry, honey, I forgot I woke you up. I just called to remind you that we will be there this weekend." Okay, I'm wide awake now.

"You and Dad are coming this weekend?"

"Yes, Loch, as we've discussed several times, your dad and I are coming this weekend. We had to miss Ashley's birthday because we were at the church conference. So, we're coming now for a late cele-bration. I thought we might stay with you, but Dad wants to get a hotel and make it a little getaway for the two of us."

I'm not hiding my child or Mercedes from my parents. I just haven't found the right opportunity to tell them that I'm a father. But it looks like the opportunity has found me. "Mom, I'm glad you called. There's something I wanted to talk to you and Dad about. Is Dad there?"

"Loch, it's 5am here, where else would he be?"

"Is he awake, Mom?"

"He's up. He had an early prayer shift this morning. I just heard him in the kitchen. He's probably making coffee. Hold on, let me walk downstairs with the phone." My mother has a bad habit of forgetting to move the phone away from her ear before she talks to someone so she basically yells in my ear.

"Neil, Loch is on the phone! He wants to tell us something." There's some commotion on the other end of the line. "Neil, how do I work the speaker phone thing?"

Two things happen at the same time. I hear my father's deep voice say, "Good morning son," and my own son decides to wake up in a very dramatic fashion. Liam sits up in the bed, looks around and starts wailing.

"Is that crying, Lochlan? Who is that?"

I get to Liam and start to soothe him. I almost have the situation under control when Mercedes comes bursting into the room. I understand this is completely inappropriate but everything going on around me temporarily ceases to exist when I see Mercedes wearing nothing but a short T-Shirt and hot pink lace panties.

"Oh, thank God. I heard him crying and then he wasn't in his bed. I thought maybe he got up and hurt himself looking for me or-" She stops mid-sentence when we both hear my parents on the phone.

"Give me the phone, Neil. Lochlan? What is going on over there? Who is that? Is that a baby? Whose baby is that?" I mouth "my parents" to Mercedes. She just nods and reaches out for Liam.

He screams out in joy at the sight of her. "Mommy, mommy!"

She takes him and whispers that she is going to the kitchen to get him something for his kiddie cup.

"Lochlan!" I must be taking too long to answer. Probably because I'm staring at Mercedes' round ass in the lace boy shorts. Men really can be simple creatures. My deep sigh is the only preparation I get for this conversation.

"Mom and Dad, sorry about that. I had planned to tell you this in a very different way, but I guess there's really no point beating around the bush now. I have a 19-month-old son."

"*What*?" It's a simultaneous shout from my parents. They couldn't have planned it to be more coordinated.

"I know this is a lot to take in, but yes, I have a son. You guys are grandparents." Silence on the other end. I think this is the part where I offer some sort of explanation. "Right before I had my accident, I had a brief relationship with someone who I had strong feelings for. I didn't know until a few days ago that the result of that relationship was a son."

"Lochlan, it's your father. Your mother had to sit down. You're telling us that you're a father? Are you sure? How do you know the child is yours? There was a lot of foolishness going around when you were in the NBA."

"Hang on one second, Dad." I text a picture I took of Liam to my parents and I can hear them both gasp.

"Neil, he looks just like him. Heck, he looks just like you."

"I can't believe this. I'm not even sure where to begin. Why are you just now finding out about a child who is almost two?"

"That's a long story Dad, I would rather get into the details when we see each other."

"This is unbelievable. He's so beautiful. Look at that little face." I can hear the tears in my mother's voice and I wish I could've done this the way I had planned.

"Well, what's the little guy's name?"

"Liam Taylor Dean. I'll be changing it to Liam Taylor Rait as soon as possible."

"Wait a minute, Loch, was the woman's voice we just heard, is that Liam's mother? Are you living with her? What happened to Rachel?"

"Mom, she stayed here one night so I could spend more time with Liam. Trust me; she does not live with me. But to be honest with both of you, I hope she will one day. It's my intention to have a family with her. And I keep telling you that Rachel and I are not together. We haven't been together since I left Texas."

"But, Loch, she was just there with you. I thought you two were working on your... whatever it was. I thought you were working on it?"

"Mom, I love you, but I don't want to talk about Rachel. We're friends. She was here for Ashley's birthday, but she and I are just friends. That's all we'll ever be."

"Well, who is Liam's mother? Does she even attend church?" Yup. I knew that was coming.

"Her name is Mercedes, but please let's discuss it more when you guys arrive. You can meet her and Liam. We can talk things out."

"I never heard him talk about anybody named Mercedes. Neil, have you ever heard him mention this woman?" Has my mother forgotten that I can hear her? I doubt it. It's much more likely that she doesn't care.

"Lochlan, this is going to get out. I mean have you thought about your role in the church and what this might mean? I know you left, son, but our understanding was that you wanted to expand in a different location, not just abandon the church."

"I wanted to expand my business, Dad. That's what I've done. I know this is difficult for you two to accept, but I don't view church the same way I did when I was back in Texas."

"I don't understand. You were such an integral part of the Next Generation movement. How can you just walk away?" I know the precise answer to that question, and there's no way I'm going to get into it right now.

"Mom, Dad, this isn't the time for that conversation."

"Well, son, you've been gone for almost a year. When is the time?" Sometimes, silence is the best answer. In this case, it's my only answer. I'm done talking about this.

"I just can't believe this, Neil. We're grandparents. Would you look at this little guy? He even smiles like Loch." My father and I are too similar. If my mother didn't intervene, we would've remained locked in a battle of silent wills. I'm pretty sure my mother knows this.

"You guys will love Liam. The way he's always thinking reminds me of Connor. You can see the little wheels in his brain turning. He's not like one of those impulsive kids; he has a plan for everything.

And I don't know if this is normal, but he can already count to five. I think he's advanced." The gushing is something that happens every time I talk about Liam. I don't control it.

"Okay, son, I... I don't really know what to say. Send us some more pictures and we'll regroup this weekend."

I end the call with my parents as quickly as I can and pray that the rest of the day is less eventful.

MERCEDES

I'm mentally exhausted. I thought I needed to go home last night, but I'm grateful I stayed with Lochlan. The energy to take care of Liam, no matter what is going on, is something I developed out of necessity. But after last night, I'm not sure my reserves of super-mom would've been sufficient.

While Liam drinks from his sippy cup and drags toys from his room into mine, I wash my face and brush my teeth with a brand new set of toiletry items I found in the bathroom. The bathroom connects Liam's room with the guest room I slept in, and it's a dream like everything else so far. It's decorated in a country-rustic style with the largest walk-in shower I've ever seen. I'm not gonna lie, when I saw the claw-foot tub in the corner, I was sorely tempted to fill it up and soak in it. But, I decided the better thing to do was to get home and try to locate some semblance of normalcy. I feel like my whole world is off kilter. So, instead of taking that bath, I'm leaving.

I can't believe there's a video.

What happened to me that night?

And then, an ugly little voice whispers. *Who else has seen that video?*

I need to stop thinking about it. Every time I think about it, I feel like vomiting. Vomiting will waste time. Therefore, there'll be no vomiting. I avoid looking at myself in the mirror. All of my bad decisions in life feel like visible scars.

Lochlan saw me like *that* and went running straight to Rachel. My mental exhaustion is partially the result of being pulled between self-hatred and white, hot anger. I hate myself for letting the things happen to me that made me into the person that I am. I'm also mad as fuck that Lochlan had the audacity to decide I wasn't good enough for him. Yeah, maybe I was caught on tape, but that doesn't make all his NBA hoeing any less real. It's always like this with these professional athletes. They want some perfect near-virginal princess when they've screwed their way through half the population. Part of me understands why Jules says the things she does, especially the part about not expecting to find sex, love, and money in one person. She always said, *"You have to choose, and don't let your choice be the one based purely on emotions."*

Lochlan's talking a good game now, but I'm not fooled. Everything that's happening now is about him wanting Liam. If he wanted anything other than Liam, he would have found me before I ran into him. I have to keep telling myself that. I can't get lost in him like last time. If I let him make me feel safe only to have it yanked away from me again, that would make me the fool. One of the only things I have going for myself outside of being a hard worker and a good mother is that I learn from my mistakes. It's been my superpower, and I'm not going to give it up because Lochlan makes me feel... never mind, I'm just not going to give it up.

"Hey, you're not leaving, are you?" So lost in thought, I've just been standing with my back to the sink. I didn't even hear that Lochlan and Liam have walked up. Liam is trying to get Lochlan to discuss his airplane with him. He loves him so much that it makes my heart ache.

"Yeah, I'm leaving. I should get home. There's some stuff I want to do at the house while I have this break from work." Lochlan looks like he's trying to decide what he wants to say. Liam interrupts him by requesting to get down. He toddles past both of us into his room announcing he's going to get his trucks which sounds more like "chucks."

"There are some people who'd really like to see Liam. I was thinking maybe you guys could come to the fitness and rehabilitation fair our company is sponsoring in the park."

"When is it?"

"It's actually today from 1 to 3. Do you think you could make it? There'll be tons of stuff there for kids. Liam will have a blast."

"Who do you think will want to meet Liam at your company's shindig?"

"Well, the most important person is my brother, Connor. He's been blowing up my phone asking about his nephew."

"I don't know, Lochlan." This is one of those times when "I don't know" really means "no and go away."

I'm surprised when Lochlan gently circles both of my wrists with his big hands. They feel... secure. Safe. "I don't know how many times I have to say this. But if I have to say it every day for the rest of my life, I'm willing to do it. I was wrong to walk away from you."

I try to interrupt him. This place in my spirit feels too tender. I don't want him poking around in here. "No, Mercedes, let me finish. I know what you're thinking. You think this is all about Liam and you're not wrong. Liam means the world to me. But you're smart, you know I could be in Liam's life and not be in yours. That isn't what I want because for me, this is all about you too." I'm terrified of this, and I don't know how to respond.

"I'm not asking you to make some kind of final decision right now. But can you give me a chance to prove myself?" He sees me open my mouth to argue and cuts me off. "And before you answer, remember one more important thing. When I saw you at Ashley's party, I didn't know about Liam and I still wanted you. When I showed up at your house that first time, I was there for *you*. I didn't know you had our son. All I'm asking is that you are open to the possibility of something happening between us, something more than co-parenting."

A deep breath is barely sufficient to pull all the pieces of me back together. I want him so bad. Other than a real family and Liam,

Lochlan is the only thing I've ever wanted this bad. But there's so much about me that is fucked up. I don't know if I'm capable of being in a healthy relationship. It seems unnaturally ambitious for me to even try. But the alternative, being without Lochlan, seems just as insurmountable.

"I'm not saying no." It's the most I have to give right now.

"Kissy, kisses, kiss, kiss kiss."

Dragged out of the moment, both of us look down at Liam who neither of us heard re-enter the room. He is looking up at us with his lips puckered like he does when I ask him for 'kissy kisses.' We burst out laughing and Liam joins in like he's in on the joke. Lochlan gently kisses the area of my neck right below my ear. "We have to give our son what he wants, right?" This one eyebrow thing he does is going to be a major problem for me.

"Yes, give the baby whatever he wants. Let me know how that works out for you." He just smiles this sexy smile. "Well, if things get out of hand, I know Mommy will be there to kiss it better."

"And on that note, I'm leaving."

"You're coming later, though, right?" We stare at each other seeming to both realize the double meaning of his words. Lochlan smirks at me. I roll my eyes at him. "Send me the details and I'll bring Liam to the park."

"Do you need me to come home with you?"

"Lochlan, you know I've survived for 25 years without you? Right?"

"I just meant that it's been a rough night. I don't want to bring up things you might not be willing to talk about, but I would understand if you needed support right now."

Since my grandmother died, there has been no one but August who showed me any kind of genuine concern. Greg takes me out and spends money on me but, that's...different. August is the only person to listen to my problems and care. I have never had that in a relationship with another man. Even though I was ready to give life another chance last week, I feel out of my depth in this place. My idea had been some flirting and dating for fun, like wading in a kiddie pool. This feels more like being thrown into the deep end of emotions.

"Thank you, really. I admit... I'm having a hard time. It's humiliating to know that people have seen me like that in a way I don't even remember." I have to stop because I'm choking on the words. "I'm sorry. I can't really talk about it. I'll be okay. I just have to get through this and I'll be okay." That compassionate look is back and still threatens to jackhammer through all my defenses.

I run away from it and everything that it can do to me.

15

LOCHLAN

My company had spent a lot of time and money on this community fitness event. Our marketing group includes a partnership director who is aggressive about the community. She helped us put the event together to raise awareness about the benefits of physical activity. It doesn't hurt that it drastically raises the public profile of our company. My plan is not to get tracked into a niche for professional athletes. We are particularly interested in extending the scope of our services to work for injured and recovering veterans. That's a big deal and it should be the only thing on my mind, but it registers the same as a gnat might. I've been looking for Mercedes for the past 30 minutes.

"Bro, where's the ice cream truck?" asks Connor. Why is he asking me this?

"What?" I reply irritably, on edge.

Connor snorts. "You look like a little kid waiting for one. You okay?" A smirking Connor is not what anybody needs in a situation like this.

"I don't know what you're talking about. I just got finished networking with several folks who might be interested in our app for vets."

"Yeah, okay." Connor's laugh fades into the background when I see Mercedes and August walking towards us.

My son is asleep in a stroller. Of course, he's asleep *now*. He partied half the night away.

Everyone has heard that phrase a thousand times that something took my breath away. I don't really know what they mean. Mercedes doesn't take my breath, but every time I see her, there are a couple of seconds when I forget to breathe. They are always followed by the same question: how did I just walk away from her?

"Mercy." It's my first breath always.

Before I can talk to myself about giving her space and letting things develop naturally, as I had been doing all morning, I step up and place a gentle kiss on her forehead. She puts her palms flat on my chest and sort of sighs before she seems to remember where we are and all the other people who are here with us.

"Oh, for fuck's sake. Can someone give me a consistent message about what we're doing? Are we enemies, co-parenting, or Romeo and Juliet out here? I cannot keep up with you two." August is exasperated.

Both of Connors eyebrows are at his hairline. Mercedes looks flustered.

"Hello, you must be Lochlan's brother, Connor, right?" And that is how you change a topic.

"Yeah, and you must be Mercedes. And this..." Connor squats down to the stroller where Liam is yawning and stretching. "Oh my God, this has got to be my nephew. He looks just like the Rait men." Liam frowns at Connor like he is personally responsible for waking him up. Connor just laughs and looks proudly at his nephew. "Hey, big guy, you wake up angry just like your dad." At the mention of me, Liam turns towards me, smiles and screams, "Daddy!" We vacate the stroller and he excitedly starts telling me about the oranges he ate for lunch. When I try to introduce Liam to Connor, he still looks displeased right up until Connor produces a stuffed monkey with a potbelly. The monkey is wearing a T-shirt that says 'Uncle's best friend.' Liam can clearly be bought because he instantly bonds with his new uncle.

August is eyeing Connor like he's edible. "Does he like boys?"

"August, please don't embarrass me." Mercedes responds through clenched teeth without moving her lips.

"Well, does he?"

"He does. But he doesn't date them or sleep with them," Connor kind of announces.

"Why August? Just why?"

August bats her words away with a hand. "Oh please, Mercury. Stop being so dramatic. You're not the only one who wants a forehead kiss today."

"August, aren't you dating someone?"

"What? No. That was last weekend."

Connor is playing with Liam. Mercedes is arguing with August and my heart swells. This feels like home. This feels like the place where I finally belong.

MERCEDES

I'm glad August came with me to the fitness day. He's a kind of shield from the emotional war Lochlan's waging.

"How are you feeling about everything? You okay? You're quieter than usual."

"August, how would you know? When do you ever stop talking?"

"Don't change the subject. I'll get you back for that little dig when you're not all emotionally fucked up."

I look at Liam who is chasing the bubbles I'm blowing for him.

"I've had almost two years of hiding my ratchet language from the baby. I know what I'm doing."

He's got me there. We're both experts at hiding our cursing from Liam. I blow out an exasperated breath.

"I think I'm okay. I don't know. I'm just trying to, I guess... process? Yeah, I think that's it, I'm trying to process everything."

"I just need you to understand that what happened to you wasn't because of some mistake you made. It was rape and motherfuckers need to die. And the first motherfucker needs to be that gargoyle, Jules."

August looks ready to murder her himself. I blow some more

bubbles. "How did she let this happen?" It's odd to me that August and Lochlan focus on the same thing in that story.

"She didn't *let* it happen, August. She did the best she could to protect me and I broke all the rules. She was as fucked up that night as I was. How was she supposed to protect me?"

"Is that what she told you? It is, isn't it? She told you that she did everything she could and you believe her?"

I can't look at him because he's right.

"I know why you protect her, Mercedes. I just don't know why she never does the same for you." This is not something that I'm willing to think about. Not right now. I turn around when I feel a presence at my back. Lochlan is there. He puts a hand under my chin. "Mercy, is everything okay?"

"Don't eyeball me, Mr. Tall and Sexy. I don't have my spatula, but I will fight."

"I'm fine, Lochlan. August isn't doing anything to me."

I'm not the type to engage in casual chuckling. I've taught myself that laughter is normal, but I'm still more of a special occasion laugher. And now, I'm out here just casually chuckling. I can't help it. The look Lochlan is giving August is so severe. I think August might actually need that spatula. August leans back and looks at me like he's never seen anyone from my species.

"Well, Mercury, I do believe you just laughed in public. Huh. It might be love after all." He's still looking at me like an unidentified specimen, or an imposter. "I'll take Liam with me to go find an ice cream cone before they close down the stand. I hope it's not some low-calorie or gluten-free bullshipsailing." August reaches for Liam who is now propped in his dad's arms explaining all that has transpired in the last hour. My child is far more talkative than I am. It must come from his dad's side of the family.

"I'll go with you to get my nephew an ice cream cone. Maybe we can buy him a bike too." Connor joins the conversation. He has a mischievous glint in his eye that seems to always be there. I really like him. And can we just pause for a minute to discuss the Rait family genetics? These men are fine as fuck. It seems statistically impossible that there are two of them. Connor wears his dark blonde hair a little longer than Lochlan, his eyes are blue instead of gray and his facial hair is thicker. Beyond that, the brothers could be twins.

"I don't like the way you're looking at my brother." I feel Lochlan's warm breath when he whispers in my ear.

My intention is to be indignant, but I forget about my right to look at whoever I want, however I want, and when I'm taken over by aggressive tingles and goose bumps. Everything inside of me responds to Lochlan. Attraction would be too subtle of a word to describe it. The pull is magnetic. In my heart I know I won't be able to be around him and resist him. I can do one but not the other, not at the same time.

"I can't help that Uncle Connor is hot."

"Okay, it's time for y'all to go get that ice cream." Lochlan hands Liam to August and Connor and steers me toward the pond in the park.

I let him hold my hand. Strange mixed feelings of stark terror and complete safety define time with Lochlan. Part of me thinks as long as I'm with him, nothing bad will happen to me. The other part is terrified that I'll have to deal with him leaving me again. It's fucked up because I can't decide if it's okay for me to embrace wanting to be with him or if I should be the one to run away.

"I'm never going to get enough of seeing you smile. You're always so serious and beautiful, but when you smile, you're light and radiant."

I tuck my lips inward to keep from laughing.

"Don't you dare laugh at me being poetic. I'm trying to express myself here."

I'm leaning against a large tree trunk and Lochlan is standing over me scowling. Of course, he has a handsome scowl because of course, he does. The fitness fair is wrapping up and this is the first time I've had a chance to talk to Lochlan one on one.

"I'm sorry. It's just funny to hear you call me radiant when I'm wearing ripped-up blue jeans and sneakers. I don't even have any makeup on."

Why do I feel shy all of a sudden?

"I don't know what to tell you. You just do it for me. I don't care about all that other stuff. It's just you."

Oh, for goodness sake, I give up. When Lochlan leans down and gently kisses my lips, I kiss him back. And the floodgates open, wide. If you asked me what was under my feet, I couldn't say with any certainty. I can't feel anything but this kiss. I stand on my tippy toes and wrap my arms around Lochlan's neck. His lips sucking mine, his tongue exploring. That's all there is in this moment. Oh, oh... I remember this tongue.

"I told you. Thank you, pay me." August stretches his hand out to Connor who just shakes his hand in amazement, takes a fifty out of his wallet and hands it to August.

"You bet that I would kiss him?"

"Bro, you bet against me?"

Connor shrugs, grinning. August rolls his eyes and shakes his head.

"He bet me and had to pay double because there was clearly tongue involved. Straight men never catch a vibe and that's why they mess their relationships up." He gestures at Lochlan. "I present to you, Exhibit A."

Liam, for his part, is reclined and sleeping soundly in his stroller.

"Please ignore him," I implore both Connor and Lochlan.

"Mercy, go on a date with me later."

"I... I can't leave Liam."

"Our son? Okay, bring him."

"Ashley is dying to see Liam. She and I can come over to your place, Loch, and hang out with him," suggests Connor. I must look as skeptical as I feel about that proposal. "Hey, Ash is a professional. The chances of me losing my nephew will decrease exponentially with her in the picture."

"Do it, Mercury. Let yourself live. It's okay." August's sincerity kind of makes me want to cry.

"I guess I could. But, Lochlan, can we not do anything fancy? I'd rather just keep it low-key." I know Lochlan wants to figure out whether there's any meaning to my words. My face is purposely neutral.

"We can do anything you want to do, Mercy."

Lochlan's place rolls into view around 7pm after I spent a truly ridiculous amount of time agonizing over an outfit. Lochlan said he had the perfect non-fancy thing for us to do. Now, I feel like an idiot. What outfit says 'perfect non-fancy thing and also I'm not trying too hard?' My nerves are frazzled to shit as it is. Greg and Jules have been blowing my phone up. Jules keeps telling me that I'm a basic bitch for not getting a lawyer and locking down child support. Whatever island she evacuated to come haunt me, I pray she finds her way back there soon. Greg wants to know when we can go to the shore. I text Jules that I know what I'm doing. She texted me back a GIF of Judge Judy rolling her eyes. I text Greg that I need to figure out my work shifts because I'm a coward. I don't respond when he keeps checking to make sure everything is all right because I'm a coward. To put a truly fucked-up cherry on this whole shit sundae, my brain is completely wrapped around the memory of Lochlan's kisses.

A simple off-the-shoulder Chanel sweater with the double-C pattern in large white letters on the front ended up as my choice for the evening. I put on a different pair of light, stone-washed ripped jeans and realized that all my jeans are ripped. Sneakers would've been too casual and heels too over the top - so I compromised with some cognac-colored chunky-heeled boots. Lochlan seems fascinated by my natural hair, so I don't bother to straighten it. If Jules was losing her shit over the child support issue, she would positively die if she knew I was running around with my hair in its natural and unruly curly state.

When Lochlan opened the door, you would've thought I was dressed for prom. He has this way of looking at me that makes me feel both beautiful and whole. Sometimes, when Greg would look at me, dressed up in those outfits he picked, I would feel like a pieced-together china doll, pretty but fractured, glued and taped.

Lochlan is wearing a simple black sweater, a pair of low-slung faded jeans and boots. He looks and smells like sex. Fine, I admit it. He makes me think about sex, a lot. But I'm not going down that road. I want this to be about something else. I already did it the other way. It didn't work out that great.

"Mercy, we've called three times. He's sleeping in his bed and he's fine." Okay, I'm being theatrical. I've never left Liam with anyone but August.

"I know you're right. He's fine. I'm going to relax."

"I doubt the total accuracy of that statement, but I'll let it slide so we can enjoy the best tacos in D.C."

"Yeah, I worked up an appetite kicking your butt at fowling." My light laughter turns into a full-belly laugh when I see Lochlan is still seriously pissed about the result of our first official date.

"Whoever heard of bowling with a damn football anyway? It's a violation of the laws of physics."

"You can't be mad because you picked the place." My words are less than clear because I'm talking, eating a taco, and laughing at the same time.

"I wanted to go throw axes. I didn't know they had fowling too. I didn't hear you talking all this junk when I rolled you up in arcade hoops. You were quiet then."

"Okay, 'rolled me up'," but who was rolled up on the race cars and the zombie apocalypse shoot out?"

The place Lochlan had picked was a large entertainment arena. I never do anything like that, but I'm hella competitive and I absolutely loved winning. I feel...happy. I think I'm happy. I have no idea how, but Lochlan has devoured an entire taco while we've been talking. We're sitting out on the C&O Canal along the Potomac eating tacos we grabbed from a food truck. It's perfect.

"How did you learn to play all those games? I mean pretty girls don't usually make the best zombie assassins." So, maybe the night isn't totally perfect. There's always going to be my past.

"I, um... I used to be with a guy who was really into football and video games."

"Is that Clay Farrell?"

"Yeah, how do you know about him?"

"The very first time I saw you, I was with two of my teammates. One of them ran in the same circles as Clay and remembered you used to be with him."

"Yeah, that was a long time ago."

"Yeah, you couldn't have been more than what, eighteen, when Clay was in D.C.?"

"I was actually sixteen."

Lochlan puts down the last piece of his taco and turns his body towards mine on the bench we're occupying.

"You were with Clay when you were sixteen?"

"Yeah. I lived with him until I turned eighteen."

"Were you with him or were you just living with him?"

"What do you think, Lochlan? He's not a blood relative of mine. You know how those guys are."

"Did he know you were sixteen?"

"I told him I was eighteen, but he paid my high school tuition without asking some really obvious questions."

"Why?"

"Why what?"

"How did you get into that kind of relationship so young?"

"I was 16 and I was basically alone in the world. My grandma had passed away and I didn't really have anyone else. I was going to become a ward of the state without some help. I met Clay; he liked me, and he solved all my problems. End of story."

LOCHLAN

That is definitely not the end of that story. I don't think I've even heard the beginning of it. I knew some bad thing had happened in Mercedes' past, but it's way worse than I'd thought. What's wrong with these guys that they all thought it was okay to do those things with a teenager?

"You were just so young."

"I know. I mean I know that now. Back then, I thought I was a grown-up making grown-up decisions. But the longer I spend as a mother, the more I think about how messed up all of that was."

"No one around Clay knew how young you were?"

"No one knew or would say anything if they had."

"Not even his family members?"

"I never met any of them."

"What about when he took you out?"

"We only ever went to private parties at other players' houses or to private clubs with private entrances. Back then, I thought I was a part of some super exclusive club. I called myself a "headline chick" because I had all the most expensive stuff." Mercedes laughs, but it sounds sad. "I was just some expensive side chick he kept hidden. He had a home and a fiancée that I didn't know about until after our fake relationship ended."

"How did it end?" I'm sure by the look on her face that the next words out of Mercedes' mouth will not be true. "I broke up with him." So, she's going with a half-truth.

"Why?"

"Ugh, can we go back to talking about how I kicked your ass in basically every game tonight?"

"Yes. But I want to know about you. I feel like I step on landmines with you because I don't know your history." I actually know a lot more about her today than I did yesterday. We had talked through our time at the entertainment complex. I know all about her grandmother and what growing up with her was like. But I noticed that Mercedes stops talking when she reaches the part where her grandmother died.

"He was unfaithful and I caught him. Ironic, I know, since he was cheating on someone else with me. It turned out he was a double cheat. If you want to know about me, here's a window into my soul: I wouldn't have cared about the cheating. I didn't even like Clay. But I was eighteen and pregnant. I was finally waking up to the fact that a lot of the stuff going on around me was very fucked up. I thought I was going to be a mother and I wanted to be better than that environment."

"What happened with the pregnancy?"

"I lost it. In retrospect, it was for the best. I wanted better but I hadn't become better. I don't think I had anything to give a child back then."

I cup her smooth jaw in my hand and rub her cheek. "That's not true anymore. You are a great mother to Liam."

"Your turn, Lochlan."

"Okay

, what do you want to know that I didn't tell you in between getting my butt kicked by you and zombies?"

"Well, I still don't know why you left Texas and the church. What happened?"

When I decided to leave Texas, I also decided to leave the story of my departure there. This wasn't something I wanted to share, but I owe Mercedes this. She's given me so much of herself so I can give her this.

"After my accident, I wanted to dedicate my life to God. At that time, I thought that meant dedicating myself to the church. So, I went back to the church I grew up in, but it was old and kind of stuffy. I had this idea to try to focus on the youth and young adults and grow that part of the church. It wasn't really getting a lot of attention back then. My dad is an elder in the church. He was supposed to oversee the youth ministry. He wasn't the leader of it, just the overseer, but the leader had left recently and my dad was trying to fill in. Naturally, he was thrilled that I was interested. He let me take over programming."

"So, what? Were you like a youth pastor?"

I laugh at that. "Hardly. I was more like what I am for my company, the CEO. I came up with plans and started finding people to fill in specific roles and create programming. It exploded in just one year. We had about 30 active members when I started running the programming, it grew to 150 active members in a year. We had another 50 or so of what we called participants."

"Okay, it sounds wildly successful so far."

"Yeah. It was." I heave out a deep breath and let it go.

"I thought the ministry needed one spiritual leader. A youth pastor, like you said. There were a couple of candidates, but one was the obvious choice. It was a guy named Zack. His family had been at the church since he was a kid. He'd been a faithful member of the ministry all along. Even when it was limping on one leg, he was committed. He was also an extremely charismatic speaker whose biblical knowledge was unmatched in that group." Mercedes lays her head on my chest and tucks her body into mine. It makes the rest of the story a little easier to get out.

"I was invited to the board meeting to give my recommendation and comment on the candidates. I recommended Zack, but the board wanted to discuss the other two top candidates so we did. It was clear they weren't as qualified as Zack. I mean, Mercy, it wasn't even close. So, I pushed a little harder for Zack and things got really uncomfortable. And to this day, I can't prove what I'm about to say, but I will swear it's true. Zack was the *only* Black candidate. That by itself wouldn't be that big of a deal, but when I looked around at all the board members and all of the elders, it occurred to me that every person with a substantial leadership role was white."

"Wow."

"Yup. So, I asked if anyone could give a specific reason not to promote Zack because up until that point, all they were giving were reasons we should promote one of the other candidates. I explained that Zack had quantifiably more skills and better relationships with our members than the other guys. I was told it just wasn't God's time for Zack. And I knew Mercedes, I just knew it was about race."

"So, you left because white people in Texas are racist?"

"Not funny, Mercedes."

"I know. I'm sorry. But Loch, honey, it's Texas."

"Okay, shouldn't you be a little more offended right now? You are Black aren't you?"

Mercedes just laughs. "I am so I've been living with racism for a long time. It's just funny to see you react to it because to be honest, Black people do expect some folks to be racist. It's white people like you, who are surprised by it."

"I hear you, but it's completely unacceptable and to answer your question, that's not why I left. I left because they tried to cloak their racism in God. And I realized in that moment that I had gotten it all wrong. I didn't need to be there to do right by God and being there didn't mean that I was being a good Christian. It's just a place and those are just flawed people."

"And so, you just turned your back on it and came back?"

"Not exactly. I still fellowship here, but in a different way and with a different understanding. I'll never let people tell me how things should be between me and God. I don't need that anymore."

"You know what's so interesting to me?"

"What's that?" I hope the question masks me inhaling the smell of her shampoo like a creep.

"That you are who you are no matter where you are. You were a boss in D.C. and a boss in Texas. You return to D.C. and you're still the boss."

"Can I be the boss of you?"

She turns to face me "Is that what you want, Lochlan?" Her voice is low.

"Only sometimes in some ways. Mostly I want you to be my partner in raising Liam and in life. I hope one day you'll consider being something more."

"Lochlan, be honest, you're not put off by my past?"

"Are you put off by mine?"

"Yeah, a little. You went from NBA superstar to Jesus Christ Superstar and it's a lot." There is no response to that other than laughter.

"Really Mercedes? Jesus Christ Superstar?"

She shrugs and laughs with me. "I'm just saying, you got a lot going on."

"Well, we're not our past. I get that it's part of what makes you who you are, but it's only a part."

"Well, that makes one of us. It scares me."

"Why?"

"What if it is me? I mean what are we other than the things we've learned?

"I don't know, Mercy, but for me today, I'm more the things I unlearned. It was easy to repeat what I was taught, but I found myself, my *real* self when I chose a different way."

"You make it sound easy."

"It's not, but you have me. I'm willing to lend you my unlearning expertise." For the first time since our night together, it's Mercedes who kisses me. She tastes like everything I want. When I groan she pulls away.

"I'm sorry."

"I'm not."

"No, I'm not sorry for kissing you. I just... I don't want it to be like last time where we rushed into bed together."

"I get it." My body does not get it. Not at all. I'm speaking purely from intellect. "I've been celibate since I was with you."

Mercedes cannot mask her shock, though she tries. "Wait. You and the Blondie didn't?"

"No."

"Well, damn. No wonder she was wound so tight. Poor thing. Why didn't you?"

"I did so many things on my way to the NBA and once I was in, it was no-holds-barred. The funny thing is that I was one of the most restrained guys in the league. Meaningless sex just didn't appeal to me anymore."

"Was I a part of your meaningless sex past?"

"No. Not at all. That was the other thing. I finally knew what it was like to have something different. And as holy as Rachel supposedly was, she offered plenty. But it wouldn't have been any different than a random groupie because my feelings about her weren't any different."

"Ahhhh, okay, I give up. I swear you have a cheat sheet of all the right things to say." Her genuine frustration is funny.

"Are you really giving us a chance?"

"Yes, but, Lochlan, I don't know what I'm doing. I'm warning you. I've never been in a real relationship. And I have no training on these things. I mean I'm willing to get some books or something but I'm really not working with much over here."

"I got it, Mercy. We'll learn together."

"Okay, Pumpkin."

"Who?" I will forever love the sound of her laugh. Honestly, it's loud and a bit over the top. It's like she doesn't know how to control it. She's still learning to laugh, and I love it.

"Our neighbor called her husband Pumpkin. When I was younger, I thought if you fell in love, you were supposed to call the other person Pumpkin." Mercedes stops laughing when she sees the serious look on my face.

"Why are you looking at me like that?

"You just said that you thought you were supposed to call the man you love Pumpkin."

The pause is back, carrying a different weight than that day at Mercy's place when I found out about Liam, but it is no less powerful. It holds us still for a moment.

"Oh..." Mercy says quietly.

"So-" Her hand covers my mouth. I'm thinking about biting her.

"Don't say another word, Lochlan. Just leave it alone. Baby steps."

She can think whatever she wants.

We are way beyond baby steps.

16

LOCHLAN

"Loch, look at this one. Ash has him singing with her."

The week has flown by. It's Friday and my parents will be here tonight. Connor and I are at the office engaged in our new favorite pastime of looking at pictures and videos of my son.

"I don't know, man. The kid's got decent pipes. Should we buy him a piano?"

"Mercedes will kill you if you have any more large items delivered. Bro, you bought him a Harley on Wednesday. A Har-Ley."

"We agreed we would teach him to ride when he's older."

"Yes, we agreed, but his mother didn't and doesn't."

"Yeah, about that, how's that going? I heard your little family, including Momma Bear, has been staying at your house every night this week."

"You heard from August?" Connor shrugs. "You know he's trying to date you. You get that right?"

He shrugs again. "I'm secure in my manhood and the man is a fountain of information."

"There's nothing wrong with me wanting to wake up with my son. I've got a lot of time to make up for."

"Mm mmm, and what about your son's sexy mother? Who's making up that time?"

"Don't call her sexy."

"What other word would you use to describe that woman?"

"*Mine*. That's the word I would use to describe her. She's mine."

"Calm down, caveman. I don't think she's even capable of seeing anything but you and her son. You two are equally obsessed. And how's that celibacy thing going?" Terrible. Horrible. Awful.

"Fine."

Connor clutches his chest and nearly falls out of his chair in my office, he's laughing so hard. "Yeah, okay."

"You're not helping, Conn."

"I know." He doesn't even have the decency to be ashamed.

"We're trying. We promised we would get to know each other this time."

"And are you getting to know each other?"

We actually are getting to know each other. It's only been a few days, but it feels much longer with Mercedes. For someone who never laughed before, she loves to laugh. My house has come alive with the sound of her laughter and my son. I can't forget August, Ashley, and Connor because they are all over every night despite my insistence that they get the hell out. I can't get anyone to leave before we put Liam to bed and Liam will not go to bed until everyone leaves. So, every night is a disaster. I will never tell them this, but I'm happy with the nightly fights over who needs to go home.

It turns out Mercedes is a good cook and she loves to do it. This is a major issue for my siblings who are always in search of a meal. Ashley makes baked goods but can't put a meal together to save her life. Mercedes has been feeding the hoard every night. The only reason I let Connor and Ashley in is because Ashley brings desserts. Also, Connor has a key. We usually get everyone out by 9, but Mercedes and I have been staying awake until 3 or 4 talking to each other.

"I feel like I've known her forever. it's incredible. And you're right, this celibacy thing is on thin ice. Every night we end up in fewer clothes and we're not starting out with many to begin with."

"I don't get it. You guys have a whole child together. You've already done the thing that got him here."

"I'm aware of that. Trust me. There is not a minute that goes by that I'm not aware of that. But both of us want something different than the way we treated sex in the past. We're trying to find that different." I run my hand through my hair, trying to decide if I want to say the next thing. "I want to marry her." I guess I wanted to say it.

"That doesn't surprise me."

"Really?"

"Loch, I've seen you together. You orbit one another physically and mentally. You move in perfect sync. I see how she smooths out all your asshole tendencies."

"And what do I do for her?"

"Take out the garbage… I'm not sure."

"Ha ha."

"Okay, seriously. When I first met her, she was all closed off. But she's come alive with you. I mean she's glowing at our family dinners. Are you sure you haven't knocked her up again?"

"You really need a better filter, bro."

"Hey, is the one o'clock in the conference room?" We both look up to see Paul standing in the doorway. "Phillip is gone to lunch and the other girl, Stephanie, is covering. You need to have a talk with her. She pays no attention to who walks through the lobby."

"It's fine, Paul. You should stop being so uptight."

"Uptight is what protects us all from expensive litigation. Is this meeting happening or what?"

"You have been even more anal than usual, Paul. Did your porn subscription get discontinued? You know they have free sites now."

Conn and I are both surprised when Paul silently gives Connor the middle finger. Paul doesn't swear, drink, or party. I haven't seen him give anyone the finger since we were teenagers.

"Okay, your behavior is starting to scare even me. You okay, Paul?" I'm surprised by the genuine concern in Connor's voice.

"I'm fine, but that woman you hired for community relations is a pain in the ass. She's completely unconcerned about the liability issues associated with her grand events, she doesn't consider how certain partnerships may reflect on the company's image, and I swear she's eaten my chicken salad sandwiches twice this week. I can't prove it, but I know it's her."

Connor and I exchange a completely dumbfounded glance. Paul is the most put-together person we know. We privately speculate that he's a touch OCD because he has to have everything in a very specific order all the time. He's a lot of things; this level of flustered is not one of them.

"She...ate your sandwich?" Connor asks the question like you might ask someone about to jump off a tall building is there anything you can do to help them. The tone seems appropriate under the circumstances.

"Oh, don't worry, I will get the evidence. I won't expose us to a wrongful discharge claim when we terminate her."

"Paul, I'm not going to fire her for eating a sandwich."

"Okay, well fire her for being...I don't know, I have to come up with something."

"Are you sure you're okay?"

"Oh shit, you like her." I'm not sure where Connor got that from. Paul seems to clearly dislike her.

"I what? No. That's ridiculous."

I stand corrected. Paul definitely likes her. Uptight Paul has a crush on one of my employees who he wants me to fire. This shouldn't pose any issues in the future. I'm not wading into that quicksand right now.

"Paul, did you find out anything about the footage of Mercedes?" A subject change is in order.

"Yes, I did. I sent you a memo. Did you not read the memo?"

"Noooo, I didn't because your office is down the hall and I figured you could just tell me."

"Per my memo on the subject, I set up a meeting with you and Dexter Taylor."

"Dexter Taylor!" Connor and I shout in unison.

"Yeah, he's on the recording, so I figured you might want to start with him. He's right here in D.C. He thinks you want to meet with him about a sponsorship for the company."

"I'm going with you, Loch."

"I can handle myself."

"Oh, I'm sure of that. That's exactly why I'm coming."

"When is the meeting?"

"Sunday night. It's the best I could do. He's flying out on Monday. The details are in my memo."

Connor rolls his eyes. "Thanks, Paul. I appreciate it."

"Don't mention it. Helping you sort this out is the least I could do. Does Mercedes still hate me?"

I say no at the same time Connor says, "Definitely."

"She just needs to spend a little time around you and get to know you."

"Oh, that's for sure not going to help," Connor adds.

Thank God we are interrupted by my temporary assistant who announces the one o'clock is here in the conference room.

LOCHLAN

The meeting was very productive, but I want to get home to my... family. That's what Mercedes and Liam are, my family. It's just after 2pm, the marketing folks left the conference room. Paul and Connor stayed behind with me to chat with Greg Klein. Greg is one of the coaches involved in the new roll-out for the rehab app.

"So, Lochlan, I hear you and I have an associate in common."

You know how you sometimes have the feeling that whatever is about to happen, you're not going to like it? That's the feeling Greg's words invoke. Something about the tone sets off my alarms. Connor must sense it too because he tenses in the seat next to me."

"Oh yeah, who's that?"

"Mercedes." I knew I wasn't going to like this. I didn't know it might lead to violence.

"I didn't know you knew Mercedes. She's never mentioned you to me."

"I know the feeling. I've been dating her for almost two years. She never told me you were Liam's father."

Greg hasn't said anything out of line. But the way he uses Mercedes and my son's names is making me want to flip the table over and choke him out. There's something too familiar about his tone. Connor taps his finger on the conference room table. It gets my attention for long enough to help me calm down and think rationally.

"Two years is a long time to not even earn a mention," Connor's tone is casual, but his meaning is clear.

"That's how it is with those types." Greg shrugs off Connor's statement.

"I would be careful if I were you." The ability to casually threaten someone is a quality that most Rait men have, but Connor is the master of it. My temper has always been too short.

"Oh, no harm intended. But you know how it is. You buy them stuff; they spend a little time with you, and then they're looking for their next meal ticket. I was the idiot for paying the tuition bill for school without even securing the return on my investment."

"You paid what tuition bill, exactly?" See? No casualness in my tone, just an outright threat.

Greg loosens his tie. "I guess Mercedes didn't tell you that I got your son into private school and paid for the pre-school program."

Paul is on it. We may fight each other, but we're a united front to the outside world always. Paul stands up and walks to the door gesturing for Greg to follow him. "Sorry for the misunderstanding, Greg. If you leave your account information with Lochlan's assistant, we'll get the tuition money wire transferred back to you."

"Look, I don't want to upset Mercedes."

"Really? Is that why you walked your smug ass in here and basically called her a prostitute?" I'm vibrating with anger at Greg, but also at Mercedes. Why didn't she tell me this so I wouldn't get blindsided?

"That's not at all what I said or meant."

"Yeah, okay, all that about you "securing your investment" that was you being respectful? Okay, I hope you respect your mother with that same energy. Now, get the fuck out of my office."

Greg is not a small guy. He's at least as tall as I am and in excellent physical condition. But even with my bad leg, there is no doubt in my mind that if he doesn't move quickly, he'll need assistance making it out of here.

He holds up his hands as if in surrender. "Hey, no sweat off my back. Just thought you'd like to know who the mother of your child really is."

If the table wasn't between us, I would have gotten him before Paul basically shoves him out the door.

When he's gone, I just stand there trying to calm down and sort through all the stuff in my head.

"Do you know how much that school costs? What do you think she had to do to get him to pay for it?"

"Lochlan, don't do that."

"Come on, Connor. You know it's true."

"I know you're jealous and I know you don't know what the truth is." Paul is back and I'm surprised at his answer. "Loch, the last time you jumped to conclusions about Mercedes, look what happened. Have you really not learned anything?"

"August says Greg is a controlling asshole who Mercedes should have gotten rid of a long time ago. There was never any real relationship." Connor looks up from his phone.

"I can't believe you and August really have each other on speed dial."

"What can I say? Ash set him up with her friend. Hopefully, he's moved beyond his crush. Even though, I mean let's face it, I'm hard to resist."

"She should've told me."

"Maybe. But what difference does it make now?"

I don't know, but I need to figure it out.

MERCEDES

I don't know why I let Jules come over. She's spent almost the entire lunch criticizing me for spending time with Lochlan and not "taking care of business."

"Jules, when are you leaving town?"

"Oh, so that's how it is?"

"It's not like anything. You said you came here to help me get a lawyer. I don't need one so I figure your work here is done." I really did think that. I don't know why Jules is still here.

"Mercedes, I didn't just come here to help you get a lawyer. I came here to make sure you do what's right for you and Liam. But you insist on being super basic and making decisions because of some feelings you think you have for your baby daddy. Meanwhile, you're trying to provide a country-club life for your son with nothing to fall back on but a Boys & Girls Club salary. That's basic as fuck."

"If you're going to cuss, keep your voice down."

"I thought Liam was sleep?"

"He is, but I don't want him waking up to you yelling the F-word."

"Whatever, Mercedes. Don't try to change the subject. Why haven't you done something to make sure Liam's future is locked down? Why don't you worry about that? And why did you break up with Greg?"

"I didn't even really break up with Greg. We weren't together. We were more like friends."

"Friends? You really have lost your mind. No man like that needs a woman friend. What is happening to you?"

"Nothing is happening to me. Why do you assume I'm going through a crisis because I don't want to be friends with Greg?"

Jules shakes her head in disgust. "This is not about Greg. Look at you." She waves her hand at me as if I don't know where I'm supposed to be looking.

"You're running around here dressed like some simple ass off the rack chick. No makeup and your hair looks like you just went through a bad breakup."

"That's stupid. People don't wear their hair curly just because they break up with somebody." Yeah, way to go Mercedes, that'll show her. Pick the most irrelevant point and argue about that, super.

"Oh is that what this look is? Curly? I thought it was more a shout out to bitches without hair brushes."

Maybe I should do something with my hair. I kind of like it like this though and Lochlan seems to like it. My hand goes to my wild curls of its own accord. Stop it Mercedes, there's nothing wrong with your hair.

"I get that you think something is going to happen with baby daddy but be fucking serious. You think a rich former NBA player is going to want an Old Navy looking chick with whatever this hair is? And even if he does Mercedes, what next?"

I stand up and take the lunch dishes off the table and over to the sink. Whatever Jules is about to say next, I'm not going to like it. After I put the dishes in the sink, I turn around and face Jules. She's still sitting calmly at the breakfast nook. Dismantling my reality is light work for her, she hasn't even broken a sweat.

"What do you mean 'what next'?"

"I mean, what is supposed to happen with you and this guy? You think some bible thumper from Texas is going to be with you on some happily ever after shit." She rolls her eyes like that's the most ridiculous thing she's ever heard.

"I'm not saying you're a hoe but you definitely ain't church girl pussy. Have you met your child's grandparents? Because I'm guessing they're going to take one look at you and haul their son back to Texas. Hell, they might even try to get custody of their grandson."

Part of me rejects every bit of the venom Jules is spewing. Another part isn't quick enough to duck the toxic waste she's throwing around. I don't think anyone is going to try to take Liam from me, but Jules has at least a slight point about Lochlan's family. I can't imagine people the way he's described them as being thrilled about him being with someone like me. It does seem a little bit farfetched. Just like that, an aggressive seed of self-doubt springs up in my mind.

The sound of the front door opening causes us both to pause. I've never been so glad to hear August return home. I need Jules to leave. There might be another perspective for me to see but I'll never be able to think clearly while she's here. If anyone can help me get rid of Jules, it's August.

He walks into the kitchen with the mail tucked under one arm and his phone in his hand. He pauses mid-step when he sees Jules. "I knew something smelled bad in here."

"It didn't smell until you walked in, Augusta."

"Biiiiiiitch." August is already moving towards Jules. She doesn't budge from her spot at the table and her bored expression may as well be set in stone. I don't have the energy to break up a fight. I just need August to help me get Jules out.

"August, Liam is sleeping." We don't play about that.

August immediately lowers his hands and backs up. "She's lucky I'm saved."

Nope. I have no response to that.

"Look, I want to go get cleaned up. I'm taking Liam over to Lochlan's tonight."

"Playing house with no house. Basic." The disgusted eye roll is Jules' signature punctuation, and there it is.

"Speaking of Lochlan, head's up Mercedes, he knows about Greg."

"Wait. what? How do you know that?"

"Connor texted me. They had some meeting today with a bunch of NBA coaches. At the end, Greg not only mentioned you, but he also said he paid for Liam's tuition."

My stomach sinks. "I'm lost. How would Greg know to mention me to Lochlan? Absolutely nobody knows that I'm dating either of them. So, how did Greg know?"

"Well, let's see." August taps his chin like he's thinking. "I know and I didn't tell. You know and you didn't tell. Who else does that leave? Is there one other person who knows about both and would also know how to contact Greg? Who, oh who could it be?"

I had turned to look at August when he walked into the kitchen. Now, I turn very slowly towards where Jules is sitting. If you didn't know her, you wouldn't know anything was up. But I do know Jules and I can discern the subtle shifts in her fixed, bored expression. The current bored variety contains a subtle hint of satisfaction. It's in the eyes.

"You did it, didn't you? You told Greg about Lochlan?" If she rolls those eyes one more time, I'm going to knock them out of her face.

"So what, Mercedes? I ran into Greg at a cocktail party and I mentioned that Lochlan is Liam's father. Sue me. I didn't know it was a secret."

"You really are a miserable bitch." August might have a point about Jules but the damage is probably done.

"August, I don't know if you've noticed, but while you're living in a basement apartment in some shack in D.C., I was on a yacht last week. I flew here on a private jet and I'm staying at the Four Seasons. I might be a miserable bitch, but I'll take that over being a *broke* bitch. It's something you might want to think about, Mercedes." With that, Jules picks up her Hermes bag and walks out.

I'm no longer thinking about how happy I am to have her gone because I'm focused on Lochlan's probable reaction to finding out about Greg. No matter how I try to bend the facts in my mind, I don't see any possibility that Lochlan is going to take this well. Is Jules right? Am I deluding myself into thinking that he's going to want to be with me in the long run? Because it kind of seems like I am.

LOCHLAN

Mercedes opens the door wearing shorts and a hoodie. We look at each other for an extended beat before she opens the door wider and steps back so I can come in. I can't decipher her exact mood and it feels like that's by design, she's more guarded than usual.

"Is Liam sleeping?"

"Yeah. I put him down a while ago."

"I'm going to go look in on him and then we can talk." My face creases into a deep frown when Mercedes barely acknowledges my words with a nod. I don't know what's going on with her but we're going to figure it out.

"I need something to drink. Do you want something from the kitchen?"

"I'll take a water, please." The barely there nod again. It's infuriating but my desire for her is as great as always and it all blends together in my turbulent mood. I don't know if I want to yell at her or forget all of our new relationship rules and bury myself inside of her. In the end, I walk up the stairs to my son's room.

The sight of my Liam, the child that we made together, smooths out some of my rough edges. The night light in his room illuminates him in his crib. Connor is right, he sleeps sprawled out just like I do.

Liam's got one fist wrapped around his stuffed monkey and the other hand above his head. I relax even more when I see he's wearing the pajamas with the line "big guy" on them that I got for him. I give Liam a kiss on the cheek before backing out of the room quietly.

When I reach the bottom of the stairs, Mercedes is coming from the kitchen with two bottles of water in her hands. I stop and stand directly in front of her.

"Please explain to me the real reason why you're here and not at my place right now."

It's 11pm, I got some generic-ass text from Mercedes at around 5pm telling me she wasn't feeling well and would come by tomorrow. When I tried to find out what was wrong, she just texted back that August had Liam, he was fine and that she'd see me tomorrow. If I hadn't had to pick my parents up from the airport and take them to dinner, I would have been here right away. Luckily, they didn't think they were meeting Mercedes until tomorrow so they didn't ask too many questions about her absence.

"I told you I wasn't feeling well."

"You didn't tell me anything. You sent me a text message and it didn't tell me anything." She at least has the decency to look embarrassed. "What's going on?"

"I just figured you probably wouldn't want me over there after the whole Greg thing." I knew that's what this was about. Connor and August chat like they're girlfriends. The thread of vulnerability in Mercedes' voice makes me feel guilty for my initial reaction to finding out about Greg.

"I'm pissed about whatever that is with Greg, but why did you think that meant I wouldn't want to be with you?"

"I don't know, Lochlan. Maybe it's because that's exactly what you did to me before. You found out something you didn't like from my past and ghosted me for two years." Ouch. She has a point there, I'm careful about my next words.

"Okay, you're right. I did that. But let me ask you this. Are you the same person you were two years ago?" Mercedes doesn't answer, but I know she gets my point. "You're not and I'm not either. I thought we agreed we weren't going to hold the past against each other?"

"If that's true, why are you pissed about what you heard from Greg?"

"I..." Damn. She got me there too. I pace around a little, trying to buy time and find a reasonable answer. Why was I mad? Mercedes walks further into the living area and sets the waters on a side table next to the couch.

"Why didn't you tell me that some guy you were with paid for Liam to go to school?"

"I didn't think I had to tell you. I'd already called the school about returning that money and setting up a payment plan for the tuition. I knew you wouldn't appreciate Greg paying Liam's tuition so I was fixing it."

I don't like that she's wrapping her arms around herself. I've learned that she does that when she thinks she has to protect herself and I don't want her feeling that way around me.

"Mercy, I'll take care of the tuition and anything else Liam needs. Why would you let Greg pay for it, but you haven't asked me?"

Mercedes is quiet for a long time. I take her hand and lead her over to the sofa to sit down hoping that will make her feel more relaxed.

"Loch, first, I never asked Greg to pay Liam's tuition, He just did it. And yes, if we hadn't gotten together, I probably would've let him. But, I don't want to be connected to my past like that, not while I'm in this present with you."

"I understand that, but I still don't get why you didn't tell me about the tuition. For that matter, you haven't asked for anything for Liam. I thought it went without saying that I would take care of everything for him, but now I'm not sure I read the situation right."

"No, I know you'll take care of your son."

"So, what is it, Mercy? What am I missing here?"

"Okay, you remember we talked about unlearning?"

"Yes, I remember."

"This is unlearning for me. In my world, men have only been as good as what they can do for me. I'm really trying to see things in a different way."

"I think I get it...but you don't see me that way. I know you don't."

"You're right, Loch, but it's not about how I see you, it's about how I see myself. For me, taking money from a man that I'm sleeping with makes me feel like I'm not growing. It's like I'm just doing the same thing I've always done which means I'm the same old person."

"I hear you, but I'm going to insist on providing for my son."

"I know, but can you just give me time to unlearn and re-learn?"

"I can give you whatever you need, Mercy." When she smiles at me, it's open again, it feels like I have her back.

"By the way, we're not sleeping together."

"We've slept together every night."

"Okay, so here's an idea, let's not sleep and then you'll be okay with financial support."

"What are we going to do at night, you know what? Never mind, I see where this is going." She laughs but she also climbs onto my lap and straddles me.

"Loch, first of all, if we're honest, there hasn't been all that much sleep as it is. But just so you know, there's almost nothing I want more than to get even less sleep with you."

I lean up and stroke my hand over the smooth skin of her cheek and neck. "Just tell me when you're ready, I'm not going anywhere."

"I know but you have to go home tonight."

"Um, no I don't." The reason why she thinks that's possible while her body is pressed into the hardness of mine is far beyond me.

"Aren't your parents staying with you tonight before they check into their hotel? If you stay here all night, they'll know you were here."

"Mercedes, I'm an adult and I'm not worried about what my parents think I'm doing with you."

I frown when she stands up. "I know you're not worried, but I am. I know your parents are really into the church and all of that. I don't want them thinking, you know." She gestures outward with her hands in a nervous fashion.

"I really don't know but I'll make you a deal. I'll stay but leave early so I'm back in time to have breakfast with them before we start the lunch party tomorrow. Deal?" Mercedes rewards me with that smile that makes me want to do anything she ever asks of me.

"Deal. Let's go to bed."

There's nowhere else I'd rather be. I'm sure of that now. My anger from earlier was far outmatched by my fear when Mercedes wouldn't answer me and didn't show up at my house. I want her in my life. I couldn't care less about Greg. I know who this woman is to me and that's all that matters.

MERCEDES

"Oh my God, Mercury. How many hats did you bring? This is the third beanie you put on that little boy and it's 80 degrees out here."

I look across the center console of my truck from the backseat and glare at August fanning himself dramatically in the front passenger seat. I'm leaned over Liam's car seat going insane because I can't pick the right hat, not beanie, to put on my son to meet his grandparents. We've been parked outside of Lochlan's house for five minutes while I rotate Liam's head gear.

"Shut it, August. I don't want Lochlan's parents thinking I have their grandchild out here looking any old kind of way."

"They are not going to think that, Mercedes." I nearly jump out of my skin when Ashley speaks from behind me.

"Are you a cat? Is that what's happening, you're a cat with a sugar problem? I never even heard you walk up."

"I pulled up a couple minutes ago. I was waiting for you guys to get out so we could go in together but then I started worrying that you were never going in."

August is now out of the truck. He pulls the back door open on the passenger side and stands with his hands on his hips. "August

Childs, charmed." August flits his fingers at Ashley in a wave I know he got from some old movie he was watching the other night.

"August, this is Lochlan's sister, Ashley."

"Oh, nice to meet you. I've heard nothing but good things. And you're not alone sister, I'm also worried that we're never going in the house, especially since I haven't eaten all day and Mercedes promised me there would be food when she forced me to attend this shin-dig."

Liam snatches the plaid cap I was trying on him off his head and throws it on the ground. "No." He shakes his little head to punctuate the denial. How did I never notice how much he looks like his father when he's being stubborn? Well, I guess that hat won't work. Okay, new plan. I take a comb out of my oversized purse and try to comb his little curls into some sort of order.

"August is supposed to be on a diet, that's why he hasn't eaten, it has nothing to do with him coming over here to meet your parents." I talk to Ashley over my shoulder while trying not to let Liam snatch the comb out of my hand.

"I am on a diet, have you seen me eat any Skittles yet this week?"

Ashley steps around me and starts unstrapping Liam while I'm still combing his hair. "Really, August, a Skittles diet? That's the plan?"

"Skittles have a lot of sugar." He deadpans because he's totally serious.

"Mercedes would you put that comb away. My parents are going to love Liam because he looks just like those other Rait men they love so much. You seriously could have brought him over here in a paper bag and it wouldn't matter."

"I know, I'm probably being silly." I step back so she can take Liam out of his seat while I collect his bag from the floor. "I just feel stupid because Lochlan was at my house last night and he overslept so I'm sure your parents know he was with me. I already have a baby by him, I don't want them to think I'm just some slutty girl." That thought has been stalking me since my conversation with Jules.

What I am not expecting in response to my passionate speech is laughter but that's what I get. Ashley is laughing so hard Liam starts laughing with her like he's also in on the joke. I look at August he just shrugs and mouths "white people."

"First of all, I'm Samoan." Ashley barely stops laughing to correct August. "More importantly, I can't believe that you, Mercedes, are worried about my parents thinking that you're slutty? I assume you've met their sons, Slut 1 and Slut 2? You know like Thing 1 and Thing 2 but more promiscuous with better hair?"

August folds his arms over his chest and raises both eyebrows. "I sense some tea about to be spilled and I'm here for it. Carry on, sis." He holds his hand out like an usher inviting Ashley to continue.

While we lock up the car and move to cross the street to Lochlan's house, Ashley accepts August's invitation. "Lochlan might be all good guy now but he was a NBA player who hoed from one side of the Potomac to the other."

"Okay, okay, TMI." My involuntary shudder is evidence that I do not need to hear this and a reminder to teach Ashley about language around Liam.

"Oh girl, my bad. This was all before you. But really, if my parents try to act like they don't know their sons are a current manwhore and a recovered manwhore, I'll be the first to set the record straight. Nobody has any room to judge around here. Except me, I'm a virgin."

I almost trip over my feet at that last piece of information. Ashley just smiles sweetly when she clarifies "to the backdoor."

"Oh my God, I think I love you." Of course August would declare his affection for Ashley at this moment, he's a lover of all things inappropriate.

"Mercury, you wouldn't be tripping over your feet if you had worn the flat sandals like I told you." August looks at Ashley but continues to talk about me. "She changed her own outfit about six good times before we left the house. I sincerely didn't think we would ever make it."

Once we're across the street, it's just a few yards to Loch's front door. He told me he'd come and park the car while I took Liam in the house but I was freaked out by the thought of being alone with his parents. It's D.C., who knows how long it might have taken him to find parking?

"I don't know what you're supposed to wear to meet parents. I just wanted to look presentable." And not like some groupie who got knocked up a couple of years ago. I don't say the last part but that's what I'm thinking. I still remember one weekend when Clay's parents came to town for a game.

Clay said "*I know you don't have any parents, M so you probably don't know this. But parents are important and a big part of relationships. I don't just bring anybody around my folks. Until we know where this is going, let's just be chill.*"

I hated it that he called me "M" but I never said anything about it. We'd also been together for a year when he told me to "be chill." I was 17 at the time, I didn't really know any better. But as I got involved with other men, I noticed that nobody introduced me to family. I mean, I'd been seeing Greg for two years, I never met anyone from his family. Jules might be right about me. Maybe I'm not the type a guy brings around his parents. If that's true, it increases the chances that I'm going to mess up this whole thing with Lochlan's super Christian parents.

"Okay, halt." August holds up his hand and turns to face Ashley and I since we were walking behind him. "Mercury, you need some positive affirmations or something. You don't need to look presentable, you are presentable and you're a present and Lochlan's future." August pauses with his hand to his chest. "Does somebody have a piece of paper? I need to write that last part down. That could be my toast at the engagement party."

"I don't have any paper but I've got a great memory and I'm definitely using that if I get called on before you."

I'm about to tell August and Ashley that they're both insane when Lochlan's front door swings open and Liam screams "Daddy."

Nobody can talk over Liam's paternal excitement; I don't even bother to try. Lochlan takes Liam from his sister's arms and swings him around like they haven't seen each other in days. It's actually been a few hours.

Lochlan puts Liam on his side and draws me into his other side. I'm used to him inhaling me whenever I'm close to him. It makes me feel less like a creep when I do the same thing to him. I greedily fill my nostrils with his spicy scent and it calms my nerves, some.

"Mercy, you look exactly like a woman I want my parents to meet."

I lean back with my mouth open. He couldn't have heard us from behind his heavy ass door with D.C. noise all around us. "How do you always know exactly what to say?"

"Because I know you. And I know you've been out here obsessing about this because you don't realize how formidable you are and how I'm the lucky one in this relationship."

"Oh my God, give me some of those Skittles, Ashley. This calls for a celebration." August holds his hand out to Ashley who quickly produced a bag of Skittles after Lochlan took Liam from her.

"Why the hell is everybody standing out here? Dad is taking the steaks off the grill and I'm starving." Connor comes to the door looking confused. August drops the Skittles he was taking from Ashley and tries to look sexy or something. I don't really know what the hell August is doing but Ashley looks less than pleased that he let some of her Skittles fall on the ground."

"We're coming in right now." Lochlan looks down at me after answering his brother. "You're good right?"

"I'm good."

As we travel through Lochlan's first-floor to doors leading to his deck, Connor is having a full conversation with Liam, Ashley and August are discussing hair-care. As soon as we step through the doors and on to the deck, I see Lochlan's parents. He tightens his arm around my waist and I realize that I just tried to turn around and go back to the car. So much for being good. What was that, 30 seconds ago? It seems like forever ago.

Lochlan's mother is setting the table when we approach her and her husband taking steaks off the grill. She looks up and covers her mouth with both hands when she sees Liam in Lochlan's arms. Tears immediately spring to her eyes. I'm struck by how different Lochlan's mother looks than either of her two sons. Where the sons are fair, the mother has an olive complexion and green eyes. She also can't be taller than 5'2, how she birthed these two giants is beyond me.

"You must be Mercedes?" I have to stifle a laugh when the short woman struggles to pay attention to me. She's fixated on her grandson and I can't say that I blame her.

"I am, it's nice to meet you Mrs. Rait. Do you want to hold Liam?"

"Yes I do and please call me Sophia and Neil get the presents from the house."

"Mom, we can wait for the gifts." Lochlan exchanges a look with his father who let Connor take over the grill so he could come over and meet his grandson.

"Girl, if Lochlan is going to age like that, you better marry him tomorrow." I pray no one could hear August's loud sideways whisper in my ear, but August can't really whisper so I should probably save my prayers. I can't even be mad though, August is right. It appears as if Neil Rait cloned himself because holy over 50 fuck, this man is a more refined and just as good looking version of his sons. I'm not exaggerating, they look exactly like him and I can tell by the way his polo shirt and slacks fit that he's in as good of shape as his sons.

"Sophia, you're going to smother the child." Lochlan's father chides his wife as she cuddles Liam but it's laced with affection. For his part, Liam thinks all the attention is hilarious. He takes the opportunity to ask about cookies and various other snacks as he giggles.

"I'm Neil Rait, it's very nice to meet you, Mercedes."

"Thank you, it's nice to meet you as well."

"Do you have baby pictures? What about videos? Do you have any videos from when he was born? Did you make a scrap book or anything? It's not too late, you could start one now."

"Sophia!"

"Mom!"

All three Rait men yell at Sophia Rait at the same time.

"Mom, just take a deep breath. He's your grandson and he's not going anywhere. We'll dig all the information out of the archives that you need to satisfy your soul. In the meantime you can make some new memories now."

I don't really know what to say. This whole experience is kind of awkward for me. I've been on my own for so long, I'm still trying to adjust to all these other people being in our lives.

"Hate to be rude but can we sit and eat? I already had to wait for Mercedes and August to take an hour getting out of the car, I'm starving."

"I don't see how, you were snacking the whole time." August responds to Ashley over his shoulder. He's made his way over to the set table and appears to be eating bread from one of the baskets on the table. Between August and Ashley, food is going to be a constant issue.

When Sophia and Neil Rait both appear visibly confused by the black and Vietnamese man dressed in a pink shirt and lime green slacks, Ashley explains "That's Mercedes' good friend, he was invited." It doesn't seem like that would clear up the mystery of August but Neil and Sophia appear satisfied and we all sit down to eat.

The conversation flows pretty smoothly as Lochlan's parents ask me about Liam and my work in nursing. I'm just starting to relax when Ashley appears at the sliding door with a visitor in tow. Ashley ran out to her car. She said she left her phone but I heard her tell August she forgot a bag of peanut M&Ms. I'm not sure if she found the M&Ms but she did show up with Rachel Lawton. All heads turn in their direction. Whatever expression was on my face freezes in place when my brain can't identify an acceptable response to what I'm seeing.

"Look who I found outside." Ashley gestures to Rachel and almost runs back to her seat at the table. She's obviously not willing to be involved in explaining why Rachel is here. Lochlan, Connor and Neil

Rait all stand up. I guess that's a Southern thing. August shrugs next to me as if to say 'fuck that, I wish I would get out of this chair.'

"Rachel, what are you doing here?" Even though all three men are standing, it's Sophia Rait who finally ask the question on everyone's mind.

"Yes, why are you here?" Lochlan follows up in a far less neutral tone. He sounds pissed. I'm glad Liam fell asleep almost as soon as we started eating. I think all my primping and the excitement of new people wore him out. We put him in his bed about ten minutes ago so he's not here to see his father's temper.

"Mrs. Rait, Mr. Rait," she nods at both of Lochlan's parents in greeting before continuing. "My parents told me that you were in town for the convention and would be here for lunch. Since I'm in town as well, I wanted to stop by and say hi."

"So you just showed up to someone's house uninvited? Where they do that at? Is that like a Texas thing?" I nudge August's loud not-whispering ass under the table and give him a look that I hope conveys a command for him to shut up.

"I hope I'm not interrupting. I just get to see you all so rarely and I barely got to say bye to Lochlan on my last visit before he was hauling me off to the airport." Rachel has a feminine southern accent that makes her sound like a southern belle. Combine that with her dainty A-line dress and she looks perfect for a tea party.

I knew I should have worn something else. While Rachel looks like wife material, I went too trendy in my khaki green jumpsuit. It comes down to mid-calf which perfectly accents my strappy gold high heeled sandals that now appear really over the top next to Rachel's simple but cute flat sandals. My multiple thin layered neck-laces and bangle bracelets probably aren't helping the situation. I unconsciously pat my blown out hair, at least it looks more conserva-tive than my curls. But who am I kidding? I look like arm candy, she looks like she could be sitting next to these people in church.

"I'm sorry you came all the way over here Rachel but my parents are here to meet my son so this isn't the best time for you to catch up."

I see August try to sneak his phone off the table where it's sitting next to him. "If you try to take a picture of her face right now, I will stab you with a fork. Do not dare." August let's go of the phone and rolls his eye at my whispered threat. Rachel's face does look ridiculous but this is not the time for August's aspirations of creating a viral moment.

"I'm sorry your what?"

"I have a two year old son with Mercedes. My parents are here to meet him and spend time with him."

"What are you talking about?"

"Rachel, sweetie," she turns towards Ashley's voice. "Lochlan and Mercedes here had a child two years ago. His name is Liam. My parents are here to meet Liam but he's currently upstairs in his room taking a nap." Ashley finishes slowly explaining the situation to Rachel and nods as if to say 'okay, get it now?"

"Rach, let me walk you out and I can explain more." I stiffen in my chair at Lochlan's offer. I don't want him walking anywhere with her simple southern...

"No, Loch, you stay here with your woman, I'll walk Rachel out." Connor to the rescue.

"Wait a minute, just wait a minute." The blond girl waves her hands in front of her like what she's hearing is a stench she needs to wave away. When Rachel turns fully to face Lochlan, Sophia Rait gives me a look that I can't quite decipher. Maybe they set this whole thing up to reunite Rachel with Lochlan. It sounds paranoid as fuck but I'm used to people doing slick shit like that.

"Lochlan, when did you have time to develop a...whatever this is with whoever? You and I have been together for two years and we were just together last weekend."

"Rachel don't do this. It's been over between us, you know that. I don't owe you an explanation for anything else. Please just let Connor walk you out."

"Lochlan, don't you do this. I know you're a good guy and I know you'd want to do right by a child but do you know he's even yours?

Don't throw your whole life away because of a fling you had with some groupie."

I've done a good job remaining calm. Hell, if there's a zen award, I should get it. But the reference to my son, even in passing, catapults me right back to my adolescent days of showing chicks that I'm not the one to play with. A strong tug on my arm gets my attention and I realize that I'd been getting up from my seat. "Oh, no, let me do the fighting. You have no chill and I don't want your future in-laws seeing you in here stabbing up a little white girl." August finally achieves a whisper when it doesn't matter because there's so much other noise on the deck now, nobody would've heard him stopping me from whooping Rachel's ass.

All hell has broken loose. All of the Raits are talking at the same time.

"You need to get the hell out of my house."

"Loch, I told you she was a psycho. If you had listened a year ago, we wouldn't be in this mess." Connor's matter of fact tone is incongruous to the chaotic situation. I really like him.

"Ashley, where are your manners?" Sophia looks like she might actually swoon.

"I'm very sorry, Mercedes, trust me this is not how we planned our first meeting with you to go." Neil's words and August's super human grip on me keep me in my seat.

Ashley is the one who is most useful. I don't know if I'm more surprised by her putting her M&Ms down or by the fact that she starts bodily dragging Rachel towards the door. "Okay, it's time for you to go, Rach. You crossed the line."

Rachel has the nerve to try to argue with Ashley, but Ashley is stronger than she looks and manages to finally get Rachel out the door. We can still hear Ashley and Rachel but the rest of the deck falls silent.

"Mercy, I'm so sorry, baby. Connor is right, I should have gotten rid of her a long time ago. I hope this doesn't ruin the whole day." Lochlan looks so sincere and he rubs my cheek tenderly when he speaks but I have too many emotions and thoughts bombarding me at the same time. With everyone looking at me like they're waiting for my reaction, all I want is for the spotlight to be somewhere else.

"No, it's fine. I'm fine. Let's just try to finish lunch." When I quickly turn my face away from him and pick up a piece of fruit on the plate in front of me, I can feel his frown probing my profile. But all I hear are Rachel's words ringing in my ears. These are polite people, I get they probably didn't want such a scene but I wonder if they have similar feelings about Lochlan throwing his life away on me.

When Ashley returns from disposing of Rachel, or whatever, lunch continues without any other major disruptions but everyone except August seems to have less of an appetite. For his part, August is still pissed he missed his viral moment when Rachel stood there with her mouth open looking like a stupid caught fish.

When everyone is done eating, I start clearing the dishes, Ashley and Sophia offer to help. We bring the leftovers and dishes into Lochlan's spacious farmhouse style kitchen. I automatically grab the saran wrap and foil out of the drawer where Loch keeps them and start wrapping dishes. Ashley sits down at the oversized island proclaiming "all that drama wore me out." When I look over to smile at her while wrapping up a bowl of pasta salad, Sophia Rait is watching me carefully.

"So, Mercedes, you spend a lot of time here?"

I freeze mid-wrap. It's only been a week but we spend a lot of time in the kitchen so I know where everything is, Sophia noticed.

"Oh, yes. Lochlan is a great dad, and he insists on having Liam here every day." I try to laugh off the observation. Great, I should've just stayed my ass on the deck. How have I managed to fail so badly at looking wholesome? First, Loch oversleeps and probably comes wandering in wearing yesterday's clothes. And now, I'm all in the cabinets and wrapping dishes like this is my kitchen. Anybody would think we're sleeping together, even though we sort of aren't.

Well this is not going to make me look like southern Christian wife material.

"Lochlan hasn't said much about how the two of you got together, how did you meet?"

"I um, I, well actually I accidentally picked up his sandwich at the deli. We started talking after that and kind of hit it off. It was the day of my college graduation and I was kind of um, well, it wasn't a great day. August couldn't make it so I didn't have many people there." It's too embarrassing to say I didn't have anyone. "Lochlan cheered me up and -" I stop mid-sentence because how do I say and then I let your son raw dog me, make a baby and disappear for two years? I can't quite find the words.

"And then voila, magic, baby. Come on Mother, you know how this works." Ashley interjects and saves me from having explain the rest.

"Thank you, Ashley, I'm sure Mercedes can speak for herself. Why don't you go bring in some more of the leftovers to be wrapped since you're not actually doing anything else."

"I think we got them all, we're good." She doesn't move while purposely missing her mother's point. "But since we're asking awkward questions, why Mother, did you tell the Lawtons about lunch today?"

Sophia Rait pats her perfect chin length hair as if a strand might be out of place, it's not. "We were just talking about the convention and I mentioned how excited I was to see all of you at the same time for lunch today. I had no idea Rachel was back in D.C. I mean, she was just here? Why is she back so soon?"

"Because she's just a tiny bit nuts, Mother. Connor and I have been telling y'all that for years. You just kept on acting like her father being a pastor mattered on her mental health index."

"Oh stop it, Ashley, she's a nice girl and there's nothing wrong with coming from a good family."

Ashley folds her arms across her chest. "She might be nice but she's manipulative and if we're being honest, she used Loch's injury to worm her way back into his life. Then she used her support during that difficult time to guilt him into being with her when it was clear he wasn't interested."

Sophia sags a little. I'm fascinated by the entire exchange.

"Mercedes, look out. One day your kids are cute and think the sun rises and sets on your word. The next they're stubborn and arguing with you about every little thing." I can't relate about the first part. I didn't feel that way about my parents. I didn't even know one of them. But the second part, I hate to break it to her but her grandson is already stubborn.

"Oh to heck with it." Sophia throws up her hands. "Rachel is a bit, I don't know the right word, she's just very focused on having things a certain way. And sometimes she can take it a little too far. I'm sure meeting you, Mercedes, and finding out that Lochlan has a son was not in her plans. And I don't think the girl can deal with anything she hasn't specifically planned. Okay, maybe she is nuts. But she got it honest, her mother is a bit special too."

I must really be a sight to see standing by the counter, mouth hanging open with a bowl of fruit salad suspended mid-air. Setting the bowl down seems like a good first step towards not looking insane.

"I thought you and Mr. Rait, I mean Neil, I thought you two loved Rachel and thought she was perfect for Lochlan?"

"Nah. She was good companionship for Lochlan after the accident but there were no sparks. It was nothing like the way he is with you." Sophia Rait fans herself and gives me a sneaky smile. "Now you two, you remind me of Neil and I when we got together and we still got it if I may say so myself."

"You absolutely may not. Stop it right now, Mother. God is not pleased." Ashley is disgusted but a smile slowly breaks through the barrier of uncertainty that has been swirling around me all day.

"I really do like him, I'm glad that's okay with you."

"Okay with me? Oh honey, all I want is for these boys to be happy and disease free. I still worry about Connor but at least now I know Lochlan is good."

"What about me? You don't want me to be happy?"

"Dear I don't worry about you, I worry about the man who has to worry about you one day." That response is met with an eye roll that would make August jealous. But my smile gets bigger and feels deeper.

All day I've been worried about looking like a certain thing and acting a particular way but Sophia Rait seems to think me being the woman her son wants is enough. Maybe she's right.

17

LOCHLAN - SUNDAY NIGHT

"Conn, you really didn't need to come with me."

"Yeah and I really don't need you to tell me that again. I don't know what this guy is going to say and I'm not going to let him say it without being here to stop you from doing something you might regret."

"You act like I can't control myself."

"Is that me or you, "red streak?" Tell me again, how many fights have you been in, little brother?" Connor uses air quotes around my old nickname. He knows I hate air quotes.

"Fine, Connor. And, Paul, why are you here?"

"For all the reasons Connor just said and also because I don't trust Connor. I left y'all alone for that family lunch yesterday and there was almost a fist fight."

"Fuckin Rachel. Paul, you might seriously need to get a restraining order. No matter what Loch does, she will not take the hint."

"I think him having a whole entire human child might finally do the trick." This seems like an accurate observation from Paul.

Connor and I both nod in agreement. Thank God everything

turned out okay after that disastrous lunch. My parents seem to genuinely like Mercedes and they are obsessed with their grandson. That's why this trip to Dexter Taylor's obnoxiously large Chevy Chase, Maryland mansion is so important. I need to deal with the ghosts of Mercedes' past so that she can be at peace in the present.

If Dexter's personality is like this house, he's a gaudy jackass. If class whispers, this house is yelling at us through a bullhorn.

"Are those actual Roman pillars? Who the hell does that in real life?" Connor eyes the architecture with palpable skepticism as we emerge from my truck.

"Apparently, this guy does." Paul rings the doorbell.

Dexter Taylor is smaller and leaner than us as a group, but I've seen him on the field. I don't doubt his agility or his ability to handle himself. He'll need all of those skills if I don't like his answers tonight. So maybe, Connor was a little right about me. But Dexter answers the door with a friendly smile.

"Lochlan and Connor, right?" He extends his hand and we shake it in turn.

"Yeah, man, and this is our cousin and attorney, Paul."

"Right, I think it was Paul who reached out to my people about this meeting. Come on in. My wife left some food out for us in the kitchen. Do you want some appetizers or cheesecake? Carmen makes amazing cheesecake."

Dexter is interrupted by something that sounds a lot like banshees. It's not banshees. It's his twin girls who go streaking by us with swords. They can't be more than 5 or 6.

"Hey, hey, slow down you two. When one of you falls, you're getting no sympathy when I keep telling you to stop running through the house. Where's your mother?"

One of the twins yells out, "Mom is on the phone with Auntie Mina!"

"Oh great, that's her sister. Who knows what shit pot she got boiling somewhere. My wife might be on the phone all damn night. My apologies in advance, fellas. Without their mom to keep them in line the twins can get out of control. They've already figured out that dad's a pushover. I can't get them to do shit that I say."

I'm speechless. I had a whole image in my mind of how this was going to go. None of it included two adorable little girls in pigtails, a flustered dad, or a room with toys scattered all around. Do you know how hard it is to be angry when you're seated across from a tea set where a stuffed frog is sipping tea with a stuffed panda in a football helmet?

"No, man, we're good on the food. We don't want to keep you too long. It looks like you've got your hands full." Connor should have been a diplomat instead of a tech genius. He might've missed his calling.

"Listen, Dexter—"

"Please call me Dex. Nobody calls me Dexter."

"Okay, Dex. We can talk about the sponsorship another time, but there's something I need to ask you."

"Oh... okay, I guess. I didn't know there was anything else."

"Yeah, that's my fault. I left this part out."

"Okay, well what's up? Don't leave me hanging in suspense."

"Do you remember a young woman named Mercedes?" At first, Dex shakes his head, no hint of recognition appears on his face, so I keep going. "You would've met her about 10 years ago. She was with a friend, Jules." Instant recognition at that name. Dex leans back in the chair he's sitting in and glances towards the stairs in the entryway. I assume his wife is upstairs.

"I definitely remember that fucking viper. Why y'all here on a Sunday night asking about her? It can't be no good reason." It's interesting how Dex's entire body language shifts at the mention of Jules. Where he was once relaxed and open, he now looks guarded and somewhat hostile. I've met the subject of his hostility and I get it.

"Jules brought another girl with her to a party with you about 10 years ago. The other girl was Mercedes."

"There were a lot of parties and a lot of girls. You're going to have to be more specific." I pull my phone out of my pocket and pull up a picture I took of Mercedes in the kitchen. She's holding a wooden spoon and laughing at something. She probably doesn't even know I took this picture. Every time I catch her laughing, I snap a picture if I can. I show the picture to Dex.

"Fuck. I do remember this girl. Why did I have a feeling this would be the girl you were talking about? Sometimes, I feel like I'll never get away from that night."

"Tell us about the video. What happened with her that night?" Dex looks towards the stairs again and back in the direction where his twins can be heard laughing and talking.

"Let's step outside. I don't want anybody accidentally overhearing this. Kids are like the streets, they always listening."

We all follow our host out the back doors to a stone patio area featuring a fire pit. Dex can still look in and see his twins playing in the house.

"How do y'all know about that video? Jules was supposed to have destroyed it."

"Come again? Did you say Jules destroyed it? As in, Jules had the recording?"

Dex heaves out a huge breath. "The girl in the video with me, how do you know her?"

"Her name is Mercedes. She's my son's mother."

"Fuuuck. You're really not gonna like this story." I'm sure that's true. I don't like it already.

"That bitch, Jules, set us up."

"What does that mean?"

"Jules partied all the time. We all knew her. She would bring other chicks with her. It wasn't nothing unusual about that. The girls were always up for anything, and I do mean *anything*. So, it wasn't like no big deal when she showed up with your girl. We knew they were wasted, but so were we. *Everybody* was."

I feel like I'm going to be sick. I look at Paul and Connor. Paul is kind of slowly shaking his head. Connor's expression is difficult to read and frozen in place.

"Jules brought the girl to us."

I lean in, "What do you mean she brought her to you?"

"Man, I mean exactly that. We had a room we partied in. Jules physically brought your girl in. They were walking hand in hand, laughing or talking, I can't remember anymore, but I remember they were holding hands. She did a little sexy thing where she helped take her friend's clothes off. We were all young, horny, and stupid. We thought it was just the usual game. So, we did what we always did, no big deal, right? Wrong! A week later Jules shows up with a video she had made. She tells us that her friend went to the hospital the next day and had the date rape drug in her system. But the catch was, the girl didn't remember anything. Jules basically had the only evidence linking us to her." Dex is clenching and unclenching his fist. Anger is vibrating in every word of his horrific story. "Maybe that wouldn't have been enough, but that witch had a trump card. She said she'd just met the girl and didn't know her well, but she found out she was a minor, under eighteen. I swear we had no idea about that shit. We had plenty of legally available women to choose from. We didn't fuck around with high school girls. We weren't *that* crew. You know, Lochlan. There were guys who did that shit, but that wasn't us."

"If you thought the girl you were with was an adult, why'd you take Jules' word that she was underage?"

Dex kind of grunts and shakes his head. "I didn't take her word, but I swear she had this shit all planned out. She showed us the website for this private school. There was a picture of the girl on the site. She was one of the finalists for the ninth-grade science fair or some shit like that. She looked different in the picture. Her hair was long and she had on a school uniform. She looked like a little girl, but it was definitely her. Man, this shit still makes me feel sick to my stomach. Do you know how fucked up it is to know you did that..." Dex trails off and covers his face with both hands. We give him a minute. We need one too.

"My twin girls are six years old. I pray every day that my fucked-up karma don't come back on them. Carmen wants to have more kids, but truthfully, I don't want to worry that a girl turns out like the ones I did wrong or that a son will make the same mistakes as me. Two is enough to worry about. Anyway, back to that bitch, Jules."

"She wanted money." It's clear where this is going now.

"Yeah, she wanted money all right. From me and my boy, Brian. Brian had a lot to lose. He had just gotten engaged, his girl was pregnant, and he was already on some three-strikes shit. If she'd found out he was still doing dirt, she was gon' call the wedding off. So, we paid Jules. It was twenty thousand at first. She blew through that and came back for another thirty. By the time it was all said and done, we paid that bitch seventy stacks."

Paul is the one to ask a question that had been burning in my own mind. "How did you get the footage back?"

"Oh, we didn't. Jules never gave it to us. The only reason she didn't get any more money is because Brian's wife found out. Home girl didn't like cheating, but she wasn't 'bout to let no other bitch run her man's pockets. And they were married by then with a kid and she didn't wanna be embarrassed by some old stuff. Brian's wife is the daughter of, well basically a mobster. They sent a "representative" to visit Jules and we didn't hear shit else from her. We got a message that the situation was taken care of." That part of the story makes Dex get close to smiling with satisfaction. "Do you know for a while, I thought she was dead? But I guess that's not how it works. Evil don't die."

"Hang on. Who drugged Mercedes?" This is an important issue because no matter what Dex thought, *somebody* drugged my Mercy.

"I know it wasn't me or Brian. We didn't get down like that. I figure Jules was lying about that part."

"She wasn't. Mercedes was drugged. She doesn't remember what happened that night."

"Fuuuuuuuck. I was 22 with my head up my ass. I swear I had no idea." Dex clenches his fist. He looks like he wants to punch something. "If I had to guess, my money would be on Jules."

"You think Jules drugged Mercedes?"

"Hell yeah, I do. That bitch had everything planned. Why else would she have left that part to chance? She knew we weren't rapist. If the girl wasn't a willing participant, it wasn't going down. How else could she have made sure her plan would work? I'd bet all my NFL salary and endorsement money that Jules drugged her so-called friend."

I think he's right. It makes sense when you hear the whole story.

"So, who has the recording now?"

"If it's still out there, I would assume the only person who ever had it still has it and that's Jules."

LOCHLAN

"I need bleach for my ears. That's the most fucked-up thing I've ever heard." Connor sums up how we all feel in the car on the way back to Woodley Park.

Mercedes is always defending Jules as if she owes her some debt for being there in her childhood. Everybody else can see how toxic Jules is except for Mercedes. But none of us guessed that she was a rapist and an extortionist.

"What do you want to do, Loch?"

"I would really like to strangle Jules. That's what I want to do. But it's more important to me right now to get that footage and destroy it and keep Jules away from my son and Mercy."

"Here's what I'm thinking. We can't do anything without some kind of leverage over Jules. If we just go to her and ask for the footage, she'll either lie about having it or try to sell it to us and we'd never actually get it."

I nod. I instinctively agree with Paul. If Jules sensed any advantage to her, she would milk it forever.

"Holy shit. If Jules is the only person with the footage, that means she's got to be the person who sent it to your investigator, Paul."

"Nah, I would've remembered that. I'm telling you it came from some big music producer."

"Who's the music producer?"

"Hang on. I think it's still in my Google Drive." Paul scrolls through his phone until he finds what he's looking for. "Here it is. The producer is DJ Diesel. I don't know his music, but he's huge in New York."

I text Mercedes: "Mercy quick question, did Jules ever associate with someone named DJ Diesel?"

Mercedes text back the green sick face emoji followed by "3 yrs. ago. Loser w big $. Y???"

I quickly answer "no big deal, her name came up in conversation. I'm on my way home. Did you wait up for me?"

Mercedes responds "always" with a pink heart.

"Loch, keep the head above your shoulders in the game. What'd she say?" Connor is looking at me impatiently.

"It was her. It had to be Jules who sent that footage." I can't figure out the situation with those two.

"It doesn't make sense. Why does her friend secretly hate her?"

Everyone is stumped by that question. We lapse into silence until Connor speaks.

"I don't know what's up with Jules, but I know who we can ask."

18

MERCEDES

"L och, are you sure about this?"

"I'm sure."

"But it's the middle of the day. Don't you need to be at work?"

"I'm right where I need to be."

"Ummm, excuse me. Don't think because you brought a babysitter, I'm foregoing my customary fee." August interrupts what had been a discussion between Lochlan and me when he walks into the lower-level den and gives Ashley the stink eye. Loch is trying to convince me to go on a day date. Ashley showed up with him and volunteered to stay with Liam. The man always comes prepared.

"I'm not the babysitter, I'm the aunt and you are not excused." Ashley challenges August with a look that has probably humbled many men.

Ashley and I have become real friends in just a few days. Her honesty is new to me, but I'm learning that I really like it. I don't feel like I'm trying to figure out a game with her and there are no rules. I can just be myself. We cook together and laugh at all the dumb stuff Connor and Lochlan argue about when they're together. She has also introduced me to the Twilight series, which she proclaimed a must read. I wasn't going to tell her I kind of hated it. Jules always said *"Never let these hoes know what you're thinking."* When I remembered that, I told Ash how I really felt because hello, unlearning. She just laughed and handed me her Hunger Games series. I like it. It's fucked up, but I like it. So now, I'm the girl who eats with family and reads young-adult fiction. I'm still getting used to it.

"I'm not impressed, but if you have some of that banana bread, I might let you slide." August is trying to win a stare down with Ash and also asking for banana bread. Who begs and tries to be tough at the same time?

Liam looks at his aunt who is holding him like a little baby. It cracks me up to see it. I know how independent Liam is and I honestly think he indulges his aunt's need to baby him. If I tried to hold him for this long he would be saying "I get down, Mommy. I get down."

"Nana bed?" Liam checks to make sure he heard right. "Don't tell Grandpa August, but I might have brought you some nana bed."

"Excuse me, all of you, I was trying to take my woman on a date. Can y'all all kindly go away?"

I cover my mouth to keep from laughing at Lochlan's frustration with August and his sister.

"Grandpa!? Aw hell no. This better be the best batch of banana bread you ever made in your whole life." When Ashley laughs but doesn't move, August follows up. "Um hello, what are you waiting for? To the kitchen please." August gestures toward the entrance to the den and back towards the kitchen.

"Oh my God, why do I put up with you?"

"Because you love me and pray that I'll share my hair-care routine with you one day." Laughter, I never would've thought it possible, but it's become a regular part of my life. Ashley and August have loved each other from the first time they laid eyes on one another. If August went that way, they'd be dating by now.

Lochlan wraps his arm around my waist and presses my back to his front. Sneaky bastard, he knows what this does to me.

"Come on, Mercy, say yes." I close my eyes and inhale him. My whole body is pulsing in time to the throb between my thighs.

Lochlan presses his lips to my neck. When I push back into him, he scrapes his teeth along my neck and I moan out loud.

Apparently, it was too loud because August yells "Y'all know these walls are thin! Please knock it off! My mouth was open when you did that."

I feel Lochlan shaking behind me and realize he's now laughing into my neck. Thank God for August because it was about to be on right under the hanging airplane and on top of the toy trains.

"Fine, Loch, you win. I can't believe I'm saying this, but let's go kayaking."

Lochlan turns me around to face him. "Why can't you believe it? You'll love it."

I feel so goofy sometimes when I'm with him. I want to giggle and agree to everything. I've never been so silly in my whole life. I don't even remember being this carefree as a child. "I've just never done anything like this before."

"Really? Where do you usually go on dates?"

"Just normal stuff like restaurants or clubs."

"Where else?"

"What do you mean?"

"You said restaurants and clubs. Where else do you go on dates?" Lochlan twists one of my curls around his finger.

"That's it."

He stops twisting the strands. "What do you mean? You've never been anywhere else on a date?"

"Nope."

"Oh, because that—"-

"I went ax throwing with you; we also went hiking with Liam, and to the conservatory."

"I'm your only real dates?" I open my mouth and then shut it. "Oh, I didn't know...So what? Restaurants and clubs don't count?"

"No, they do. Well, maybe not clubs. You can't even talk in a club. How's that a date?"

"So, where did you take Rachel? You guys went kayaking?"

I'm kind of relieved when he shakes his head "Nah. We didn't go out much unless we were with a group. I didn't have any pressing desire to be alone with Rachel. But if I had wanted to get to know her, yeah, I would have done the things with her that I'm doing with you."

"Well, Loch, I guess you're the first guy who's wanted to get to know me." Is that true? It's kind of sad and pitiful. Now, I'm pissed. Why the hell didn't anybody else take me kayaking? I've gone to the shore with Greg and there's lots of water, but it's the fucking shore. And still, no kayaking. That's why his ass got dumped via short text. If he had taken me kayaking maybe he would've got a call.

"I'm glad."

"You're glad about what?"

"You're a date virgin. I'm popping your date cherry."

"Oh God, please stop talking."

"You have to kiss me to shut me up." The words are barely out of his mouth and my lips are on his. I had to. He was being corny, so I'm helping him out.

"Kissy kiss kiss." Liam is back to narrate our affection.

When I break away from Loch, I chase Liam so I can get kissy kisses from him. He shrieks and runs through the house like he doesn't love my kisses. And I'm as happy as I can remember being.

LOCHLAN

This was all a ploy to get Mercedes into a swimming suit and while her yellow bikini with ruffle accents was worth it, I'm enjoying her excitement just as much. We're out on the water in a double kayak.

"Loch, row harder; those guys in the orange kayak are trying to beat us."

Even though we're rowing on a river and there's no actual endpoint, I paddle harder because I'm not a punk. If my woman wants to win, I'll win for her. Mercedes laughs that crazy laugh as we speed by the confused kayakers in the orange kayak.

"Whewwww! Yay, babe, we did it."

It's never going to get old, her calling me babe. It's always going to make me feel like Super-man. I don't care if I'm 80 and decrepit. I'll leap a tall building for her when she addresses me with so much affection.

"I hate to ruin the moment, but we have to turn around now."

"Aw, do we have to?"

"I promised Liam on a stack of 1,000 bananas that I would be there to tuck him in super tight. That gives us an hour to dry off and 30 minutes to get back home." Our home. I don't say that part, but I don't have to. We have a home together in each other.

"Okay, I'll race you back."

"Mercy, we're in the same kayak"

"Well, you better get to paddling, suckaaaaaaa." My woman is crazy. Just how I like her.

Once we're back on shore, we lay out on a beach towel and hold hands. We're on our backs with our heads turned towards one another. Mercedes's hair is fanned out around her; the sun glows on her face accentuating her freckles.

"So, at what age did you become a competitive psycho?"

"I'm a psycho? Me? Have you met yourself? You raced me up the stairs last night and then wanted to do a best out of three when I kicked your ass."

"To be fair, it was raining and my bad leg was acting up."

"Oh, bad leg, schmad leg." She waves her hand dismissively. "I didn't hear you claiming a bad leg when you were dusting me in basketball at the gym the other day. If I recall correctly, you jumped over me like you were in a NBA dunk contest. So, just admit I beat you up the stairs."

I'm not admitting anything. The only reason she won is because I got caught off guard watching her run up the stairs in some tiny jogging shorts. She basically cheated.

"So, Mr. Fake Bad Leg, real slow going up stairs, where did you get your competitive streak?" Mercedes turns to the side and props herself on one elbow.

"I always felt like I was competing for my parents' attention. It was so difficult to get them to focus on anything other than the church that I had to be the best and then some. So, I was a star athlete, an honor-roll student, a trivia champion, and I'm fluent in sign language."

"*Sign language?*"

"My mother had a deaf Sunday school student. It's a long story."

"I get it."

"You do?"

"Yeah. It's weird, but I think the same thing kind of drives me in a different way. At first, there was of course, my grandmother. She was just so convinced that I was the smartest and the best at everything. She kind of made me believe it. She worked so hard to give me bigger and better opportunities. Once she was gone, Jules acted like that proved that my grandma was wrong about me. Like, if I was really as good as she thought, it would've kept my grandmother alive. I don't know. It pissed me off. I think that's what gives me my psycho edge."

I bristle at the mention of Jules. Interesting how her name shows up in every nightmare story Mercedes has to tell.

"Mercy, what's the deal with Jules? She seems like a stone-cold sociopath."

I'm proud of the amount of restraint I've exercised. As soon as this Jules thing is figured out, she's done being around Mercedes.

"She might be. But it's been her and August for a long time. Orphans can't be picky."

I cup her face in my hands and look in her eyes. "You're not an orphan. You belong to me and you are loved by me. I love you, Mercy. So, you can be as picky as you want now." I kiss the single tear that rolls down her cheek before placing a kiss on each one of her eyes.

"You love me?"

"Yeah, I do. I think I've loved you from the first night I met you."

"I'm so glad. I didn't want to be the only one thinking I was in love. I mean I love you too."

"I knew that."

"Because you're cocky."

"You like my cocky."

"I do. You're right again...Just promise me you'll try not to break me."

"I'll do better than that, Mercy. I won't let anyone else break you either." When I seal my lips over hers it feels like so much more than the end of our date. It feels like the beginning of our lives.

19

LOCHLAN

I didn't think it was going to take quite this long to talk to August. But Mercedes went back to work and things have been hectic all week. I want Mercedes to stop working and go back to school. It's what she wants to do, but she refuses to let me pay for it. I'm still working on that project.

The 12-hour shifts Mercedes works every Monday through Wednesday are probably the only thing that has kept us from screwing like bunnies. The deeper our emotional connection gets, the harder it is to resist the physical connection. In my mind, I've accepted that it's only a matter of time. And maybe we need to just get it over with so we stop getting caught in compromising positions when the lust boils over at some unexpected point. Yesterday, Connor found us in the kitchen. Mercedes had on some skimpy shorts and a tiny tank top. I was in a pair of basketball shorts. I'd been in my workout room trying to get rid of my sexual energy, but when I came in the kitchen and saw her making a snack, all rational thought flew out of my head. By the time Connor came in, we were well on our way to the point of no return.

"Oh, for fuck's sake, you two! People eat in here."

"Connor, why can't you knock like a normal person? I'm getting my

locks changed and turn your head so Mercy can get down." As soon as
Connor turns around, Mercedes unwraps her legs from around my waist,
jumps off the counter and runs out of the kitchen.

"Where is my nephew while you're down here defiling his mother?"

"Connor, just worry about all the women you defile on a regular basis.
My son is tucked in and sleeping soundly."

I got the locks changed because Connor was never going to give
the key back. And that's why he has to knock on the door today
instead of just barging in.

"Hey, is August here yet?"

"No, you know August is never on time. Ever."

"How'd you get Mercedes to detach from your side? I thought you
two were permanently connected."

"She's with Ash. They took Liam and went shopping."

"Yeah right. Ash probably has her going from bakery to bakery,
sampling shit." I can't argue with that logic. "So, you haven't said
anything to Mercedes about what we found out from Dex Taylor?"

"Not yet. She told me Jules left town with some guy on a trip. If
she hadn't left, I was going to have to say something to Mercedes. I
don't want her around Liam."

"Agreed."

We hear the doorbell ring loudly, reminding me that I need to
change that thing. "That must be August."

Once we're all sitting in the den August gets right to the point.

"What has Satan done that made you have to call in backup?"

Connor and I exchange a glance. I explain to August what we
learned from Dex Taylor. I can only describe August's reaction as
completely stricken.

"Are you two sure about this? Jules drugged Mercedes, set up the
whole sex thing, recorded it, sent the recording to you, and still has it?
You are positive these things are true?" There is a tremor in August's
voice that matches his hands shaking.

"We can't be sure where the recording is now, but I'm confident
the rest of the story is true."

August stood up and started pacing as we recounted our meeting with Dex. Now, he puts his hand over his heart and collapses into a chair with tears in his eyes.

"I get it, August. We've been trying to figure out how to get the footage back. We need some leverage on Jules."

August dabs at his eyes and laughs with no humor at all. "No, Lochlan, honey, you don't get it at all."

When August doesn't continue, I prompt him. "Help us out, August. Tell us anything about Jules that might help us get that footage back. Or better yet, tell us why Jules hates her own friend so much."

"*Friend*? Jules is not Mercedes' fucking friend. She's her mother."

LOCHLAN

Silence. Sometimes, it's the only reasonable answer.

"Jules had Mercedes when she was fourteen or fifteen. Her mother, Mercedes' grandmother, didn't even know about the pregnancy. Before Ms. Liv, Mercedes' grandmother, before she died, she told me that she thought Jules was going to throw Mercedes away. She gave birth in her bedroom. Ms. Liv came home from work and heard Mercedes crying. She was sitting on top of a large trash bag with all the birth stuff still attached to her. Something went wrong. Jules lost too much blood and passed out. Ms. Liv had to rush both of them to the hospital. Probably saved Mercedes' life."

"Does... does Mercedes know this?"

"Mercedes knows Jules is her mother. She doesn't know any of what I just told you about the day she was born." Dear God.

"Jules would never tell who the father was, but Ms. Liv had suspicions. There was a family down the block that had a daughter Jules's age. Jules spent a lot of time at their house. Then one day, they just disappeared. The family packed up and moved out of state. Jules would barely come out of her room for three months. Ms. Liv thought it was because she missed her friend until she came home and found

Jules and Mercedes. Jules, being the sociopath that she is, gave Mercedes the family's last name."

"Wait. Was there like an older brother or someone?"

"You guessed it. But older as in eighteen, an adult."

This is like unraveling a rotten onion. There are just layers upon layers of bad stuff.

"Jules ran away when Mercedes was about Liam's age. I think she went looking for the boy. She hadn't been taking care of her anyway. Ms. Liv had. Jules always acted like Mercedes was a sibling, an adopted one. She never once did any parenting. According to Ms. Liv, Jules returned a few years later, but she never stayed for long. She was in and out for years."

"I'm not understanding." Connor is standing up now too. "What is the hatred about?"

"I didn't come into the picture until Mercedes was about fifteen. I have to piece together a lot from what I observed over the years. In my opinion, Jules partially resents Mercedes for, I don't know, *living*? And the other part of her is so jealous of Mercedes until it eats her alive. Mercedes was a beautiful little girl and she was smart. I'm sure Jules could see how much potential she had. Jules tried to infect her with all of her sick bullshit at every turn. She called herself schooling Mercedes about life, but she was really trying to poison anything good Mercedes might get. And it worked a lot of times. Mercedes didn't really have anybody else so she took in a lot of the poison Jules pumped into her."

So many things make so much sense now. Mercedes' persistent opinion that there's something wrong with her, her history with men, her fear of losing relationships. It's like, all the pieces are clicking together. And as terrifying as it is, August is not even done yet.

MERCEDES

I vow that I will never let Ash convince me to take her anywhere near sweets ever again. She said we were making a quick stop at this new specialty donut shop before we headed to Tyson's corner. Ash proceeded to OD on donuts and get ill. I had to bring her back to her place, make her gulp down some Pepto and lay down. I have one child. I'm not trying to have two. And I didn't even get the new outfit I wanted to pick up to go out with Lochlan next week.

I creep into the house as quietly as possible. Liam is sleeping and I'm hoping to get a couple things done before he wakes up. I don't even take him upstairs to his room. I just lay him on the sofa and cover him with a throw blanket. I'm struck for a moment by how I don't think of this as Lochlan's house anymore. Liam and I have been here for over two weeks. Every time I suggest we should return to southwest, Lochlan pretends to understand, but he always finds a way to convince me that leaving at another time would be better. If he can't use an argument about Liam, he uses his hands or his mouth or both. And I'm embarrassed to report that I'm extremely weak. I can't get enough of Lochlan. I don't think I ever will.

I'm surprised when I hear voices coming from beyond the kitchen in the den. I thought Loch and Connor were going out today. I creep away from Liam, so I don't bother him and head for the den. I'm even more shocked to hear August's voice. I didn't think August was capable of speaking in such a hushed tone. Something about the sound of his voice makes me break out in a cold sweat. His actual words rip my chest open and it's not a clean cut.

"I think that's why she made that video and why she sent you that footage. Jules has been there to sabotage every good thing Mercedes has achieved. She knew about Mercedes' graduation from college. I called that bitch and told her I got detained and I begged her to come so Mercury wouldn't be alone. She just laughed and said she was busy. The joke wound up being on her because Mercedes met you that night. You could tell that Mercury fell in love with you. I don't know how but Jules must have figured it out and she still found a way to ruin that. She doesn't want Mercedes to be happy. She's a vile snake."

I'm standing in the entrance to the den. Connor, Lochlan, and August's backs are to me. Thanks to my stealth sleeping-baby skills, they don't know I'm here. I am unilingual and well versed in the single language I speak, so on some level, I understand what August just said. But I feel like I'm trying to understand the words like you would understand a picture seen through dirty glass. The edges of it appear, I have a general sense of the size and shape, but I can't quite bring the whole image into focus.

"What do you mean when you say she made that video?" I step down into the sunken den and I feel like I'm sinking in more ways than one.

"Mercury! I thought you were out shopping. What are you doing here? We didn't hear you come back." August talks fast when he's nervous and right now he's going a hundred miles a minute.

Lochlan walks towards me slowly, I feel like I'm seeing him from outside of my body. He's being cautious of my feelings but I don't have any. The way dead people don't get hurt or sad, that's me, just sinking with an open empty chest. This feeling is not unfamiliar, I was like this for a week after I woke up at 15 with a torn body and no memory of what happened. It's not so bad, a place where there's no pain is a safe place.

"What are you talking about August? Jules made what video?" There's only one video he could be talking about but for some reason, I need confirmation.

"Oh, Mercury, I'm so sorry. I wouldn't have wanted to tell you like this." My long-time friend is more emotionally appropriate than me. August looks devastated while I just stare blankly at him and Lochlan hovering carefully over me.

"Mercy, I wanted to make sure that video was destroyed so we did some digging. We found out that Jules made the video of you when you were a teenager. Apparently it was something she had done before."

"What else?" The coldness in my voice is met with a wary expression from Lochlan. "What else were you guys talking about before I walked in?"

Even through my numb haze, a slight tug of irritation penetrates when Lochlan looks at August. August shakes his head almost imperceptibly. What the fuck are they hiding from me? What is worse than this?

Lochlan takes my hand "Mercy, why didn't you tell me that Jules is your mother?"

I look at him blankly. So that's what they were talking about. I see August is in here telling all my business. "Her pushing me out of her vagina 24 years ago does not make her my mother. I'm a mother to Liam. Sophia Rait is your mother. Don't insult us by calling Jules my mother. I wouldn't even know Jules gave birth to me if I hadn't heard her and my grandmother arguing when I was little."

"I know it was hard when she was born Julissa but she's eight now. She's not a little baby. No diapers, no formula and she sleeps at night. Maybe you couldn't take care of her back then but now is your chance. She's your daughter." They're in the kitchen. I was coming to ask for a popsicle when I heard my grandmother's voice.

"I'm 23 years old, what makes you think I want to drag an eight year old kid around with me?"

"Oh Julissa, she's not just some kid. She is your child. Mercedes is your child, you're her mother." I pull on my ponytail and bite my lip. It's what I do in school when I'm feeling nervous or scared but it doesn't help me now. I didn't think I had a mom, it seemed like there was just grandma. And this is all really confusing because I thought moms were supposed to love their kids. Jules hates me.

"Just because I pushed her out eight years ago, doesn't make me her mother. That's it. I don't want to ever talk about this again."

I hate the way the words feel on my lips when I explain to Lochlan how I found out Jules gave birth to me. Telling them this stuff makes me want to rip my own mouth off my face. This is why I don't talk about this. I wasn't keeping anything from Lochlan, there's nothing to tell.

"Where's the video?"

"We're not sure yet but we think we know how to get it. Just let me take care of that."

My nod is one of acknowledgment, not agreement. I don't need help with this. I got this.

"Liam is sleeping on the couch. He ate lunch, but he'll want a snack when he wakes up. Can you get it for him?" Lochlan looks from me to August as if he needs help deciphering my continued blankness. I try to show some expression, give him something that will make him feel comfortable letting me go, because I need to go now.

"Of course, I can, but Mercy where are you going?"

"I need to clear my head for a little bit. I'm just going to walk around and breathe and think."

"Mercy, let me come with you. August will stay here with Liam. I don't want you alone right now."

"It's fine, Loch. I need to be alone. I can't digest this with you all here. I just, please, I have to be alone." He doesn't want to let me go. I can tell from the look on his face. "Please Lochlan, just give me this." In the end he relents thinking that I'm just going for a walk. I'm going to walk but I have a very specific destination in mind.

LOCHLAN

"She's been gone 20 minutes. Should I call her?"

"Give her a little more time, bro." August nods his head in agreement with Connor.

"I think we should have told her the other stuff we found out about Jules. She knows about the video but it's more than that."

"I know, Lochlan but damn, how much can the girl take at one time. Maybe we just let her digest that, as she said, before we feed her another heaping serving of evil."

I don't know what to do with myself. The only other time I've seen Mercedes instantly shut down like that was when she first found out about the video. It's like one minute she's there and the next minute, nothing. The lights are on, but nobody's home.

Another 10 minutes go by with all of us tense as we try to decide what to do next. August is Googling psychological trauma when his phone rings.

"Hello? Yeah, Ted, I remember, but now isn't the best time." August listens to the person on the other end before responding "You saw who?" He frowns at whatever the other person says. "Just now, you saw her there now?" Connor shrugs when I look at him as if to say 'I'm as clueless as you.'

"Do you know what room she's in? Ted, hold on one second." August puts the phone on mute and looks at us with a horrified expression.

"Ted is a very old associate. We keep in touch. He's the head concierge at the Four Seasons. I used to take Mercury up there to meet Ted for dinner and drinks. There was a whole crew of us. Anyway, he's on the phone. He says he just saw Mercedes in the lobby."

"Why would she be at the Four Seasons?"

"Jules is there."

"What? She told me that Jules left for the Riviera."

"Well, that was either a mistake or a lie because Jules is there in room 12B."

"I'm going to get Mercy. This can't be good."

August agrees. "No, it definitely can't be good."

"I'll stay here with Liam. Hang on." August unmutes the phone. "Ted, if I send a friend to the hotel can you get him into 12B?"

"I know, yeah, I'll definitely owe you."

"Okay, I'm texting you a pic. He's hard to miss." I roll my eyes at that last part. "Yes, thank you again, I owe you."

"Ted will be looking out for you so get going. I know Mercedes in a different way than you guys do. She's had to fight a lot so she's no stranger to it." August talks as we all move toward the front door. My little boy is still sound asleep. He has no idea of the evil in this world and I promise myself I'll protect him as long as I can.

"I don't know what Mercedes will do to Jules, but when she blanks out like that, it's hardly ever a good sign."

MERCEDES

I'm thankful for random D.C. Saturday traffic. When I first walked out of Lochlan's house, there was only one thing in my head: I'ma fuck this bitch up. I planned to get a bottled drink from the bar, break the bottle, and slash that bitch's face like the girls used to do when I was in middle school and high school. Let's see her find someone to take care of her when I fuck her face up. But, while my Uber navigates some street festival, I start to really absorb what August was telling me. Jules, my fucked-up surrogate, seems to want one thing more than anything, to drag me down to her level and see me miserable. What if I take that away from her? What would that look like? Slash her face or play 3D chess? What's it going to be?

I have more time to decide when I get to the hotel and text Jules. She's in the spa, her appointment will be done in 15 minutes and she'll meet me at her room.

Slash her face or 3D chess? Slash her face or 3D chess? Slash her face or 3D chess?

Jules decides for me. She opens the door to her suite 25 minutes later and I follow her inside. She barely even glances at me before she turns to get a bottle of water out of the refrigerator.

"I hope you're here because you decided to take my advice and stop being a basic bitch."

I look at her back as she gets her $20 bottle of water and I know what to do.

"Nah, I'm not going to take your advice, but I wanted to share some fantastic news with you." I force enthusiasm into my voice.

Jules rolls her eyes and for just a second, I teeter towards slashing her face.

"I'm in love with Lochlan. Well, we're in love with each other. Liam and I are moving in with him and we're going to be a family."

I don't know how I missed it before. All these years and I couldn't see it right in front of my face: envy and malice. Jules is dripping in it. I think me talking about love is making her physically ill.

"I owe a lot of my happiness to you, Jules."

"I don't see how because you aren't listening to a damn thing I say."

I laugh lightly "Yeah, I'm not. But I still owe you. I owe you for not trying to be my mother. I owe you for letting my grandmother raise me. I owe you for all the time you spent away from me. Maybe it's not much, but you gave me just enough to have a chance to find happiness by not being there."

Her practiced bored expression slips for once. Jules' beautiful, almost slashed face, morphs into an ugly sneer. "Don't forget about how you owe me for all the dicks you've been on and everything it got you."

This bitch really wants door number 1. And that, more than anything, is why I will not give it to her.

"I know what you did, you rancid, miserable bitch. I know you made that video." I could be talking about the weather I keep my voice so carefree.

"Oh is that what you think, little Mercedes?" The sneer on her face is accented by a glint of satisfaction in her eyes. That gives me pause. If Jules feels like she has the upper hand here, something very bad is about to happen." She walks towards me in her stretch pants and crop yoga top. It reminds me of an animal stalking prey which makes me the prey. Her momentary lack of balance has been restored.

"How would I know to record you? How would I have known that would be the night when you'd start spreading those pretty little legs?"

My brain sputters like an old engine threatening to give out. What am I missing? "Wait, did you know they drugged me?" Jules is just a few feet away from where I'm still standing in the entrance to the suite.

"Did I know? You fucking idiot, I did you that particular favor. Nobody was going to want some uptight little girl hanging around, including me; I just helped loosen your shit up so you could stop acting like it was made of platinum when it was just regular pussy."

When people talk about hating other people, they don't really know what they're talking about. Most people can't muster the emotional strength required to truly hate someone. But Jules is a case study in it. She doesn't wish me dead, she wishes me alive and in agony.

The woman who birthed me drugged me, raped me, filmed it and used the film to destroy the one good thing in my life. I don't have the capacity to identify or sort the emotions warring for control of me. Jules just watches me and licks her lips like she's preparing to savor a delicious meal. The expectation on her face catapults me back from the edge of a pitch black void. This bitch has to be dealt with.

"It's in the past, Jules and honestly, I couldn't give less of a fuck."

The sneer finally cracks and a fission of worry emerges. I'd chosen right. She isn't bothered by my reactions. She's bothered by my lack of reaction.

"Lochlan knows *everything* about me. He got the little video you sent and he knows all about my past. It's water under the bridge for us. We're in love and none of that shit matters."

"So he knows I'm your mother?"

It's my turn to laugh. "Bitch please, you're not nobody's mother just because your dumb ass got knocked up and pushed a baby out."

"Fuck you, Mercedes. Fuck you!" All signs of neutrality have disappeared. Jules' chest heaves up and down with her heavy breaths, she's enraged and there's no hiding it. "Unlike your ditzy ass, I was happy with the man who got me pregnant."

"So you do know who my father is? You don't tell the truth about shit."

"Your grandmother thought it was my friend's brother but it wasn't her stupid ass brother I was fucking. I been up on game, I never go for the small fish. I tried to teach you the same thing but you've always been simple. It wasn't that dumb ass little boy I was with, I knew back then only a man could handle me."

My legs feel like they might just say fuck it and give out on me. Jules is not just crazy, she's depraved. How did I come from this trash heap?

"You were sleeping with your friend's father when you were fourteen?" I guess where this is going and Jules actually looks satisfied with herself when she nods.

"He was in love with me. We were going to be together and you fucking ruined everything. I would've had an abortion but I thought he'd be more likely to leave his wife if he knew I was pregnant. But I had the game fucked up back then. Pregnant pussy might be good but nobody wants a bitch with a baby." I don't even know if she's talking to me or herself. Jules paces around as she drags me down into the heart of darkness with her, she's not even looking at me anymore.

"He just disappeared one day. I had no idea he was leaving. I just looked up and the whole family was gone. I thought if I could just get rid of you, I could get him back but even that got fucked up by you."

"Yes, that's right." Jules responds to me shaking my head like I can dispel her words.

"I planned to throw you out like a pile of trash and you even messed that up when you were born."

Lochlan was telling me something the other day about God knowing how much we can take and not giving us more. I'm thinking somebody is sleep at the off-button when the door to the suite burst open. I don't question why Lochlan is here with Connor, somebody must have finally flipped the switch and I'm grateful. Loch opens his arms and I walk right into them. His gentle squeeze feels like it's infusing light back into me.

"I'm right here, Mercy. I love you and I'm right here." I cling to him tighter until Jules' words claw my back like talons.

"You're so fucking stupid. You think some church boy who left your ass when he saw a dick in it is going to want you?" Jules' laugh sounds like the dying breath of a movie villain. I turn back to face her for the last time. She's moved back and is standing by the breakfast bar. I go to her.

"It eats you up, doesn't it? All the time and energy you put into making me like you and I still wound up happy with my Prince Charming. You're 40 now and well on your way to a sad lonely death. I'm not even 25 yet and my future looks bright as fuck." I can see her searching her mind grasping for anything, but I'm not done yet. "I just wanted to say thank you for being gone and now thank you for staying gone. Because if I ever see you again, I might forget how sublimely happy I am and fuck your face up beyond all recognition."

"Damn. Even I'm scared." I forgot Connor was here until he speaks from somewhere behind me.

"I never fucking wanted you anyway. You think it's a problem for me to stay away from you? I—"

Jules never gets to finish that sentence. I take a heavy coffee mug sitting on the breakfast bar and smash it into her face. I wasn't sure where my limit was but Jules found it. I close my eyes and force breath into my lungs. It's all I can do to stop myself from swinging again. Jules is bent over, blood spurting everywhere.

"Oh my God, you broke my fucking nose."

I bend down next to her. "Your video doesn't matter Julissa. You can put that shit on Pornhub or on the nightly news. I don't give a single solitary fuck who sees that video. The only thing you need to worry about is me seeing you again. I will not kill you but you'll wish I had. You know enough about me to know I'm dead ass serious. Stay the fuck away from me, forever."

Lochlan puts his hand on my shoulder while I'm still bent over a crying bleeding Jules. I look up at him and I'm surprised he's blurry. I'm crying.

"It's okay now, baby. Let me take you home."

"Yes, please take me home now. I'm done here."

When I leave with Lochlan I make up my mind. I'm not taking any of this shit with me. I want to hurt Jules as much as I can. The only way I can do that is to be happy so that's exactly what the fuck I'm going to do.

EPILOGUE

"Kahri, are you sure this is a good idea?"

"Yes, it is." Lochlan answers for Kahri.

"Thank you, Pumpkin but you're biased, you think I can do anything."

"And I'm right, so you should listen to me."

Lochlan kisses me right there in the middle school hallway we're standing in surrounded by black history facts. We're here for a career day with an 8th grade group that Lochlan's community engagement director, Kahri Fletcher, set up for about twenty adolescent girls who are interested in a career in the health-care industry. Rebound is launching a youth rehabilitation program and expanding their reputation for working among that demographic.

Kahri drops the bag of company swag she's carrying for the participants and puts her hands on her hips. "Mercedes you are the perfect person to talk to these girls. You're from where they're from and you've overcome all this shit. You don't have to do anything but walk in there and tell them the truth."

Kahri and I have become pretty good friends. When I found out at one of the Rebound company events that Paul couldn't stand her, I knew I liked her. When she told me that Paul could stab himself in the eye with a spoon, we started talking on the phone and going to lunch. Kahri is my first girlfriend since I was a teenager. I'm having a lot of first these days.

I went to my first of many therapy appointments the week after the horrific day at the Four Seasons. For the first time, I'm aware of all my toxic thought patterns and I'm really working to unravel them. I went to church with Lochlan for the first time. Unfortunately, we felt so good afterwards that we came home and screwed like bunnies. Mixed results there but I'm still going and it's been a good experience.

"Okay, I can do this." The man that I love smiles at me in a way that is not appropriate for a school where children are waiting for me on the other side of a door.

"Don't look at me like that."

"Like what?"

"Like you want to eat her for lunch." Kahri shakes her head in disapproval at her boss. The Rebound executive team is more like a family and Kahri is very much a part of it despite Paul's nasty attitude.

"It's already past lunch time, but how about dinner, Mercy? Will you let me eat you for dinner?"

"No, no, you two. I've worked hard on this school partnership. We're not messing it up because you can't restrain yourselves around one another." Kahri didn't miss the effect Lochlan's words had on me. I was ready to forget all about the poor eighth graders. "You," Kahri, points at me, "it's show time, go in there and do your thing."

"Mr. Rait, you and I will be in the audience."

Lochlan raises one eyebrow at me, "You good?"

"I'm good."

"Okay, let's go."

Standing in front of the class full of young girls who remind me of me at their age, I tell them what I wish someone had told me, the truth.

"You can do anything you want to do. Nobody can stop you but you."

AUGUST

TWO MONTHS LATER

The good ones are always straight. I mean look at this fine specimen here, 6'2ish" with jet black hair, green eyes, and a jaw made out of ivory. The Rait cousin is fine, straight. and repressed as fuck. Oh well, it wasn't meant to be anyway. Mercury still kind of hates him so I can't dip into that pool.

I lean back and enjoy the Christmas music blasting from the speakers in Mercedes and Lochlan's sitting room. We're here for a pre-Christmas dinner and I'm pretty sure a proposal. Lochlan has asked me 80 ring questions, sent me 30 photos and 15 videos. At this point, I'ma need a ring too.

The gangs all here, Connor and whatever disposable girl he's on this week, Ashley and her sugar stash, the sexually-repressed cousin, Liam, Lochlan, and even Lochlan's parents. They still often and loudly express their discomfort at Lochlan "shacking up" with Mercury, but they're obsessed with their grandson. I was ready to fuck both of them up if they acted funny towards my Mercury, but surprisingly, from that first meeting, they seem to have taken to her too.

My little Mercedes found herself a good therapist. I keep asking her if she's fixed and she keeps telling me it's a process. But if you ask me, she's well on her way. I only have to remind her monthly, instead of weekly, that she deserves love. With some more self-care and self-confidence she will get there.

Mercedes finally gave in and decided to go back to school so that she can become a nurse practitioner. That was always her goal. She wants to run her own clinic. I was shocked as hell to find out that she's even gone to the little church group meetings with Loch a few times. I was going to go until she explained the food situation to me.

"August, this is not an alcoholics anonymous meeting. They don't have donuts and coffee but there are snacks."

"Well, Mercury if they don't have donuts and coffee, what is the point? I'm confused."

"It's just a group of supportive positive people."

"Who don't have sex? I'm still confused. Where's the support?"

"Well you know, Loch and I have been failing at that so I guess we support each other but, you know what, Never mind, August, I'll just pray for you."

"Okay well I'll pray for you too because I know you and Lochlan were supporting each other in the laundry room before everybody got here."

Mercedes' face was priceless. Poor thing, she's trying. But, whatever, if they don't got donuts at the church, count me out. I'll keep attending TV church, thank you very much.

Nobody has heard from Jules and as much as I hope it stays that way, I still owe that python these hands and one day I will deliver. But not today. Today, Lochlan is down on one knee and Liam is saying "Mommy, Daddy wants you to be his life."

"That's right, buddy, but it's wife."

Liam looks his father dead in the eye and says, "That's what I said, Daddy."

Mercedes is crying, I'm crying, and Ashley is eating the Christmas cookies and crying. But these are all happy tears now. Happy tears for the woman who had a choice and chooses her present and her future over her past. If it can happen for her...naaaah, I'ma be shaking ass and taking names until they wheel me up outta here. But for now, I join in the celebration for my friend who deserves all of this happiness. Mercedes.

Follow Lola Joy on Social Media:
FACBOOK: www.facebook.com/lola.joy.9003
INSTAGRAM: @authorlolajoy

Made in United States
North Haven, CT
27 November 2021

11580538R00148